Sun Child

Sun Child

ANGELA HUTH

LITTLE, BROWN

A *Little, Brown* Book

First published in Great Britain in 1975 by William Collins & Co Ltd
This edition published by Little, Brown in 2003

Copyright © Angela Huth 1975

The moral right of the author has been asserted.

A CIP catalogue record for this book is
available from the British Library.

ISBN 0 316 72458 0

Typeset in Berkeley by M Rules
Printed and bound in Great Britain by
Mackays of Chatham Ltd, Chatham, Kent

Little, Brown
An imprint of
Time Warner Books UK
Brettenham House
Lancaster Place
London WC2E 7EN

www.TimeWarnerBooks.co.uk

For Candida with love

'Children begin by loving their parents. After a time they judge them. Rarely, if ever, do they forgive them.'

Oscar Wilde *A Woman Of No Importance*

'Childhood is measured by sounds and smells
And sights, before the dark of reason grows.'

John Betjeman *Summoned By Bells*

One

*F*rom where she sat in the long grass Emily Harris could see her parents laughing. She couldn't hear the laughter because the kitchen window was shut, but their inaudible joke added to the niceness of the afternoon.

Out here it was sunny, very bright, after the husky brown light of the loft in the barn. It was only after lunch Emily had found this new loft. She was still finding new things most days, but the loft was the best discovery yet. The barn itself she already knew well, and loved: the piles of mouldy hay, the rusty bicycle, the rotting tyres, the donkey cart with *Ada loves Charlie* on its side, and the wobbly ladder that led up to the hole of impenetrable blackness.

This afternoon Emily had dared at last to climb that ladder. At the top, she stayed for a while on her hands and knees, cautiously feeling about the floorboards. Her fingers bumped over scabs of dried pigeon dirt and flinched away from splinters. When she became accustomed to the light she stood up and looked about her, knees trembling a little. There wasn't much to see. A pile of empty sacks, a page of yellow newspaper, a small plastic boat, a horrible red even in the gloom. The place, Emily felt at once, had prospects, but should be contemplated elsewhere. Quickly she climbed back down the ladder and returned to the garden. There, crouching in her hideout of grass, she listened to the small jet zooms of bees, drunk on pollen, as they flew indeterminately back and forth from flower to flower. She felt the sun, and she felt the warmth of her parents' laughter.

Last summer, it had all been very different. Then, they were still living in a stuffy London flat with long white moiré passages and aubergine carpets. She didn't see her parents much, just the early mornings, some evenings before bed, the occasional whole weekend. True, they all had breakfast together, every day. Idle, Emily's father, insisted upon that. They ate in the blue silk dining room – mostly in silence. Idle would read the newspaper as he ate, very neat in his dark suit, a perpetual frown on his kind, creased face. Fen, her mother, would be in her dressing gown, hair unbrushed but shining, gazing out of the window, taking a long time over a triangle of anaemic toast. Occasionally she would break the silence by asking Emily some impossible question: what was she going to do at school today?

Some mornings Emily felt that her mother was really interested, genuinely wanting to know that sums, dictation and painting were the order of the morning, and she would reply conscientiously. Other days the question sounded automatic, and Emily would hear herself saying peevishly:

'You must remember by now it's gym on Tuesdays. I've told you.'

'I always forget,' Fen would smile. In London, her mind was on so many things.

It was at breakfast one morning that Fen had found a perfect country house advertised in the paper. She gave a wild yelp of pleasure, startling both Emily and her father. From the three line description of the house she could tell, she said, there was no possibility of there being anything wrong with it. Wouldn't it be marvellous? The solution to their lives? She would go and see it at once, this morning. No point in delaying. She jumped in the air, shouting with uncontainable delight.

'*Really,* Mama,' said Emily, who was used to her mother's exuberances, but never quite used to the speed with which they came and went. Idle merely smiled and encouraged his wife to go, at once.

2

The following day breakfast was no less dull. Fen had made an offer for the house. It was now only a matter of planning and impatient waiting.

Emily was pleased by the thought of leaving London. For her, it had always been a bleak life there. She was looked after by a devoted but stupid Danish au pair girl called Angelica, who had a heavy gold moustache and smelt when she moved her arms. Emily and Angelica spent every afternoon after school together. As Angelica's idea of adventure was limited to the Round Pond, they went there each day. Emily came to hate park life: the prim, clipped sheet of water crowded with its miniature yachts, just as she grew to hate the feeble sound of wailing Nannies – at least Angelica was better than *them* – whose cries of warning nagged the air.

Every afternoon the routine was the same. After three turns round the pond (two on rainy days) Emily and Angelica would return to the flat. While Angelica screwed her key round in the lock Emily dreaded the silence, and the smell of central heating, that she knew awaited them on the other side of the door. Angelica would prepare the sliced-bread sandwiches – Marmite one day, peanut butter the next, with a few chocolate biscuits and a dreary bought cake. Because Angelica was on a permanent diet, Emily was forced to eat by herself. Angelica sat at the other end of the white formica table, enviously watching her every mouthful.

'Not more than two biscuits,' was her daily admonition, 'or you'll get big and fat like me.' Sometimes, Emily shuddered.

Occasionally, she would bring a schoolfriend home for tea. Although they anticipated interesting games on the way home, when they actually arrived at the flat something of its deadness subdued them. They would abandon their plans and, disconsolate, watch television instead.

Occasionally, Fen would be home. Usually on the telephone. If she wasn't on the telephone, and had nothing else to do, Emily would be treated to the best hour of her day.

'Let's *do* something, Em,' Fen would say. 'What shall it be today?' (As if they were confronted by the problem *every* day.) Then, gay and enthusiastic, she would think of something. They would paint huge pictures together, water colours. Fen was particularly good at skies. She showed Emily how to wet the paper with a large brush, then run blues and greys into the water, leaving natural clouds to form. Emily was better at reflections. She liked to do castles with lighted windows beside lakes. She would turn the picture upside down and draw the reflection, rather more shakily than the actual castle, and make the lights smudgy in the water. Sometimes, they combined on a painting. Storms were their favourite subjects. Fen would streak a thunderous sky with silver lightning, while Emily purpled the hills with shadows, and put in one tiny old man, alone in all this violence, bent double by the rain. Between them, they would make the kind of mess that turned Angelica to despair. And then, with one accord, at precisely the same moment, they would abandon their paints, turn on loud music and dance. Fen would kick off her shoes, twirl Emily around, sing in a funny voice which Emily tried to imitate. The room, so often dormant, would come alive.

Best of all were the occasions when Fen let Emily come and help her dress for the evening. In London, Fen and Idle were out most nights. Emily would stand at the dressing table and watch the mysterious process of her mother transforming herself from a near-beautiful, uncared for woman, to a woman of almost haughty grandeur. Fen would pile up her hair, leaving little wisps to curl about her ears. She would ponder about earrings.

'Which ones, tonight, do you think?' she always asked, most seriously, convincing Emily that she required her choice. Emily would run her fingers along the spiky shapes of jewels in the velvet-lined box. She never knew which ones she liked best.

'The purple ones.' She handed her mother a pair of amethyst earrings surrounded by diamonds.

'Why not? They're Papa's favourites. He gave them to me years before we were married. He sent them to me in a parcel with no note. But of course I guessed.' She pierced the earring through the invisible hole in her blue-white lobe.

4

'Were you and Papa together years and years before you were married?' Emily was forever trying to pierce together her parents' past.

'Only two years.'

'Did you have any other boyfriends?' Fen smiled at herself in the glass.

'One or two. Well – lots and lots.'

'But none so good as Papa or you wouldn't have married him?'

'None so good as Papa, or I wouldn't have married him.' This time Fen smiled at the reflection of her daughter, as well as herself. A proper smile, with teeth showing and tiny lines round her eyes.

Idle came into the room. He stopped at the door. He seemed amazed, confused, by the reflection of his wife's beauty through the looking glass.

'I hate to have to tell you to hurry,' said Fen, 'but we're meant to be there by eight thirty.' She was at once apologetic and beguiling. A look of extreme weariness passed over Idle's face, but he hurried off to change.

Later, when Emily was in bed, they would come and say goodnight before leaving. In the semi-darkness of her room they would be glamorous figures: Idle tall and wide in his dark velvet jacket, his marvellous face and silver hair patterned with shadows; Fen in a wispy dress of peacock colours that floated like underwater plants when she moved.

'Night, darling. We'll tell you all about it in the morning.' When Fen stood up from kissing Emily she left in the air a smell of stephanotis. Emily would wrinkle her nose with pleasure.

Before going to sleep, she would try to imagine their evening. What sort of people would they talk to? What would they eat and drink? She had a hazy picture in her mind of a kind of pantomime palace in which tables were crusted with brilliant food and golden goblets filled with wine. Her father, for some reason, wore a powdered wig, and his trousers had turned to knickerbockers. The light of a huge chandelier full upon him, he would run down a flight of curved stairs, and begin to search among the masked dancing women. Suddenly he would notice a shy lady by herself, hiding behind a pillar. He would drag her from her hiding place, unmask her. It was Fen. They would both begin to laugh, and to dance, faster and faster, old fashioned waltzing, till everyone else stopped to watch as they spun round the empty floor, and applause came in a great burst, almost drowning the orchestra.

But next morning, Fen and Idle always forgot to tell her what it had really been like. Their warmth of the night before always seemed a little frozen in the morning It wasn't their time for concentrating on her. In London, they were forever preoccupied by other things. They didn't laugh, there, nearly as much as they did now.

The church clock struck five. Emily knew that at any moment her father would come striding out to find her, hoist her on his shoulders, and quickly involve her in one of his innocent conspiracies.

As she expected, he came. He wore a blue silk shirt, the colour of the sky. It was open-necked and the sleeves were rolled up, but it couldn't be disguised. It was a London shirt. Idle hadn't yet been able to bring himself to wear country clothes.

'Emily !' He strode towards the patch of sunflowers, some taller than him, that grew near the barn.

'I'm here!' He changed his direction. She could see him, still he couldn't see her. The grass crushed under his feet, making a quiet cracking noise.

'You're always changing your hiding places. You confuse me,' he said. He helped her to her feet. 'Where did all those cobwebs come from?'

'I went up to the loft in the barn.'

'Don't you remember? I told you. That ladder's dangerous.'

'I was very careful.'

'You mustn't go again till I've tried it.'

'I was trying it for you.' She looked at his momentarily stern face. 'All right.'

'Promise?'

'Promise.' Idle stooped down and began brushing the cobwebs from her shoulders and long gold hair.

'Now listen. I've something to tell you.' His voice lowered conspiratorially. 'Mama has made a chocolate cake – the most dreadful chocolate cake you ever saw.' Emily giggled at his seriousness. 'But the thing is, she tried very hard, and we don't want her to think we don't like it, do we?'

'No,' said Emily.

'So the plan is this. We eat it. We might even ask for more. And we tell her it's delicious. You understand?'

'Yes.'

'You'll stick to the plan?'

'All right, if you do.'

'Of course I will.'

Emily giggled again and braced herself for secrecy. She always enjoyed her father's plans.

'I promise,' she said. 'It'll be a secret.'

'Right, then. Up?' With a practised leap Emily bounded on to his wide shoulders, feeling the warm, soft silk of his shirt beneath her bare legs. 'You high in the sky?'

'Highest ever!' With one hand she grabbed hold of a clump of her father's hair. The other arm she whirled round like the sail of a windmill. 'I've never been so high,' she shouted. She let the clouds spin dizzily about her head, holding her face up to them, feeling their whiteness right through her eyes. These rides had become a habit since they had been in this house. They were always exciting, but best on days when the clouds were hard-edged, racing against a taut blue sky, undisturbing it, like today.

At the kitchen door, which opened on to a rough stone terrace, Idle let Emily slide to the ground. The stone was warm under her bare feet. Bantams jerked about, clucking, pecking. She stood quite still for a moment, getting used to the ground again. Then she followed her father.

After all the sun outside, the kitchen was dim, the quarry tiles cool. Fen, also barefoot, was bending down by the Aga, two tins of deflated cake in her hands. The sun, low in the windows, had outlined one side of her long, honey coloured dress, making it shimmery with gold until Emily had refocused her eyes. Fen laughed when she saw them.

'We'll be having a thin, crisp cake,' she said. 'A sort of giant biscuit.'

Emily and her father exchanged a private look.

'Good,' said Idle. 'If there's one thing I really hate it's a professional cake.'

He didn't care one way or another about food of any kind. Triumphs or disasters in the kitchen left him equally unmoved. But his wife's reactions to both amused him. He was smiling down at her, arms folded, eyes tired. Since eight that morning he had been writing a report on the economic situation of one of the underdeveloped countries into which he was researching on behalf of the government. He wrote slowly, laboriously, by hand, reading each page as he finished it and crossing out the occasional adjective. His English master at school, he remembered, said that unless you had a flair for adjectives they were dangerous. So Idle took no risks in his reports. Now that he had finished this one, thirty pages, he had writer's cramp. Also, his head ached.

'Can I do anything ?' he asked.

'No, leave it.'

He liked coming into the warm mess of the kitchen, where he was never expected to help, after the solitude of his study. He liked the unconscious placing of things that seemed to go well together on the dresser – the bowl of brown eggs, the huge washstand jug of tumbling dried flowers and whiskery corn, the basket of bright wools bought by Fen in a one-day fit of wanting to crochet. In spite of being almost obsessively orderly himself, here, he enjoyed the chaos. Occasionally, perhaps to please him, Fen had days of inspired tidiness. She would wake full of good resolutions, and spend the whole day scrubbing, polishing and dusting. By evening she was exhausted and depressed. The resulting neatness did not please her. She found no pleasure in

8

Idle's praise. By nature she was untidy, and happy in her untidiness.

Now she went to the kitchen table, pushed away a pile of unwashed plates, a lump of melting butter and a dish of cold sprouts, and dumped down the two cake tins. She began to edge round them with a sharp knife.

'Have you finished for today?' she asked. She wasn't concentrating very hard on either the question or the cakes. 'You must be starved. Only those filthy sandwiches for lunch. I wish you didn't have to work *every* weekend.' She turned the two frazzled discs of cakes on to the table and looked up at Idle smiling. 'Well, you can't say I'm not trying, can you?'

'You're doing very well.' He stepped towards her, pushed the long tousled hair out of her eyes, and ran his hand over her face. 'Why's your face on fire?'

'Frustration.' She pouted, childlike, for a moment. 'You see I like the idea of cooking – I never thought I would, but I do. In practice, though, it never seems to work out. I mean look at this mess. Would you believe it, for one cake?'

They both looked at the sink high with saucepans, chocolate streaked spoons and bowls. Idle began to laugh. Fen could never resist his laughter. In response she flung herself against him, threw back her head, lifted her arms round his neck and laughed too. They stood like that for a while, clutching each other, rocking back and forth, till Idle pushed Fen gently away to look at her again.

'You most beautiful prize ridiculous idiot,' he said.

'Certainly I'm not a cake maker,' Fen replied. Emily, at the table, was picking up crumbs of chocolate sponge, tasting them.

'Oh yes you are,' she said.

Later, they heard outside the unmistakeable sound of Uncle Tom's car in the drive. Uncle Tom, Fen's brother, was fiercely loyal to his car. It was a shabby old blue Mercedes, its limp exhaust pipe held up with a leather belt which once had had as aristocratic origins as the car itself. One of Emily's greatest pleasures was to be taken for a ride in it, alone with Uncle Tom, the hood down, hair blowing in the wind.

With a shriek of delight she ran from the kitchen to greet him. Idle followed her.

'Why have you come, Uncle Tom? What a surprise!'

'I was just passing.' Tom got out of the car and enveloped Emily in a hug. He wore jeans, and a wispy Indian scarf round his throat. His hair was almost as long and wild as Fen's, but curlier. His narrow face, beautiful in repose, was endearingly impudent when he smiled, as he did now.

'How lovely, lovely, lovely,' Emily was chanting.

In the confusion of her greeting she didn't notice a man get out of the other side of the car, a very large man with a white face and startling grey eyes.

'Idle, I'm sorry.' Uncle Tom extracted himself from Emily's clasp, went over to his brother-in-law and indicated the stranger. 'This is Kevin. Kevin McCloud. We were in Oxford for the afternoon. Didn't think you'd mind if we came over.'

'Of course not, my dear chap,' said Idle shyly. For some reason, with Tom, he always felt his age. Formality overcame him, and he found himself using phrases he would not normally use. He turned to Kevin. 'How do you do? Come on in. Fen'll be delighted.'

Idle and Tom led the way into the house. Emily lingered behind for a moment to look at Kevin. He was leaning against the car, gazing up at the house.

'You must be Emily,' he said, his eyes on the upstairs windows. 'I've heard about you from Tom.'

He had a nice voice, but Emily didn't answer. She resented his presence. She wanted Uncle Tom to herself. Kevin followed her indoors.

In the kitchen Tom was being welcomed as happily by his sister as he had been by Emily. Again he introduced Kevin.

'You remember, I brought him round in London.'

Fen responded with a blank look. She had a streak of chocolate on her chin and shining eyes.

'You must remember,' Tom went on. 'You argued for an hour about *Cyrano*. I couldn't get a word in edgeways.'

'I have a totally immemorable face,' said Kevin. 'My mother always said that.'

Fen suddenly smiled.

'Of course I remember. But you had a beard, didn't you? Idle was in Africa.' Kevin smiled back.

'With or without a beard, just as immemorable.'

'Kevin being modest is only slightly worse than Kevin being arrogant,' explained Tom. Fen, standing on one leg by the Aga, concentrated on Kevin.

'You were negotiating for a factory in the North,' she recalled.

'I got it,' said Kevin. 'Spare parts. They're better than the stage, I can tell you. They're doing all right.'

'Won't everyone sit down?' asked Idle, sitting himself in the rocking chair.

'Uncle Tom, please can I have the next bit about the owl?' Emily had hoisted herself on to the dresser. She was plaiting strands of scarlet, yellow and orange wool, which she had taken from Fen's basket.

'Later,' said Tom. 'I'll have to think of something.'

'What's the owl?' Kevin went over to Emily. He leant against the dresser beside her, and let his huge fingers run through the mound of coloured wools.

'Oh, just an owl who hasn't got a hoot. It's a *serial* Uncle Tom tells me.'

'An owl who hasn't got a hoot? Well, I don't know much about that. But would you by any chance care to hear about a hippopotamus who wanted to be a photographer?'

'Not particularly.' Emily hoped she didn't sound mean. She was set on the owl.

'I could tell you about him before tea.'

'Where?' Emily looked at Kevin with suspicion. 'Not in here. Mama and Tom are making too much noise.'

'Anywhere you like.'

'Why don't you take Kevin into the garden, Em,' suggested

Fen, 'and hear the story there? By the time it's finished I'll have tea organised.' She seemed suddenly flustered by all the people round her.

'Well, all right,' Emily agreed with some reluctance. Kevin followed her outside. 'I'm always the one who has to take people for walks in the garden,' she said. 'I suppose I know it all by heart by now. Those are the sprouts, and that's the cutting border.' She pointed to an untidy row of chrysanthemums the colour of autumn fruits, and a few soggy marigolds, their flaming heads bent low over the earth.

'Very nice,' said Kevin. 'Do you pick the flowers?'

'Sometimes I help Mama. It's one of the things she likes doing – sometimes. Other times, it bores her. But actually, this year, do you know what? She says she's going to make apple jelly. We're going to pick up apples in a big basket tomorrow.'

They paused near a heavily laden tree. Emily stooped and picked a fallen apple from the long grass. She cupped it like a ball in her hands, and put its glossy yellow skin next to her cheek.

'It's quite cold,' she said.

'I can't believe,' Kevin was saying, 'your mother is the kind of person who likes making jam.'

'What I don't like,' answered Emily, not really listening to him, 'is when apples get all creased up skins like old people. It'll be awful when Mama gets lines on her, even on her legs.'

'But that won't be for years,' said Kevin, very serious. 'She's pretty young, your mother.'

Emily looked up at him, handed him the apple.

'I've warmed it a bit for you. Do you want to see the field? It's not much of a field. Just a scruffy old place, but I'd better show you.' She turned away from him and began to walk down a path. 'Last year,' she said, 'Mama was a very grand lady.'

'I remember. When I met her in London she had earrings, and her hair all piled up. I hardly recognised her today.'

'That's right. She had lots of grand clothes. But down here she doesn't bother and she likes it very much. She tries out all sorts

12

of new things, like the jam. She's very good at things,' she added.
Kevin caught up with her and walked by her side.

'How about the hippopotamus?' he asked. Emily was climbing
a low grey stone wall into the field. She swung one leg over the
top so that she could sit astride. Like this she was only a head
shorter than Kevin.

'Well, actually, you needn't bother if you don't want to,' she
said. 'I only really like stories by Uncle Tom and Papa. Papa tells
me all about Africa, real things that happen to him when he
goes there. Uncle Tom does very funny voices for all the different animals and people and everything.' She paused, taking in
the slight look of disappointment on Kevin's face. 'Thank you
very much all the same,' she said. 'Perhaps another time, if you're
going to come again. Will you get over first and jump me down?'

Kevin obliged. They walked round the field in silence. Emily
felt no need to talk. Kevin seemed to be one of those people you
didn't have to try to entertain, he was happy to be quiet. She
liked that. Some of her parents' friends were quite different.
They asked boring questions and pretended to be interested,
and asked her to show them things, paintings or stories. Then
they always said they were good, even if they weren't. They had
funny judgement, sometimes, her parents' friends. Or else they
were being dishonest. Anyhow, she hated ever to be asked to
show things: she liked to choose her critics. Mama and Paper
were always good and honest, and so was Uncle Tom. Kevin, she
suddenly felt, might be good too. One day, perhaps, she would
ask his opinion about something she had done.

He walked beside her and she studied his huge boots, muddy,
worn, pressing footprints in the longish grass. She betted he
never cleaned his shoes, or washed his shirts very often, or his
hair. He didn't look dirty, exactly: just uncared for, or as if he
didn't bother about himself. Emily glanced up at him. He was
taller than Papa, tall as a tree, looking about him as if everything
he saw was important. It would be good to marry a man as big as
Kevin because he would frighten burglars all right, and even if
you had three children he could carry them all at once. She

13

could quite see why Uncle Tom had him for a friend, and hoped her parents would come to like him too: he seemed a nice kind of man.

At tea he was very complimentary about the chocolate cake, although Emily hadn't told him the plan, and ate three slices. He made everybody laugh at a story he told about some play he had been in when he was younger. Emily didn't completely understand the jokes, but she saw it was funny the way he stomped about the kitchen, imitating someone, bashing his cup down on the table and flicking at things, making his big hands look like the spiky delicate hands of a dancer. She joined in the laughter, though she wasn't consumed by it like her mother. Fen's chair was pushed back from the table, she was doubled over, weak, the tears shining on her cheeks. Idle was enjoying it too, head thrown back, throat moving, tired face shifting with delight. Then the telephone rang. Uncle Tom went to answer it.

'A Marcia Burrows for you, Idle,' he said, when he came back. 'Sexy voice.'

Fen smiled.

'I forgot to tell you she rang this morning to ask when you wanted her to come down,' she said. 'Idle's new secretary,' she explained, as Idle left the room. 'Wonder how long *she'll* last ?'

'Why, does he work them too hard?' asked Kevin.

'Yes, but they also fall in love with him. Quite desperately. The amount of girls I've had on the telephone to *me* . . .' Her voice was scathing. 'He's tried them all shapes and ages, and never gives them any encouragement. But the more he ignores them the more they tear their hearts out for him. Until I met Idle I never knew there were so many lonely women ready to suffer unrequited love. A time wasting, humiliating experience *that* is,' she added. 'Something I'd never allow myself.'

Kevin frowned at her.

'You speak with the arrogance of a beautiful woman who's probably never had to,' he said sharply. 'You could afford to be a little more understanding.'

'Oh, I *understand*.' All Fen's laughter was gone. 'I understand unrequited love to be an indulgence that consumes useful energy. A form of masochism that blurs sensible judgement. And sensible judgement should only be confused by mutual love. That's what I believe, anyhow.' She smiled at herself, then her voice rose, lighter. 'Look at Tom, now. He's another one with Idle's problems. All his silly blondes fall in love with him, cling to him like leeches. And you know why? Because he's too kind to shake them off harshly, and above all because he *listens* to them. The great way to guard yourself against a woman's love is never to listen to her. Especially,' she added, 'if she's inclined to reveal some of her most private feelings.' This time she smiled at Kevin. He smiled back.

'Must remember,' he said.

'What's got into you ?' asked Tom. 'Can't think why you get so cross about something that hardly concerns you.'

Fen flushed.

'The general indignity of women concerns me,' she said. 'The way they go throwing themselves at men's feet in the humiliating fashion they do these days. Women's Lib doesn't advocate women should make fools of themselves. And heavens, how they do that! For a start they confuse sensitive listening for sensitive understanding. Most of the time, listening has nothing to do with loving.'

Emily slid herself down from the dresser and went to stand by her mother's chair. She didn't precisely understand what was being said, only that Fen seemed to feel strongly about something, and the others seemed not to comprehend her. Frequently, Emily knew, Fen was misunderstood. She was a critical woman (equally of herself as of others) and spared no one her judgement. On the occasions she made her more critical observations of her friends, she did so in a flinty voice and with brittle eyes: she was often funny, speaking with malice but not malevolence, although frequently her audience confused this relish with bitchery. They called her merciless, sometimes, then were confused by the fierce and generous appraisals she would make, the next moment, about the same people. At times, even Idle, her most loyal supporter, would claim she had gone too far, and defend the subject of her attack. When this happened, almost against her will, Fen would become more outrageous, daring people to disagree with her, to attack her. Emily, if she was present, unable to understand the facts of the situation, understood her mother's mood, her mother's sense of defiant aloneness in a crowd. Then, as now, she would go to her. Simply stand by her, a silent supporter.

Idle returned from the telephone.

'Marcia Burrows,' he announced, 'is willing to start any time. She'll come down here, sometimes, to save my going to London.'

Fen's previous gaiety, which had only briefly been shadowed by her small outburst, returned at once.

'Oh, darling! When?' she asked. 'When can she come? I want to watch the whole thing from the beginning this time. What's she like? Blonde? How many days will it take her?'

'You're absurd.' Idle was smiling. He liked being teased. 'You exaggerate so. I haven't seen her myself, but I hear she's quite presentable. Perhaps, when she isn't typing for me' – he twinkled in the direction of Tom – 'she might come in useful to you.'

Tom smiled.

'She might indeed. I'm on the look out. I lost Gillian – the one the week before last, you remember? – to Proust. My fault for having introduced her.' He stood up, picked up his mug of tea from the table. 'The very name, Marcia Burrows, arouses all sorts of possibilities as a matter of fact. Don't you think so, Kevin? Marcia Burrows. "The very name is like a bell upon mine ears."' Fen began to giggle. Tom put on his John Gielgud voice. '"Marcia Burrows? That is the question . . ."'

Kevin, too, rose from his chair.

'Let me be the one to propose the toast to her future.'

Fen and Idle both held up their mugs of tea.

'The toast,' said Fen.

'The toast,' said Idle, near her.

'To Marcia Burrows. To the possibility of her and Tom.'

All four grown-ups took a gulp at the remains of their tea.

Emily looked up at them. They were quite solemn. They had forgotten her, and she wanted to ask what this strange ceremony was about. It seemed to be almost a child's game, and yet they were all old. And what, then, caused the sudden laughter? For they were all now laughing, sharing some mutual and incomprehensible joke about the absence of Marcia Burrows, a woman none of them knew. Was it simply her name that was so funny?

Emily said the name over to herself. Marcia Burrows. No smile came to her lips, but the pattern of the words, like the pattern of some poems, or songs, or names of foreign countries or Greek gods or wild flowers, engraved themselves in a special way on her mind, so that in future the very mentioning of the name would, she knew, bring about a feeling of strange familiarity.

Much later, when she was in bed, Uncle Tom came up to say goodnight. He sat beside her, legs crossed. She appreciated that, in his extraordinarily busy life, he always seemed to have time for her.

'Are you liking it better here than in London?' he asked. He only asked questions if he really wanted to know the answer. Also, he would never ask any such question in public. Emily liked to answer him as seriously as he asked.

'Yes,' she said, 'much more. Much.'

'Why?'

This time Emily thought for longer. Eventually she said, 'I like the mornings here, and the afternoons and the evenings. And I like it because when I'm at school I can imagine what Mama and Papa are doing. I know Mama's in the house or garden, cooking or reading or something. And I know even if Papa is in London for the day, when I'm coming home from school, he'll be getting on a train to come home too. Except of course when he's abroad, and I wish he didn't have to go away so much.' She paused. 'I like to be able to imagine what they're doing, where they are, all the time I'm not with them. I could never do that in London. Then I like it all being more untidy than it was in London, and the animals and eating in the kitchen and having the garden and everything You know, all that sort of thing.'

'I know,' said Uncle Tom.

'I expect we'll be in this house for ever and ever, don't you think? As Mama and Papa seem to love it too.'

'I can see no reason why not,' said Tom. He went over to the window. 'There's a goldcrest in the apple tree. Do you know what a goldcrest looks like?'

'Of course,' said Emily. Then she added: 'Uncle Tom, do you think, you and Marcia Burrows?'

He kept his back to her but she knew he was smiling.

'I dare say,' he said. 'I'm apparently vulnerable to almost any pretty woman.'

'What does that mean?'

'That means I can never say no to a girl who wants me to say yes.'

Emily giggled.

'You mean love them?'

'Not exactly. More, cheer them up.'

'Perhaps you'll be able to cheer up Marcia Burrows.'

'Perhaps.'

'Why did you all think it's such a funny name?'

'Because it is, really, isn't it? Absurd. Some names are almost entirely responsible for their owners' characters, I've always thought.' He turned away from the window, faced Emily. The sky was thinly dark behind him. 'Any moment there'll be swallows gathering on those telephone wires, you know. Something you never see in London. Doesn't the church clock keep you awake?'

'Heavens, no. I'm used to it.' Wriggling down in the bed Emily felt quite proud, used to the clock already. 'But I expect you all will, tonight. I've never heard such a noise.'

Tom stood listening.

'When grown-ups laugh they make even more noise than children,' he said.

'Still,' said Emily, 'I don't mind.' She meant: I like it. I like these sort of days: the sun, the loft, Uncle Tom turning up surprisingly, the warmth of the kitchen, the knowing there's tomorrow. But her eyes were shut. She couldn't be bothered to say the words out loud. She watched them merge in her head, bright, peaceful shapes, shimmering in the wake of the downstairs laughter that still reached her, even here beneath the sheets. Drowsily, she realised this was the kind of happiness you could put out your hand and touch, and store away for winter nights, and no one could take it away.

Two

One of those nebulous autumn mornings: no sun, mist colours, the shape of trees printed palely on a pale sky: cobwebs, still, on the hips and haws. Emily and Wolf, her new friend, squatted by the banks of a small stream that ran through a watery meadow behind the house. Their thick jerseys, their gumboots, and their hair glistened with a drizzle so fine it only became perceptible when netting something solid. Wolf tested the depth of the stream with a stick.

Emily had met Wolf some weeks ago in the churchyard. He was kneeling by a gravestone scraping at the ancient crusts of granite with a penknife. Beside him was a jam-jar half full of snails. Emily, to whom the graveyard was a place of some awe (walking through it was a private act of slight courage) and to whom snails were a positive horror, was impressed. She watched him in silence for some moments. With the point of his knife he stripped off a small slither of moss and tossed it into the jar. He looked up, uncurious, at Emily, then returned to his work. Something about his concentration – nose almost touching the moss – gave the impression that he was enjoying his silent audience. But so great was his renewed effort that it spent itself unexpectedly soon. Emily was surprised when he broke the absolute quiet.

'Will you come up the church tower with me?' he asked. 'I can never find anyone who likes going up church towers.'

Half-way up the spiral stone staircase Wolf became aware of a restless tingling in his limbs, a new energy, a nameless pleasure. Here at last was someone to come with him. She might not like it, but at least she was there. Exuberant, he climbed fast to the top, leaving Emily far behind. When she joined him on the roof he felt the slouch of anti-climax uncomfortable within him. Perhaps it wasn't so great after all. Emily didn't look that impressed. They stood far apart. Diffident, Wolf pointed out the chimneys of his house.

'We're quite high up, really,' he said, knowing he lacked conviction. Emily made a quick decision not to observe that it was nothing compared with the Eiffel Tower, where she'd once been, and agreed. They listened to the crows for a while, then went back to the stairs. There, with a gallantry that surprised him, Wolf suggested he should go down first, knowing every step as well as he did, in case Emily should fall.

Since then they had become devoted companions, meeting for as long and as often as they could. Now, they were in the act of carrying out a major plan they had been plotting for some time.

Wolf took from his pocket a small, steamed up polythene bag and untied it. Gently he lifted out a bunch of watercress. Some of the leaves, limp for all their careful preservation, were freckled with small spots of congealed gravy.

'Wolf!' Emily sighed. 'Where on earth?'

'They had steak last night,' Wolf said. 'I sneaked it off the plate afterwards.'

'Golly gumdrops,' said Emily, quietly. She never ceased to be impressed by Wolf's ingenuity and imagination and, further, by his apparent casualness in face of his own achievement. For several days they had been planning to plant a watercress bed which would bring them riches, employment, and perhaps even a certain fame in the village. The stream was the ideal location: the procuring of the first bunch of watercress the only problem. They had immediately rejected the idea of a packet of seeds because of the slow time they would take to grow. Waiting for fruition, they just might become bored by the idea, or just might have established some other kind of project which would then leave them no time for the watercress. What they desired was instant results and immediate occupation of a serious nature. And in anticipation of their end product they were not idle. Emily had collected a variety of old paper bags and carefully printed on them the words *Wolfem's Watercress Farm: directors Emily Harris and Wolf Beasly*. Underneath she had drawn a single watercress leaf which might also have been a four-leaf clover, as Wolf observantly pointed out. It should bring them good luck, he said. Meantime he spent two weeks' pocket money on cash books in which he neatly went through the pages marking them *Paid In* and *Paid Out*. But still they found no watercress in the village shop or even the local town. Its scarcity was frustrating, but to have requested grown-up help would have spoilt the surprise the mature watercress farm was going to be. As the days went by their hopes wavered a little. Alternative plans were even being considered to ward off increasing dejection. And then their lucky break: the sudden steak for dinner in Wolf's house.

'Will the gravy matter?' asked Emily.

'Course not, silly.' Wolf was rarely scathing to Emily, whom he respected in many ways, but the fragility of his plan combined with the excitement of having at last acquired the watercress made him nervous this morning, irritable.

'What exactly are you going to do?'

Wolf rubbed his short, freckled nose, thinking. Now the time had come he was not entirely clear.

'I'll put it in a ring of stones so that the current can't carry it downstream. Why, can you think of a better plan?'

'No.' Emily was positive.

'Let's find some stones, then.'

They sank their hands into the icy water, wetting their sleeves, their fingers prying through the soft cold mud for large stones. They drew several on to the bank and made their choice. Then, in the shallowest water, Wolf formed a small circle of the stones. Carefully, he placed the bunch of watercress in the middle, splaying out the leaves like flowers in a vase. When he withdrew his hands the moving water of the stream bent the leaves a little, but not enough to dislodge them. Wolf sat back on the bank, contemplating. He ran a muddy hand through his long, matted hair, gold on top from last summer's sun, sable coloured beneath.

'How exactly will it grow?' Emily was careful to eliminate any note of doubt from her voice. She appreciated Wolf knew best about things like biology. She hoped he wouldn't think her silly, wanting to know the facts.

'Well.' Wolf's arms were folded over his knees. He shrugged, moving his whole body. 'I expect it'll just germinate, in the water, somehow.' He paused for a moment. 'On the other hand, it might not. In fact we shouldn't be surprised if it doesn't.'

'No,' said Emily.

'We'll be able to tell in a few days, I should think.' He looked down at the bunch of watercress still firmly lodged in the stones, the gravy washed from its leaves now. 'As a matter of fact, I think it's flourishing.' Emily followed his gaze, to see if she could see what he meant.

'What's flourishing?' she asked eventually. Wolf released his knees from his arms and lazily stretched a leg over the stream. He slowly lowered it till the water whirled round the heel of his boot.

'According to my stepmother, everything's flourishing. "How are you, darling?" people say – (he imitated a woman's high voice) – "flourishing," she says. She tells people my father's business is flourishing and the new puppies are flourishing and the rhodedendrums are flourishing.' Emily giggled. 'Flourishing,' added Wolf, 'is anything that flourishes.'

He stood up, suddenly, legs planted astride in the stream, muddying the water.

'What shall we do now?' asked Emily. 'I mean there's no point in just sitting watching it, waiting for it to spread.'

'Absolutely not,' said Wolf, 'especially as I don't think it's going to. In fact I'm sure it's not.' He kicked at the circle of stones, tipping the bunch of watercress on to its side. A few stray leaves escaped their enclosure and sailed downstream to clearer waters. Wolf bent down and picked up the remains of the bunch. With a violent gesture he threw it in the same direction, then kicked at the stones, splitting their carefully constructed circle. Then he stepped back on to the bank, not looking at Emily.

'Why did you do that?' she asked. A sense of failure too soon: the wet wool of her sleeves stung her wrists.

'Anyone could see it wasn't going to work. We didn't think it out well enough.' He didn't sound as if he much cared: he never minded if things went wrong. It gave him a chance to replace the idea with a new one.

'I suppose. But what shall I do with all those bags?'

'They'll come in useful some time. You could put your *sewing* in them.'

'That's being sarcastic. I don't sew.'

'Perhaps you'll learn.' He sounded quite cross – with himself more than with Emily. A pause between them. Emily felt no inclination to take offence. A new project, perhaps, would cheer him up. She asked him what they should do next. Wolf folded his arms, stared into the haze. In the moments while he waited for inspiration he went a great distance from Emily. His silence was formidable, not to be interrupted. Emily waited patiently.

'A bird table, I think,' he said at last. 'A really interesting bird table that would amuse the birds.'

'*That's* a good idea' Emily was glad now they had abandoned the watercress, really glad, not just pretending to herself.

'A kind of *Gothic* bird table.' Wolf made an elaborate design in the air with his wet muddy hand. Emily wondered the meaning of the word Gothic, but decided to ask another question instead.

'How would we carpenter it all ourselves?'

'We wouldn't. We'll get an old wooden tray from somewhere and then make turrets and towers out of old boxes and papier mâché. Then we'll stick them to the tray. They'll have doorways and windows and everything, and *private* places for the birds to go. It'll be more of a bird town, really.' Wolf looked at Emily's excited face. She deserved some gesture of generosity to make up for his past unkindness about the paper bags. 'You can paint all the buildings,' he said, warm, magnanimous. 'You're good at that.'

The luminous field and shadowy trees shimmered in Emily's delight at the prospect. She jumped up and pulled at Wolf's sleeve.

'Come on. Let's start straight away.' Her enthusiasm was always rewarding, but Wolf had learnt from watching his father that to keep up an appearance of coolness in face of female exuberance was the wisest reaction.

'Hang on a bit,' he said, shaking her off, still thinking. 'And then we'll get my father to nail the whole thing to a pole.'

'Whose garden shall we put it in? Yours or mine?' So far Emily had never been to Wolf's house: so far there had been no invitation.

'Yours. And I dare say your mother'd give us bits of bacon and stuff.'

'What about your stepmother?'

'Oh, her. She never has leftover bits. She's so careful.' With one accord, they began to walk slowly up the slope of the field towards the house.

'Why have you got a stepmother anyhow? What happened to your mother?'

'She died.'

'Did she?'

'Having me.' Wolf jerked his head in the air so that his tousled hair moved all in one bundle. 'So my father married Coral. *Coral.* What a name. Can you imagine?'

'What's she like ?'

A crowd of epithets came to Wolf's mind. He picked those that would seem least disloyal.

'She's not too bad, I suppose. Very fussy though. Always patting the cushions when you get up, and telling you to wipe your feet. She makes those dried flower arrangement things and sells them in London. Once, she sewed blue bows all over the bedspread, but my father was furious and made her take them off. She cried quite a lot.'

'Gosh,' said Emily. The drizzle, harder, more visible now, was cold on her face.

'Also,' said Wolf, struggling with his conscience, 'she's not very brainy. She can't begin to help me with my homework.' One day, when he knew Emily better, he might tell her a lot more.

As they reached the garden they saw Fen driving the Morris shooting brake through the front gate. There was a woman in the passenger seat beside her.

'I forgot to say,' said Emily, 'my father's got some secretary woman coming down for the weekend to help him.' She and Wolf and Fen had had many a happy Saturday lunch together: it wouldn't be the same with the addition of a strange woman. Emily hoped Wolf wouldn't be cross.

'We can always mob her up if she turns out to be an old faggot,' said Wolf, and Emily, relieved, giggled.

Fen, getting out of the car, opened her arms to her daughter. Emily ran towards her. She was suddenly in a whirling hug, spinning round, her feet off the ground tangled in Fen's long flowery wool skirt; she smelt the brief familiar smell of stephanotis on warm skin, heard the squeak of a rubber boot as her mother slipped in a puddle, laughing. Firm ground again: Fen's hands still on her shoulders, steadying her, looking at her.

'You're *soaked*, you nut. And Wolf too.'

'We've been in the stream.'

'Go and get changed quickly. But first come and meet Miss Burrows. She's coming to work for Papa.'

Miss Burrows walked stiffly towards Emily, spindly legs beneath a longish brown mackintosh. On her head she wore one of those folding plastic rain hats that spends most of its life compressed into a remarkably small plastic sheaf and is often described by its owners as handy. Through its pleats, only half unfurled, Emily could see Miss Burrows' hair was a similar colour to the mist: a small clump of it had escaped the cap's protection at her temples and seemed to be of the same indeterminate texture as the drizzle that swept about them. Miss Burrows extended her hand to Emily.

'How do you do,' said Emily.

'What a cold hand,' said Miss Burrows. Her own was small, warm, papery.

'And this is Wolf who lives nearby.' Fen was pushing him to Miss Burrows. He shook hands silently, suddenly subdued by the suitable smile that the woman arranged on her face.

'And now you two hurry up and wash before lunch.' Fen was sweeping towards the house, a child each side of her, anxious to get things going. She didn't look back at the reticent figure that followed her.

Upstairs, his arms deep in warm brown water that left interesting different ridges round the basin as it moved, Wolf said:

'I should think she could do with a going over.'

'You bet,' said Emily, snatching the soap from him and lacing it through her fingers.

'Still, to be fair, we'd better just give her a chance.'

'Just one chance, then.'

'And after that,' said Wolf, taking the clean white towel and hand printing it with perfect brown finger marks, 'and after that, well, she better be warned. Anything could happen to her.'

The children came slowly down the stairs that led into the kitchen, observing Miss Burrows before she saw them. She stood stiffly by the dresser, pretending to lean against it, holding a small glass of sherry in one hand. A thin, pale, rigid figure, she gave the appearance of slipping from youth directly into old age. Youth was not as yet entirely gone from her: its signs were in the narrowness of her hips and the soft curve of her powdered neck – but it was on the decline. Two deep clefts of real old age appeared between her light eyebrows, and the skimpiness of her frazzled grey hair reminded Emily of her grandmother. She wore a neat grey worsted skirt and a pale blue blouse, intricately tucked and pleated, and fastened with a dozen pearly buttons. In the kitchen full of warm colours, bright fruits, flames, vivid wools, Fen's energetic shape radiating from stove to sink, hands full of steaming casseroles, Miss Burrows was an almost pathetic contrast. It was as if she was a brittle manifestation of the dark climate outside: a pale stalagmite of mist broken off and set in an alien place. She stood, aware of her own incongruity, waiting to melt.

'Boo,' said Wolf mildly, uncertain how his joke would be received. Miss Burrows, against her will, gave a small start.

'Oh,' she said, 'it's you.' She laughed slightly, showing teeth that matched the pearl buttons.

'Come on and sit down.' Fen was terse. Her voice said they had to behave. Miss Burrows dabbed at her bag, a very neat square navy blue bag with a gilt M stuck in one corner. She took out a small gold-mesh sack of chocolate coins wrapped in gold paper.

'I've brought something for the child,' she said, handing it to Emily. 'I'm sorry' – to Wolf – 'I didn't know there were two of you.'

Wolf was abashed by her decency. Then, on a sudden inspiration, he pulled out her chair for her, contrite. It was the kind of extravagantly polite gesture that caused Coral overwhelming pleasure. If it worked on her, it was worth trying on Miss Burrows.

It succeeded. Smiling, charmed, she sat at the table opposite Emily. She looked vaguely about her, for a napkin perhaps. Then, quickly, acclimatising herself to this unfamiliar atmosphere in which serviettes represented laughable formality, she let her hands fall into repose on her lap.

While Fen dished out plates of stew and baked potatoes Emily studied Marcia Burrows' face. In close-up it had a soft, hairy bloom, like that of an English peach. It was heavily powdered with old-fashioned loose white powder and the flat mouth, neatly lipsticked with unshining plum, was minutely jagged at the edges due to the powdery down that encroached on the lips. The eyes were grey, bland, stamped into the face one at

28

a time rather than as a pair. They were younger than the mouth, unclouded with powder, clasped by nice wrinkles when she smiled. Emily couldn't stop looking. She wondered, when it came to the gravy of the stew, if the lipstick would run. She stared, waiting.

'*Eat*, for heaven's sake.' Fen was kicking her under the table. Miss Burrows, aware of the friction she caused, did her best to make a go of things.

'And do you two go to school together?' she asked neither child in particular. Wolf, always bored by such questions but feeling he still owed Miss Burrows a small measure of politeness, dismissed it as quickly as he could.

'No, but we met, and this afternoon we're going to make a very complicated sort of bird table. In fact, I wouldn't be at all surprised if the zoo didn't want to copy our idea.'

'It's going to be more of a bird town, you said,' Emily corrected him.

'Well, yes, a bird town with streets and squares and things. And a hotel, where they can fly in and out of the windows for the night. And a restaurant with a bag of peanuts outside.' He enjoyed being carried away by his own flights of fantasy.

'Goodness me,' said Miss Burrows. Fen spluttered over a mouthful of stew. Emily giggled. Everyone but Miss Burrows felt easier.

For her the time had come when, in her napkinless state, she was acutely ill at ease. She either had to search in her handbag for her paper handkerchief, thus underlining Fen's oversight, or let the threads of lipstick, loosened by the greasy stew, course down her chin, veining it with red. In her predicament she paused, digging at a carrot, dreading to eat it for fear of increasing the wild state of her mouth. Had she not then been rescued by Wolf, she did not know what polite action she would have taken. But he, remarkable child (as she then immediately assumed him to be) suddenly sensed her despair, and decided it a propitious moment to exert a little of the tact he knew he possessed.

'Mrs Harris,' he said, his eyes purposefully avoiding Miss Burrows' chin, 'hadn't we all better have napkins with this stew?'

As Fen jumped up to get them, all apologies, so great a spasm of relief surged through Miss Burrows that it revealed itself in a blue-mauve flush on her pale cheeks. The next problem, therefore, so minor in comparison to the last one that it made her quite lighthearted, was how to disguise this blush. But this time the solution came to her quickly. Between courses – if there was to be a sweet, that was – she would make use of her compact.

Once again, she was saved by an outside force. The telephone rang. Fen left the room to answer it. Miss Burrows took her plastic tortoiseshell compact from her bag, and set about tidying up the dreadful redness of her chin. Then she patted the small floury puff over her cheeks and nose, rubbing at the hard edges of the bluish flush as if by so doing she could exchange them for a more admirable pink She was closely watched by Emily and Wolf.

'Why do you wear that stuff?' Emily asked.

Miss Burrows widened her eyes at herself in the mirror. Wolf thought that if they stayed that shape they would be remarkable. People would say: *What big eyes you've got, Miss Burrows.*

'When I was a little girl like you I had lovely skin, fresh as a daisy. Nothing but soap and water in those days.' She sighed, and snapped her compact shut. 'But when we get older our skin gets tireder and not so – well, not so pretty. So we have to go on making them look as nice as we can with make-up, don't we?' She smiled and braved the carrot with the fork in her right hand, while in her left she clutched the secure-making clump of her paper napkin. 'I expect even your Mummy, with her lovely skin, wears a little something, sometimes.'

'She doesn't,' said Emily. 'Except at night. Then she puts stuff on her eyes. She lets me put it on for dressing up.'

Miss Burrows fluttered her own pale lashes.

'Unfortunately I'm allergic to mascara. I'm afraid that's one thing I've never been able to wear.'

30

Wolf was leaning forward, hunching his shoulders against the table.

'I think you've got nice eyes, anyhow, with nothing on them,' he said suddenly.

'So do I.'

'Oh thank you.' Miss Burrows felt the rising heat of the blue blush again. Strange how two children could be so unnerving.

'Actually,' Wolf went on, boldened by his successful flattery, 'I've been thinking, and I can't imagine what sort of place you come from.'

'How do you mean?' Miss Burrows shifted a little in her seat.

'Well, I mean, where do you live?'

'I have what they call a little terrace house near Olympia. But my family comes from Edinburgh.'

'What's your house like?' Emily asked.

'Well, how can one describe one's own house?' With all this talking Miss Burrows wondered if she would have managed to finish her stew before Mrs Harris came back. She didn't like to be the only one left eating. 'It's a very manageable little house. One bedroom and a bathroom upstairs, a nice sitting room and kitchen downstairs. Then out at the back there's a small court-yard, no bigger than a pocket handkerchief, really. But I like to call it my garden.' She smiled. 'I put out crumbs for the sparrows in the winter, not that there are many sparrows in the Olympia district. And next summer I'm going to try my hand at planting a tub of geraniums. But I'm rather afraid I haven't very green fingers.'

'And do you live there all alone?' Wolf rather liked the sound of her house.

'Quite alone, yes.'

'No brothers or sisters?'

'Two sisters, but they're in Edinburgh. Married sisters,' she added.

'Heavens,' said Emily, 'that must be lonely.'

'Oh no. I have my work. I'm kept very busy. In fact sometimes I hardly have a moment to myself.' She sounded quite brusque.

'What do you do when you *do* have a moment to yourself?' Miss Burrows turned to Wolf, a little suspicious. But the child wasn't merely being polite. His face was intent with curiosity. She would answer this one last question.

'Well, what does anybody do? I go for a stroll in Holland Park – it's lovely there in the Spring. Or I read my library book or do a little shopping, or go to the Odeon in Kensington if there's something I want to see.'

Nothing else immediately came to mind.

'Nothing very different from anybody else,' she said.

Fen came back into the room fast, glowing, smiling, the gold of her shirt reflecting up into the brown-gold of her face. She began to sweep away the plates, apologising for her absence.

'Who was that on the telephone?' Emily was still resentful of people ringing her mother up, though here the calls were far less frequent than they had been in London.

Fen laughed. 'Nosey. You wait till people start ringing you up. You'll hate it if I ask you who it was each time.'

'I won't,' said Emily.

'You wait,' said Fen. She brought a bowl of trifle to the table, its custard top encrusted with an extravagance of silver balls. 'They all came out of the tube in a rush,' she explained. 'I tried to put them back, but I couldn't.' The children laughed.

'It looks delicious: I've always loved a trifle,' said Miss Burrows, entering into the spirit of the thing, and half-stifled her own delighted laugh with her paper napkin.

Idle arrived back just as they were finishing lunch. As always, he seemed huge in the kitchen. He carried a large brief-case and bundles of papers: he looked tired. His silver hair and the velvet collar of his dark coat glowed with the damp. Emily threw herself upon him, smelling station platforms and dark, city cold.

'Why didn't you come earlier?'

'I missed the train.' He smiled wearily. 'I'm sorry, Em.'

'But this afternoon you can help Wolf and me make things for our bird table.'

'Bird town,' Wolf corrected. 'It's even going to have a Piccadilly Circus.'

'Maybe later,' said Idle. 'But first I've got to work with Miss Burrows. There's a lot to do.' He tapped his papers, avoiding the disappointment on Emily's face. 'But I tell you what . . .' He paused. 'I tell you what. After tea we'll light the bonfire we made in the orchard. We won't wait till tomorrow. It'll be more fun, when it's getting dark, than in the morning. How about that?'

'Yes . . .' Emily had a high-pitched scream in moments of delight.

Fen cleared a place for Idle, but he had no wish to eat. Just coffee. He seemed melancholy, preoccupied. He watched the children play noughts and crosses on a paper napkin. The fire took the chill off his clothes. Eventually, he told his news.

'They want me in Africa again on Monday.' Emily, looking up from the game, watched his eyes on Fen's face. Miss Burrows gave a little cough.

'Oh, darling, not again. Not so soon.'

Fen was behind his chair, arms round his neck, head bent over his for a moment. Miss Burrows looked away.

'I'm afraid so.'

'How long for, this time ?'

'Three or four weeks, I should think.'

Fen straightened herself up, her body a little slacker, less alert than it had been before the news. She sighed.

'That means you're only with us tomorrow. And we had so many things planned for next week.'

'I know. I'm sorry.'

'You're away too much, Papa,' said Emily.

'One day I'll retire, then I'll be here all the time. Promise.'

'Will you send me a postcard every single day?'

'Every single day, starting with the airport.' Emily smiled. That would be some compensation. At school her father's post-cards from distant lands earned her a certain notoriety.

'*My* father,' said Wolf, 'wouldn't *think* of sending a postcard, if he ever went away, that is. He hasn't got that sort of mind.' Idle raised his eyebrows and glanced at Fen. She responded with the flicker of a smile. 'On the other hand, Coral, my stepmother, only has to go as far as Paris, and she comes back with a whole load of rubbishy old souvenirs nobody could possibly want. She brings me back hideous badges to sew on my anorak. I'd rather die.' Wolf knew when he had an audience with him. Their laughter stimulated him, spurred him to think of a dozen more anecdotes to keep them happy. He could have gone on all afternoon. But Idle had to go off to his study to work with Miss Burrows. Fen began to peel large yellow apples from the orchard, in preparation for apple jelly: she had mastered the art of slicing off their skins in one unbroken snake. There was a certain satisfaction watching the cold yellow ribbons try to curl back into their old apple shape as they dropped into the sink. Wolf and Emily brought out paints and cardboard boxes and pots of glue. They cleared a space among the chaos on the table and began their work. Soon, from Idle's study, came the monotonous tap of the typewriter.

The church clock struck six. In the orchard, an unplanned gathering of apple and pear trees between the barn and the meadow that sloped down to the stream, the mists of the day gathered more thickly among the greenish branches, flaky with grey lichen. For all Fen's fruit gathering, the grass was scattered with large, chrome apples, many of them seared with soft brown patches, and smelling faintly of rot in the dew. In a clearing among the trees Idle and the children had raked a pile of dead branches and leaves. At the time they had collected them these multicoloured leaves had been crisp, frail, newly dropped from trees on a sharp dry day. Now, affected by their wait in the damp, they had become soft and floppy, unresilient in their pile. But the mists had not managed to suck from them their testudinarious colours. In the smoke-colour of the air, they made a still-life bonfire of unflickering flames.

Emily came out of the house, Wolf close behind her. She shivered: the inarticulate pleasure of knowing that after the adventure into this ghostly mist was over, the warm life of the kitchen awaited their return. Fen and Idle followed, Fen in a long football scarf and a torn old mackintosh, Idle still in his incongruous London coat, its small velvet collar turned up round his neck. He carried a box of matches, looked pessimistic.

'I think it may be too damp after all.' He kicked at the pile of soggy leaves.

'Oh, *no*, Mr Harris. Leave it to me.' Wolf took his own box of matches from his pocket. He was a proud and able Cub.

'Leave it to Wolf, Papa. He can do anything like that.' Confidence made her warm, warm and shivery. She watched Wolf bend down, light a match. Its flame sizzled out. He tried again, and a third time, with no luck. Fen and Idle remained silent, side by side. Wolf stood up.

'Tell you what, Emily, you go into the house and get some fire-lighters and dry kindling,' suggested Idle.

'All right.'

'That's hardly the point of a bonfire,' said Fen.

'It'll never get going, otherwise. Go on, Em. You might as well.' Idle gave his daughter an affectionate shove. She ran off, brought back a bundle of dry sticks and a couple of firelighters. Then, it was easy. Two small flames, hesitant at first, wavered up, grasped at the apple branches, ate into the soft lichen, and increased their strength. There was a creak of twigs, a movement among the dead leaves. A spire of smoke rose into the mist: smoke, mist, smoke, blue unfurling into grey. The two became indistinguishable.

As the flames increased and cast their heat, Idle, Fen, Wolf and Emily stood back a little, staring, solemn, transfixed as people are by a peaceful fire, fascinated by the slight element of danger. In one pocket of her duffle coat Emily's fingers twiddled with a piece of fluff, and she thought that when she grew up she'd have a dress the colour of a flame. Fire colour was her best colour. Not orange, but definite fire colour which sometimes surprised you with a twinge of purple or green or blue, but was never pure orange. She wondered if Wolf would bother to say, as he nearly always did when they were by the kitchen fire, that if you looked hard enough you could see dragons in the flames. Of course there weren't dragons: anyone knew that. But he liked to tease her. The first time he'd said it, very seriously, she looked at him wondering how to react. If she'd agreed, or even pretended she could see dragons, he might think she was silly. If she contradicted him he might not like it either. In the end she said nothing, just laughed. Luckily, Wolf laughed too, and explained it was the kind of rubbish Coral expected him to believe. Now, when he referred to dragons, he imitated Coral's voice and it always made them both laugh. A pretty soppy woman Coral must be, really. She'd like to meet her one day.

And one day she wouldn't mind seeing another real fire, like the one they'd seen in Norfolk a few summer holidays ago. They had come across the fire driving along a small country lane, and were held up in the congealed traffic for a long time while more and more fire engines, sirens screaming, raced to the flames with their useless hoses. A whole forest was on fire. The tall black evergreens had melted into one gigantic tree of flames: they were all bent to one side in the wind, flapping at the edge of the evening sky, much taller than the tallest fire-engine ladder, and puffing huge clouds of black smoke at the poor firemen. In the back seat of the car, Emily had whispered to Angelica that it was the most exciting thing she'd ever seen, and Angelica had said: how could you say that? But then Angelica never liked anything out of control. She missed all sorts of excitements, Angelica did, what with not liking strong winds or Big Dippers or dogs that jumped up at you. She would have got on very nicely with Coral, from what Wolf said.

Wolf nudged her. He was squinting up at the darkening starless sky. He gave a little leap towards the fire, making his fingers into the shape of a nozzle, and letting off a hissing water sound from his mouth.

'Careful,' said Fen.

'Wouldn't mind being a fire fighter,' said Wolf.

'You want to be something different every day.' Emily was half scornful, half admiring.

'Not true. I'd still like to have a traction engine museum, but I could be a part-time fire fighter as well.'

Emily bent down and picked up a couple of apples from the grass by her feet. She threw them gently to the edge of the fire. Wolf wasn't the only one to have ideas.

'Roast apples,' she said. 'They'll have a lovely smell.'

'They'll burn,' said Fen. Her eyes were staring far past the apples, a tiny flame in each pupil, a bigger flame flickering on each cheek.

'Bet they won't,' said Emily.

'Bet they will,' said Idle. He put his hand on the back of Fen's neck, tugging at the clump of hair tied back with a scarlet ribbon, which fell over her scarf. But his gesture didn't stop her eyes staring. He said he'd go and get a drink to christen the orchard, and wandered away.

He came back with two glasses of champagne on a tray, and two bottles of coke. This made Fen laugh. She laughed a lot, a marvellous sound, bending over at the waist, teeth glinting. When she straightened up again, she took one of the glasses in her hand and smiled as she sipped, trying to control herself.

'You're mad,' she said to Idle. The champagne made a small arc of gold bubbles beneath her nose.

'Probably,' said Idle.

'It's my champagne era,' said Fen. 'You're always suddenly producing champagne as if you were a millionaire.' Idle laughed, then, too, and kissed her on the forehead.

'What's so funny between them?' Wolf whispered to Emily.

'Grown-up jokes.'

'Barmy.'

'Barmy old grown-ups.'

'Coral can only laugh through one side of her mouth. The other side's paralysed.'

Emily giggled, making the coke in her straw bubble noisily. Her knees, unprotected by boots and coat, felt hot.

'Here, Em. Come and have a try.' Fen was bending down, pushing away the long dewy grass, offering her glass.

'Hate the stuff.'

'Come on. Don't be silly.' Near to her mother, Emily took the chilly glass. Through the wood smoke she could smell stephanotis. She sipped cautiously: her parents loved giggled.

'Run and fetch the rest of the bottle for Mama and me, then,' said Idle. 'It's on the kitchen table.'

Inside, the warmth was quite different, Emily noticed at once. Still and flat rather than glowing and shifting, like it was round the fire. No cold edges. She intended to hurry back, and snatched at the icy bottle on the table. Then she became aware of the ceaseless, muffled tap of the typewriter. Miss Burrows! Poor thing: she must still be working.

Still holding the bottle, Emily crept to the study door. Quietly, she turned the handle. She had no idea what she would say if Miss Burrows saw her, but some instinct made her continue to push the door.

Miss Burrows was sitting, back to her and very upright, at her father's desk. A pale blue cardigan, to match her blouse, hung over the back of her chair. Like the blouse, it had pearl buttons. At the back of her head her greyish hair watching her try their drinks. It made her sneeze. She ended in a neat roll. If she let it all fall down, Emily thought, the back of her head, at least, would look much younger.

Although Emily made no noise, Miss Burrows suddenly stopped typing and turned round.

'Oh, hello dear,' she said. 'It's you.'

'We're all outside by the bonfire.' Emily leant on the doorpost. 'It's lovely out there.'

'Mind you don't catch cold. It's getting quite chilly these evenings.'

'It's lovely and warm round the fire. Why don't you come? Mama and Papa are drinking this' – she held up the bottle – 'and having all sorts of jokes.'

'I've got all this to get through, dear,' said Miss Burrows, indicating a huge pile of letters at her side. 'But it's very nice of you to think of it all the same.' She slipped a new piece of paper into the typewriter.

Emily paused. 'Do come,' she said. 'Just for a bit. I'll get you a glass. Would you like a straw?'

'Well.' Miss Burrows smiled and slipped her cardigan over her shoulders, feeling the draught from the door. 'Why do you want me to come?'

Emily paused again.

'I just do.' Miss Burrows rubbed her hands together, kneading the knuckles.

'Very well,' she said, standing up, 'since you're so insistent, just for a moment. I could do with a few minutes' break.'

'Goody. Come on, then.' Emily darted away ahead of her. While she fetched another glass from the kitchen Miss Burrows put on her long brown mackintosh. They went together into the garden. In silence they walked side by side towards the orchard. The figures of Fen, Idle and Wolf were silhouettes against the untidy triangle of flames. Miss Burrows sniffed the air.

'What a lovely smell. I haven't smelt anything like that for years.'

'My roast apples,' said Emily. 'You might have them for dinner.'

Fen and Idle welcomed Miss Burrows: said what a good idea it was of Emily's to have brought her. Idle poured her a quarter glass of champagne – all she would allow as alcohol didn't agree with her, she said. Glass in hand, she stood a little away from the others, further from the fire.

Emily found a stick and tried to poke one of her apples out of the ashes. It fell apart as she did so, a charred grey ball brightened with just one stripe of unburnt yellow. Fen said she would get some potatoes instead. Miss Burrows smiled gently in the firelight. Wolf ran to fetch the potatoes. Emily whispered to her mother she felt quite sorry for Miss Burrows. Out loud, she asked if they could cook sausages on sticks, as well. Idle threw more branches on to the fire, shifting its position. The flames pointed higher into the night air, cold now, and Miss Burrows, shivering, sipped politely at her iced champagne.

*

39

Emily's bedroom was at the top of the house, the attic floor. Its small window overlooked part of the garden, the barn – whose thatched roof sagged under its weight of old moss, and badly needed renewing – and the solid tower of the church. The room itself, with its sloping ceilings and low-slung white-washed beams, hazardous to grown-ups, was a delight to children. The walls were papered with a small pink ragwort, old-fashioned and pale. Emily had pinned some of her own paintings to the beams – crowds of brightly coloured, active children all with their names and ages floating above their heads. In a tooth-mug on the pine chest was a sprig of bronzed beech leaves and a couple of white chrysanthemums – Fen's doing: this autumn every room, every corner of the house was lit by a random clump of flowers and leaves. The arm chair by the window was piled with old stuffed animals whose heyday was long since past, but whom out of loyalty Emily could not bear to throw away. Only her two special bears – quite opposite characters, one tall and skinny, one fat and fluffy, both called Patrick – were allowed on her bed. On the table beside the bed were a pile of E. Nesbit books, an alarm clock with a funny luminous face that Idle had given her when she was six, and an old bottle of scent, with just a trace of scent left on its bottom, that had once belonged to Fen.

A rod of early sun shone directly on to Emily's bed, waking her. She stirred, rubbed her eyes. The small square of the sky in the window was bright blue, the mists of yesterday all gone. She pulled the two Patricks into bed with her, their early morning treat. They were too big to sleep there all night. Their fur was cold, the inside of the bed soft and warm.

It was Sunday, Emily remembered. She liked everything about Sunday except for the church bells. No school, an hour or so in her parents' room before they got up, roast beef, a whole afternoon with Wolf. There was just one thing wrong with this Sunday, though: it was Papa's last day.

Remembering this, she reached under her bed for her sketch block and Caran d'Ache felt pens: she would do him a picture to take to Africa. Guy Fawkes' Night: a bonfire bigger than theirs last night, with an ugly guy and people with smiling red faces. She started off with the flames, brilliant on the white paper. It was almost irresistible not to do the best bits first.

Emily drew carefully: Idle liked her drawings. When she gave them to him on special occasions, such as going abroad, he would take them with him, folded small in his wallet. Then when he came home, he would add them to the collection in the special drawer in his desk. Sometimes they would get the whole lot out and laugh at Emily's earliest attempts, things she had done when she was three and four. Idle himself had never been able to draw, so he couldn't help her. Fen was the best one at that. Only last week she'd shown Emily an easy way to draw a horse: draw box shapes first, then fill in the curves. But Idle used to write poetry he said. Once, he'd had something published in his school magazine, and a magazine he worked for when he was at Oxford published several of his poems. He'd show them to Emily one day, he promised, when she was older. She probably wouldn't like them much at the moment: they were about love and people running away from each other and things like that. He still wrote poems, sometimes, for Emily: she kept them locked up in her writing case and only showed them to her three best friends, who thought they were very good. Once Idle had sent her a letter addressing the envelope in rhyme: it had taken five days to arrive from Scotland because, she supposed, all the postmen had taken so long to read it. Emily was proud of her father: he gave the best advice she knew, about anything you asked. This morning she must remember to have a word with him about her play. He'd never been in the theatre himself, like Uncle Tom, but he seemed to know about everything.

When Emily had finished the drawing she crept downstairs to the kitchen. It had become a routine, in this house, to take up her parents' Sunday breakfast on a tray. Every week they seemed surprised and pleased. Every week the planning of this surprise was an especial pleasure.

The kitchen itself was warm, but the tiles cold under Emily's bare feet. Sun glittered on the draining board and through a pot of chives. There was a faint smell of last night's garlic, and apples, and the smoke from Fen's French cigarettes. The kettle was still warm: Fen must have been down to fetch coffee and the papers already. Emily went to the larder, to the shelf crammed with different cereals. Which should she choose for them this Sunday? Every week, whatever her choice, Fen and Idle were marvellously pleased. Taking her time, enjoying the luxury of the decision, Emily reached for two packets. Then she went to the fridge to fetch the jug of cream. She opened and shut the door quickly, so that only for a moment was she struck by the cold blast of refrigerated air.

Fen and Idle's room, beneath Emily's, was a disorganised clutter. Books were piled everywhere, between faded antique jugs full of dried wheat and pheasant feathers, between dull brass oil lamps that had never worked. Long necklaces of jet, coral, amethyst and quartz, entangled with crude plastic beads, hung down the sides of the dressing-table mirror, whose dull silver glass was speckled with black spots. On the chaise-longue under the window lay a muddle of Fen's bright clothes: velvets, soft leathers, wools rich with cornflowers and emerald leaves. The low window ledge itself was crowded with pots of flowers: rust crysanthemums mixed with orange and scarlet poppies made of tissue paper, their petals fulgent in the sunlight, their layered shadows very precise, very pale.

Fen and Idle were propped up in bed against a mass of untidy pillows: Idle in his Londonish pyjamas, almost uncreased blue silk, Fen in a Victorian nightdress of cream cotton, lace ruffles up to her neck. She leant against Idle, her turbulent dark hair awry on his shoulder. Both read papers: both held mugs of coffee.

Emily, so silent at the door with her tray they didn't notice her, thought that if they had an oval gold frame round them they would look like her grandmother's miniature paintings of olden days people. She didn't want to disturb them, in a way, but she needed their attention. She could wait no longer.

'Mama and Papa?'

'Em!'

'You were so quiet!'

'How long have you been standing there?'

'Only a minute.'

They put down their mugs and papers simultaneously. Emily went to the bed and gave them the tray. Fen took the Grape Nuts and kissed her.

'I was just hoping for Grape Nuts, this morning. You are a clever one to have known.'

Idle dug his spoon into the Rice Krispies swamped in thick cream.

'Just what I wanted, too,' he said.

Emily curled herself upon the warm, faded old patchwork quilt that covered the bed, watching her parents eat. She gave a small, comfortable shiver, thinking of the day ahead: all of them helping her and Wolf with the bird town. Of the weeks ahead: snow and holly, and stockings she would fill for them at Christmas with painted fir cones they were making at school, tangerines, and paperbacks from the bottom of the piles so that they wouldn't remember, and think they were new.

When they had finished eating, Fen and Idle put down their plates and shifted nearer together. Idle had his arm round Fen, now. His fingers stroked her ruffled shoulder. She was warm, deliquescent, beautiful against him.

'Wolf says his father and Coral his stepmother sleep in separate beds,' said Emily.

'Do they?' Fen sounded curiously sleepy.

'Wolf says Coral says it's because she doesn't like being so near his father's snoring.'

Idle smiled at his daughter.

'Tell you what, Em. Why don't you go and see how Miss Burrows is? Find out what she'd like for breakfast. Perhaps you could even take it up for her.'

'That's a good idea.' Fen nodded, eyes shut, her hand climbing to Idle's shoulder.

'All right. Then I'll come back.'

She climbed off her parents' bed, went to the door. In the lesser light of the passage outside their room, the impression of her parents, so close together, became a shining banner in her mind.

Miss Burrows' brown mackintosh covered her narrow bed. She must have been cold in the night. The room, sunless on this side of the house, wasn't warm. Emily crept over to the window and shut it.

The noise woke Miss Burrows. She sat up quickly, surprised and confused by Emily's presence.

'Sorry if I woke you.'

'Oh, dear, have I overslept? What's the time?'

Miss Burrows pulled a crochet dressing-jacket from under the sheets and arranged it round her bony white shoulders. Unlike Fen's, they looked as if they would be uncomfortable to grasp.

'It isn't very late. I just came to see if you'd like me to bring you any breakfast.'

'Breakfast? Well, at home I just manage with a cup of tea and a Ryvita.' Miss Burrows touched her hair. The roll had come undone. It hung, thinly, to her shoulders. Stripped of its powder, her face shone palely. Her mouth, without its dark lipstick, was a gentle curve, a little tight at the edges.

'I'll get it for you,' said Emily, 'if you like.'

'Oh, don't bother. I can easily come down.'

'No, really.'

'Very well.' In face of such kindness Miss Burrows shivered again. 'I'm not used to such spoiling,' she said.

When Emily returned to her parents' room an hour later, the previous mood had disappeared. The bed was a choppy stretch of newspapers, empty mugs, dressing gowns. Fen was in it alone, reading. Totally absorbed, as she always was by the printed word, Emily didn't disturb her as she crossed to the bathroom, where Idle was shaving. His face was a snowman's face of soap: just two black holes for eyes. Emily sat in her usual position on the edge of the bath.

'I suppose that's why Miss Burrows is so thin,' she said. 'She only eats Ryvita for breakfast.'

'I dare say that's it.' Idle braced his chin in the mirror and made a skilful track of skin across it with his razor.

'I think she's *too* thin.' Emily paused. She liked to prolong these Sunday morning conversations with her father. Steam rose up from the emerald water he had already run in the bath. There was a smell of pine essence. 'Thinking of green,' Emily went on, 'I was wondering. Do you think in my next play, the children should wear green or brown? I mean, they do live in a wood. In a tree house, you know.'

Idle fidgeted his razor round the crevices of his nose. His decisions on such subjects were always very serious. Even now, Emily was sometimes shy of asking him: but each time she remembered she need not have been, so thoughtful was he in his answers. He'd been a great help over her last play, *Daisy, Daisy*, the first one she'd actually written down. It had been performed in the drawing room in London, two friends and herself in the cast. Her own part had been Mrs Lemonheart, a fussy old woman with a bun. She'd stuffed her jersey with a cushion to make a huge bosom and stomach, rouged her cheeks and spoken in a gruff voice. And Idle hadn't known it was her till the very end, when she let down her hair at the third bow. He swore positively he hadn't known it was her: he thought she was just the producer and writer. It was amazing. He was the best ever audience, Idle.

'Couldn't you dye their clothes greeny brown, like camouflage?' Idle suggested. 'That way, when they were being chased through the forest, like you said, they'd stand a better chance of not being seen.'

'Oh, Papa, that *is* a good idea. I'll do that. Wolf'll like that because it'll be more boyish, camouflage. It'll be the first play he's ever been in, you know. He's going to be the murderer.'

'A child murderer?'

'I read about one in the papers the other day. Oh, he'll get punished all right.'

Idle raised his grey brows, cracking the drying soap on his forehead.

'And will you help us a bit with our bird town this afternoon?'

'Of course.'

'I wish you weren't going away.'

'So do I. Still, it won't be for too long.' Idle cleared his mouth of soap. He came over to her, bunched his lips through the circle of white froth, and kissed Emily on the forehead. He was expert at doing this, without getting the soap on her. Emily tried to smile. She supposed it wouldn't be that long, really.

Three

'Emily Harris, please. Come forward, Emily.'

From the shadows of the hall, Miss Neal's bossy voice. Up on the stage Emily stepped from the security of the line of Children by the Manger. She had been chosen to speak a solo poem. A double-edged honour, fear and excitement combined to make one of her knees tremble. She took a deep breath. You should always start off with a deep breath, Miss Neal said. Like opera singers. Otherwise, how would your voice carry?

"'The *Star* that shone on Bethlehem,'" Emily began.

"'Its bright, ethereal *ray*,

"To guide three kings and show to them

"The place where Jesus *lay*,

"*Shine* on your path all through the year –'"

"'*Your* path,'" Miss Neal interrupted. 'How many times have I told you, Emily? You've got to get this message to the parents, down here in the audience. *Their* path, you must make them feel. Try again.'

Emily tried again.

'And once more, shall we?'

Behind her, Emily could hear Sandra Buckle tittering. Someone else shifted, restless. She sensed Miss Neal's patience, limited by her keenness, was expiring. If she didn't get it right this time, someone else would be asked to replace her. She'd have to tell Papa, who'd known for weeks she was going to do it, they'd changed their minds.

Deep breath. Dig toes into polished wooden floor boards that were becoming warm under her cold feet.

"'. . . Shine on *your* path all through the year'" – Emily gritted her back teeth –

"'To *guide*, to *com*fort and to cheer and *bless* you'" (sweetly)

"'On'" (pause, smile) "'your'" (pause, smile) "'way'" . . . (smile, smile, smile).

'That's it. There we are at last.'

Miss Neal snapped together her small hands. They remained locked, like a clip. Together they bounced up and down, eager. Miss Neal was blessed with a superlative enthusiasm, every Christmas, for producing a Nativity Play whose strength and tradition were built on lack of change. Over the years these plays had achieved a considerable reputation in the locality. The consistently high standard of fine emotion with which the school wrung from its version of the Christmas story had been known to cause tears in the most cynical father's eye. More, one old girl Virgin Mary had had a screen test with MGM (outcome still unknown), and possibly as a result of attributes developed since her Virgin days. But still. It was common knowledge that anyone who rose above an extra in the Nativity Play was certain of a solid beginning in the real theatrical world, should she choose a histrionic life.

'Now.' On her particularly small feet Miss Neal trotted across the hall to the pianist, Miss Curtis, whose only resemblance to Beethoven was her deafness. '"The Holly and the Ivy," girls,' said Miss Neal. She took a slight hop in Miss Curtis's direction, unclipping her hands and posing them above her head to indicate she held a garland of imaginary ivy. 'And the ivy, dear,' she mouthed. The partnership had been a long one: Miss Curtis understood.

The children descended the squeaky steps from the platform and formed themselves into two rings of eight. Miss Curtis, eyes alert for signals, played a chord, bending her whole body forward. She was always moved by Christmas carols, no matter how often she played them.

'Ready! Eight to the right, then. Begin.'

The music, the singing, the skipping began. Emily concentrated hard. This was her best time of the week at school. The excitement of rehearsals was like climbing a slow hill to Christmas, being quite positive of all the glitter at the top. Besides, she loved dancing and acting. This year, being a junior, she had to put up with her minor role as Child by the Manger, although the solo verse gave her a slight taste of the stardom to come if she tried very hard. If she tried very hard there was even a chance, next year, she would be a Dancing Angel. The year after, perhaps, a Speaking Shepherd, followed by a Singing Wise Man. (Each Wise Man had to sing a whole solo verse walking up the hall through the audience. If ever she was one, she'd keep her fingers crossed to be Myrrh.) After that . . . Well, she didn't like to think about it, really. Her hands might get too big, or her nose. And according to Jennifer Plomley, this year's Mary, it was quite a drag keeping still all that time, staring unblinking into the strong torchlight shining from the manger which, from the audience's point of view, was merely a gentle halo.

Meantime, she skipped well. Glancing critically about her, she realised this was no small talent. Although she herself found it easy, there were plainly others who didn't: those to whom music, rhythm, beat, had no meaning, couldn't take you up and down with them like bossy waves. Also, some of her friends didn't seem to realise they were dancing on their heels instead of on their toes. Joanna, for instance, so good at maths, would never be more than a hopeless skipper, heavy and out of time. No wonder Miss Neal was forced to keep on and on with the sing-song chant . . . 'And *up* with those heads. *Up* with those knees. And *stop* a moment. . . .'

A heavy silence. The girls unclasped their sweaty hands and Miss Neal gave a small pat to her hairnet. She looked pained. She could look pained very quickly in rehearsals. Considering the torment they caused her, it was noble of her to struggle on, really, trying to keep the reputation flying. Sometimes she almost despaired, squeezing performances from the mostly untalented lumps she was faced with year after year. But she had to go on trying, of course, for the sake of the school. Gently, now: 'Girls, what have I been telling you ever since rehearsals began? Anybody?'

Silence. A few guilty wriggles. Girl with plaits raised her arm: anything to alleviate Miss Neal's pain quickly.

'To point our toes, Miss Neal.'

'To point our toes, Belinda. Exactly.' More silence: scathing, uncomfortable. '*And have we been pointing our toes?*'

'No, Miss Neal.' The dancers in unison, with far greater alacrity than they ever managed to begin a carol. Emily stifled a smile. Papa would think all this funny if he was a fly on the wall. He'd think it quite funny, even, on the day, when they'd all learnt to skip quite well. He'd be bound to ask a lot of questions: he always did. 'Who was that fat girl opposite you? Why did they leave out verse three?'

Oh, she'd have to explain it all. Not many weeks, now. They'd laugh about it going home in the car (snow, perhaps). Mama saying it was marvellous because she always liked all school plays, you could be sure of that. Maybe Wolf'd come too, if she warned him it wasn't going to be too soppy. Tonight she'd tell Papa about how she couldn't get the 'your path' bit right, with Sandra giggling away behind her like that. It was all Sandra's fault. It was difficult enough to concentrate, knowing all those eyes were behind you, seeing your knee tremble, without anyone giggling as well. Very unfair, really, she'd tell Papa. He'd understand. Except he was in Africa. What a nuisance. She wished, suddenly, he would come home. Tonight.

'One more try, then, girls? Garlands up. Miss Curtis? Are you ready?'

Emily pointed her toe.

Arriving back home a couple of hours later, Emily found the gloom of the November afternoon had eaten into the kitchen.

No lights, just a smouldering fire. Fen was curled up in the arm-chair smoking, a full ashtray by her side, a fat paperback – *Lytton Strachey, a Biography* – on her knee. She didn't stir when Emily came into the room. Her heavy eyes moved slowly.

'Hello, Em. How did it go ?'

'Oh, all right.' Emily flung off her satchel. It wasn't the moment to tell. Besides, now the danger had passed, it didn't seem so important. Often, by the time Emily got back from school, events she had meant to recount had lost all their zest. Suddenly they weren't even worth telling.

'Why's it so dark in here?' she asked. The dark oppressed her.

'I was just sitting reading. Couldn't be bothered to get up.'

'I'll do it for you.' Emily went round the room lighting the lamps. From the record player next door came the sound of Dory Previn. Fen and Emily listened to her melancholy voice.

> *Whatever you give me*
> *I'll take it as it comes*
> *Discarding self-pity*
> *I'll manage with crumbs . . .*

The room was pooled with light and shadows now. Better. Fen bent down to throw a log on the fire.

'I've brought you an invitation to the play, Mama.' Emily searched in her satchel for the stiff white card. *Mr and Mrs Harris*, it said at the top, in her own neatest hand writing. They'd spent the whole of English Language doing the invitations this morning. Emily had embellished hers with two holly leaves and three scarlet berries in the top left-hand corner. Each berry was chipped into with a small highlight, as Fen had shown her how to do years ago. Highlights brought things like apples, and balloons, and berries to life.

Emily handed her mother the card. Fen looked at the date.

'I don't absolutely guarantee Papa will be back in time,' she said.

'Oh, Mama. Why ever not?'

'You know what he's like. He has to work so hard. They always keep him so long.'

'That's not fair.' Emily's voice was tight.

'I know. Still, he might make it. Just don't hope too much. – Come on, cheer up! Here.' She patted the broad arm of her chair. Emily went and sat down. 'Don't look like that. It's a smashing invitation. Your best writing. Let's pin it up somewhere, shall we?'

'All right.'

'I'll get a drawing pin in a minute. Guess what?'

'What?'

'I've made you banana pudding for supper.' Fen's voice was light and cheerful.

'Thank you.' Subdued answer. Emily turned on the arm of the chair. 'Do you sometimes miss Papa?'

'Of course. Always. But being gloomy won't bring him back any faster.'

'I've made a chart of the days. I'm going to cross them off every evening till he comes back.'

'Well, why don't we pin up your chart, too? Then we can see how we're getting on.'

'All right.' Pause. 'Can Wolf come round for supper tonight?'

'Not tonight, I don't think.'

'Why? He hasn't been for two days.'

'Because Kevin's coming.'

'Who's Kevin?'

'You know, that tall man who came here with Uncle Tom the other day.'

'Oh yes. He kept wanting to tell me a story about a hippo-potamus who was a photographer. I didn't want to hear it, actually.' Emily sniffed. 'Why's he coming?'

'Because he's in Oxford. On his way back to London. He rang to ask if he could drop in for a drink. I felt I had to ask him for supper, really. It would have been mean not to, wouldn't it?'

'Suppose so. But why does it mean Wolf can't come?'

'I just think it would be better if he came tomorrow instead.

Why don't you go and ring him up right now and ask him if he can come tomorrow ?'

Fen rose from the chair. She stood in front of the fire, warming her hands and her back, stretching. A muddle of long strings of pale beads hung round her neck to below her waist. She sighed, patient.

'Go on,' she said.

'I wanted him to come today,' said Emily. 'Why should grown-ups' plans always work if children's don't?'

Fen laughed.

'Grown-ups' plans don't work out just as often as children's,' she said. 'They go wrong even more often, perhaps.'

'Doesn't seem like it.'

'Oh, stop sulking, Em.'

'It's all very well for you.'

'Emily!' Fen's voice rose, sharp. Emily held her mother's eye.

'You don't seem to mind about Papa being away!' A shout of defiance. A silence.

'Of course I do, darling. Don't be ridiculous.' Fen's voice soft and low, now.

'Oh, Mama.' Emily was by the fire too, in her mother's arms, head against the warm silk of Fen's breasts, the beads biting into her cheeks. 'I wanted him to come to the play.'

'I expect he will. We'll write and tell him he must, shall we?' Fen rocked, moving Emily with her. 'Look, stop crying. You're wetting my shirt!'

'Sorry.' Emily moved back. Fen's face was liquid through the tears, distorted like a reflection in a fairground funny mirror. They looked at each other. Both laughed at once.

'Go and wash your face, Em, before Kevin comes. You can have supper with us if you like.'

Emily shook her head, sniffing.

'I must do my homework.'

'Whatever you like. Go on, now. Cold water's best.'

Smiling like that, all the earlier bleakness had fled from Fen's eyes. Emily left the room. The short burst of tears had left her strangely weak. But already, as she climbed the stairs, she felt the strength return. By the time the cold tap was running, hope and calm were fully restored.

Kevin's presence, anywhere, was dominating. This was partly to do with his physical size and magnificence – a huge man with wide stooping shoulders, large hands, long legs. His fine head was wild with black untidy hair: accipitral eyes pranced under thick black brows. When he smiled his face would halt for a moment before laughter, but his usual expression was one of constant, restless curiosity. His face was never at peace. He exuded energy. His limbs were springs that he moved with a strange, swift coordination, so that even the most domestic gesture – reaching for something on a high shelf, perhaps – had a style so powerful that unconsciously he drew attention to himself. It was this grace, this dominating presence on the stage that had brought him remarkable success as an actor very quickly. But his histrionic career was short lived. The life hadn't appealed to him. Nervous tension made him physically sick, and an uncomfortable feeling that it had all been too easy dulled the flame within him that fed off challenge. After two years in the theatre he left to buy his electronics factory in the north.

That first evening Kevin came to dinner with Fen he seemed tired, but unrelaxed. In a vast, much-darned jersey he lay back in the armchair, one leg jogging up and down, immensely long fingers drumming the arms of the chair.

His eyes scoured Fen who stirred something over the stove. She was tense, alert, smiling occasionally as Kevin described some play he had seen the night before. He spoke so fast, in his enthusiasm, she had to listen with extraordinary care.

Upstairs, on the floor of her mother's room, Emily could hear their voices. She was struggling with an essay on the Sahara Desert which, due to her instinctive lack of concentration in Geography, for several weeks she had been quite positive was in Australia. The fact that today she had realised her mistake, and had been most firmly assured by her teacher that it was in Africa, made the essay doubly hard. She had a very clear picture of Australia in her mind: *that* she could have written about for at least two pages – easy. Africa was more elusive. Sun, there was, of course and copper mines and diamonds. But its general shape was hazy. What on earth could she say about the silly old Sahara? *I want half a page, at least*, Mrs Prism had said, her teeth skittering about her mouth in an unruly fashion because they hadn't been fitted very well. Emily chewed her yellow pencil. In half an hour all she had done was to draw a huge sun, and they hadn't even been told to do a picture. If *she* ever had to have false teeth she'd get the dentist to try out all sorts of different shapes and sizes till she found which ones suited her best, and she most certainly wouldn't take them out at night.

Once, going into her grandmother's bedroom early in the morning, she had found a smile of plastic teeth sprouting from their beds of bright pink gums and clenched together in a glass of water. She had screamed (she was only very young at the time). Her grandmother, waking up, had screamed too, a blathery sound coming from her own naked beige gums. She had reached out for the glass, but in her confusion knocked it over. The water spilt like urine down the sheets. The teeth slipped out on to the table, falling into a terrible grimace. Aware of her own cowardice in face of her grandmother's dilemma, Emily had run from the room. She had several nightmares about teeth with independent lives after that, and later she wrote a story about a ghost smile that ran clacking up the stairs of a haunted house and gave people terrible frights. *The Sahara Desert*, she wrote, *is definitely in Africa.*

Half an hour later she screwed a full stop into the page. She had written eighty-three words, big writing, not too many facts, but some original thoughts on how it might feel if you were lost in all that sand. She stood up, feeling hungry. Four fish fingers and some chocolate biscuits she'd like, now. She went downstairs.

Kevin sprang up from his chair as soon as he saw her, an electric reaction, pouncing upon her with a great welcome.

Emily remained cool, noticing the mud on his boots, and two bottles of red wine on the table. Kevin set about uncorking them, questioning her all the while.

'Finished your homework?'

'Yes.'

'What was it?'

'An essay on the Sahara Desert.'

'Never been there myself.'

Emily paused.

'Papa has,' she said. Fen glanced at her. 'Except it was when I was so young I don't really remember what he told me about it.'

'There are some photographs of camels in one of his drawers in the study, if they'd help,' said Fen. She was very calm.

'It's all right, thanks. I've finished.'

'And what else are you learning about?' Kevin was pouring the wine into glass beer mugs from the dresser. He filled them. Emily shrugged.

'Oh, about Felix Mendelssohn.'

'*Felix* Mendelssohn?' Kevin sounded as if he'd never heard the composer's Christian name before. He took a deep gulp of the wine and ran a hand through his riotous hair. 'Wasn't he the one who had a sister called Fanny who was so impressed by her brother's compositions that she learnt every one of them by heart?'

Emily paused. She had no idea. If it was true she'd be able to surprise Mr Losse with her extra piece of knowledge next lesson.

'That's right,' she said.

'Thought so. I used to like Mendelssohn. Got quite a few of his records. I could let you have one, if you like.' Emily watched his fingers fidgeting about with cigarettes and a steel lighter. She said nothing.

'That would be nice, Em, wouldn't it?' Fen turned from the frying pan of fish fingers to her daughter. Her eyes sparkled like they did sometimes when Idle came up with a good idea.

'Yes,' said Emily, quietly. And to Kevin: 'Thank you.'

They couldn't persuade her to eat with them. She took her

supper on a tray into the room with the television, asking if she could stay up till nine o'clock. She had some strange feeling that tonight her mother would grant almost any request, and indeed Fen agreed at once, adding that Emily could read in bed for ten minutes.

But when the time came Emily didn't feel like reading. She lay in the dark looking at the clouded moon outside her window. She thought of her mother at dinner, beautiful head cupped in her hands, laughing uproariously at some story Kevin was telling very fast – plate pushed back, forgetting to eat. She had looked up when Emily came in to say goodnight, and hugged her, and said Kevin was giving her too much wine. Kevin had kissed Emily too, ruffling her hair, making it all wild like his. She supposed he was quite nice, really. If he came again, perhaps she'd let him tell the story about the hippopotamus, if it would please him. All the same, it hadn't been the kind of evening she had hoped for: just her and Mama making sealing wax things for Christmas. She wondered if tomorrow there'd be a postcard from Papa – a picture of the Sahara Desert, even. *That* would be a squish on Miss Old Clicketty Teeth Prism all right. That would be funny. Emily pulled the two Patricks towards her. Somewhere miles up in the sky someone had turned out the moon.

Next morning at breakfast Fen was still in ebullient spirits. By nature she functioned lethargically in the mornings if she had slept well, but after a late or bad night a perverse energy came to her at dawn. She told Emily she had slept little and so had come down early to wash up. She had also baked a huge apple tart. The smell of warm pastry and apples, a lunchtime smell, made the kitchen a secure fortress against the frost outside.

'When on earth are just you and me going to eat all that?' asked Emily.

'Oh, I don't know.' Fen was marvellously careless. 'I just felt like *making* something.' She cupped her head in her hands again, as she had last night: smiled gaily at Emily as she had at Kevin. 'Surprise for you,' she said.

'What?'

'Three guesses.'

'Postcard from Papa?'

'Shut your eyes.'

When Emily opened them the card was on her plate. Mauve mountains in a blue sky. An elephant nearly as tall as a tree. *Went on a one-day safari in Kenya*, it said. *Nearly shot a lion. Made friends with a monkey who reminded me of Wolf. Showed your picture of the bonfire to a big-game hunter who wanted to keep it for his daughter. Of course I wouldn't let him. Much love, Papa.* Emily pouted.

'He's not working at all.'

'Oh, he is. Very hard. I had a letter.'

'When's he coming back?'

'Didn't say. Hurry up. You'll be late.'

Emily put the card in her satchel.

'Come with me to the end of the drive,' she said. This morning the short time with her mother had gone too fast. It sometimes did that, for no apparent reason. She needed a few more moments.

'Not this morning.'

'Why not?'

'It's too frosty.'

Emily followed her mother's glance out of the window to the silvered garden.

'You could put on your coat. Please.'

'No.' Fen was unusually firm. 'Go *on*, Em. You'll keep them waiting. There they are – hooting.' For a second, no more, her eyes were troubled. But she smiled as she dumped Emily's hat on her head, and kissed her.

Emily ran from the room. When she opened the front door sharp crystal air stung her face. Her first breath made a white balloon. She tried to catch it, to hold it for a moment like a bubble. But it quivered into nothingness as she raised her hand. Behind her, she could hear the telephone. It rang only twice. Then, her mother's laugh. It was infectious, somehow, that laughter. Smiling to herself, Emily ran across the frosty lawn to where Sandra Buckle's mother (a fat old thing *she* was, in a mink coat) hooted impatiently in her steamed-up car.

The only kind of magic Emily believed in was the magic of change. The transformation of normality to strangeness, due to a mood, or an addition of unfamiliar people, or a day of peculiarly violent weather, was an inexplicable phenomena. The kitchen, for instance (the room more than anywhere she liked to be), was a strangely magic place, vulnerable to disturbing changes. At its best, at its most normal, it was full of winter sun and firelight, cooking smells, an untidy jumble of brilliant colours. Fen would be its only other inhabitant, a vibrant thing whose sense of vitality gave life to the inanimate things around her. Sometimes, she would flop into the armchair, eyes shut, long flowery skirts swinging between her parted legs, and listen to Emily chatter about her day. Or they would listen to music. But even in Fen's tiredness there was vivacity. After a moment's relaxation some new thought would re-invigorate her. She'd be up instantly to chop or peel or mash, stoke the fire, or dance if the music was right, swirling about the room, an onion in her hand, laughing at her own exuberance.

Alone with Fen like that, the kitchen was normal. Should Idle appear, it shifted a little. The change was almost imperceptible, but quite definite. Then, it was Idle who occupied the dominant place in Fen's territory. For all the attention they extended to Emily, she was forced to see them through transparent bars. It was *their* kitchen, then. And for Emily all the colours dimmed, so privately it would have been impossible for anyone else to recognise or understand the fading of their tones.

On mercifully rare occasions the room became totally unrecognisable: as on the day Uncle Tom and Kevin arrived unexpectedly, spiriting away the familiar peace and quiet, and leaving restless signs of moved chairs and filled ashtrays behind them when they went. Last night, when Kevin had sat at Idle's place at the table, an instant reaction within her told Emily the magic had been at work. The kitchen was a sharper place, temporarily not hers: she resented its desertion.

But it never went for long. One thing she could rely upon was that its natural atmosphere would always be reconjured by Fen. It would always return. Her constant hope, the thing she looked forward to all day, was that when she arrived back from school no unforeseen spell should have changed the place, that normality was unshaken. The day that she received the postcard from her father was a good day at school, but she arrived home to be disappointed.

Fen's car was not there. Irritation. Why wasn't she there? Fear. Where was she?

Emily ran into the house. It was dusk, but no lights were on. In the kitchen the fire was almost out, the table was strangely tidy. Emily called out to Fen, her voice shrill. She was rewarded with the sound of footsteps overhead. Then an unfamiliar tread on the stairs. It was Mrs Charles, who came to clean the house three days a week. A middle-aged woman whose skin, in the greenish light, shone like gristle. Emily hardly knew her.

'Oh, there you are, dear,' said Mrs Charles. 'Don't look like that. Your mother's had to go to London. On business,' she added, in a mean voice, and lumbered her way into the room.

Mrs Charles was by nature an unhappy woman. Convinced she was a lifetime victim of bad luck (rather than actual hardship) she was full of constant wrath on this score. Indeed a kind of permanent indignation had settled upon her (you could tell this – something about her very stance – from a range of fifty yards) which she had not the slightest wish to abandon. It had become a habit. Extending into areas which in no way affected her own life – skinheads, Watergate, pornography – it richened her responses to almost any news. The fact that Mrs Harris had called upon her with a suggestion that was thoroughly inconvenient had ripened her afternoon. She had fortunately found the chance to get some of it off her chest to her next-door neighbour, and had muttered a good deal more to herself, which she wouldn't like to repeat, on the fifty-yard bicycle ride to the house. However, where children were concerned, nobody could accuse Mrs Charles of being anything but cooperative, no matter how great the inconvenience. If Mrs Harris had to go to London for the day (and Mrs Charles had always secretly judged her employer to be a flighty woman) then of course she would baby-sit. But it did seem to her, and her reactions to injustice were more spontaneous than most, that one of the great unfairnesses of the world was the way in which the stolid lower classes so often found themselves suffering from the irresponsible acts of the middle classes. So thinking, she swerved her sturdy jaw from side to side, indignation lending an impressive violence to the movement. Emily, slouched on a chair, thought she looked like a man in disguise.

'When's Mama coming back?' she asked.

'Later,' she said.

'But why's she *gone* to London?'

'Don't look to me for any answers, dear. I don't know what people do in London, do I? Now, come along. Take off your things, and I'll get you something to eat.'

Emily didn't move. Her arms and legs were heavy. She watched Mrs Charles turn on the light, then poke unskilfully at the fire. At her touch, the scarlet embers frizzled into grey.

'You could put on a log,' said Emily, dully.

Mrs Charles obediently threw on some wood, muttering.

'I don't know what they put in the coal, these days. Nothing burns. When I was a child, we had blazing fires. I remember, we always had a blazing fire in the grate. No trouble with the coal then. But it's like everything else, I suppose. Slipping standards. There's no quality for money any more. Even the elm trees have all got this disease, haven't they? Couldn't use them for logs, I wouldn't be surprised. It gets me down.'

'What do you think Mama might have gone to London for?' Emily persisted. Mrs Charles, upright in front of the fire now, lifted her skirt a little so that the backs of her knees should benefit from the pallid flame that began to hover round the logs. Here was a situation she'd have something to say about, later. It made her blood boil the way some people just came and went as they pleased, without a thought for their children. But it was up to her to be heroic. Otherwise, it might have a nasty effect on the child. For life.

'Don't you go worrying your head about your mother,' she said, 'She's got some very good reason for going, I shouldn't be surprised. The dentist, perhaps. Perhaps she had trouble with her teeth.' When put to the test, Mrs Charles could be quite imaginative. 'Or the bank. I know of a lot of people who have to go and see their bank managers.' This was something Mrs Charles had never been summoned to do herself – in her imagination such an interview was socially almost as exclusive as an invitation to Buckingham Palace. And as such important events outside her own experience inspired an uncontrollable envy, her voice took on the blighted tone common to those who consider themselves to be underprivileged in interesting ways. She hitched her skirts higher. 'Although they do say that getting too close to your bank manager can be a mixed blessing,' she added. When stricken with envy she was not without resources of consolation. Emily, watching her angry, working face, hated Mrs Charles. She hated her ugly body absorbing all the heat from the struggling fire: she hated her being there instead of her mother.

They spent a desolate evening. It remained cold. Mrs Charles finally inspired flames, but no warmth from the fire. Emily, having refused tea (Mrs Charles saw this to be a sign of stupidity rather than protest), struggled to read a chapter on William the Conqueror, and learnt by heart two new French verbs. It would have been a help to have repeated them out loud, but there was plainly no point in asking Mrs Charles to listen. For her part, having made the unselfish gesture of coming to the house, Mrs Charles decided against any further effort to enliven the hours. She was suffering from outrage about the quality of television. All three channels had conspired to put on programmes that held no appeal for her, and she switched impatiently from one to another. The noise of the ever-changing buttons, accompanied by threats of fury to the heads of each television station, made it difficult for Emily to concentrate on King William.

At eight the telephone rang. Its noise irritated Mrs Charles by interrupting a good commercial (the only decent things on the box, the ads). To her mind telephones should be kept for emergencies only. Crossly she stumped over to it, unsure what her telephone manner should be. The fact that it was Mrs Harris, not a strange voice – people mumbled so, on the telephone, that was another thing – gave her courage. She was determined to put up a good show. She knew what children could be, with their tales.

'Yes, Mrs Harris. All's well. Lovely. Yes, as good as gold. Well, we haven't had our supper yet, but we're going to. Would you like a little word?' She paused. 'Very well. I won't say a thing. I'll leave it to you to tell her.'

As soon as she reached the telephone Emily knew something was wrong. The brightness in her mother's voice was alarming.

'Sorry about today, Em. I had to rush up unexpectedly. I didn't know till after you'd left.'

'Why? What did you have to do in London?'

'Oh, a lot of boring things. You're all right, aren't you?'

'Yes.'

'Good.'

'Where are you now?'

'Still in London.'

'When are you coming back?' Pause. Emily felt her heart thumping very fast.

'Well, that's the thing. Look, it's like this, darling. I was asked to a party, and I said yes. I hoped you wouldn't mind. I thought you'd understand. I mean, I haven't been to a party or up to London for ages, have I?'

'No.' The word was stricken.

'And in fact it's good news for you in a way. It means you can go and spend the night with Wolf.'

'With Wolf?' That was quite a thought. A midnight feast, perhaps. But then she didn't know Coral or his father. Suddenly she didn't want to meet them.

'I've already rung Mrs Beasly and it's all arranged. She's coming to fetch you any minute. You'd like that, wouldn't you?'

'I suppose so.' Emily had no desire to disappoint her mother. She supposed it would have been mean to say no, I don't want to go. Not at all, not at all.

Fen chattered on then, relief in her voice, gay. She would be home in the morning, would fetch Emily from school herself. She might even bring her some small thing from London. She was longing to see her and hoped she really was happy with the plan, wasn't she? Yes, said Emily, she really was happy with the plan.

The conversation over, Mrs Charles grumbled for a while about having to pack Emily's night things. But Emily scarcely listened. Her heart was back to its normal rhythm, but her limbs felt dreary. She sat at the table turning the pages of her history book backwards and forwards, counting them. Where was her mother now? Why hadn't she asked? She liked to be able to imagine her at all times: she disliked the idea of knowing only that she was somewhere in the black void of London. Had she taken a special dress with her? Who would take care of her, at the party, if Papa wasn't there? A vision of Fen's face came to her, horribly clear: it was a laughing, happy face, smart London hair, piled up in curls; a filmy London dress that ended vaguely like a mermaid's tail. She spun around, dancing, and yet not seeming to move. Her eyes searched for someone. She wasn't *really* all right, in spite of the laughing.

The front door bell rang. Coral Beasly, neat in stiff tweeds, smelling of a sweet, cloying scent, was noisily cheerful. Wolf, she assured Emily, was delighted by the idea of the visit, and they were all going to have a lovely time. On the way down the black frosty path her gloved hand squeezed Emily's shoulder.

'Now cheer up,' she said. 'You know what Mummies are. You see, they do have to go away *sometimes*, don't they?' She sounded both smug and accusing. Emily tweaked her shoulder till the hand went away. Fen's face, still laughing, was still searching for

Papa, at the beastly old party somewhere a million miles away in London. Emily didn't answer.

The Beaslys' house could not have been more different from the Harrises'. Its tidy precision was claustrophobic. Detail had been thought out to the point of ridicule: picture frames the same blue as the sofa, the colour of the curtains reflected in the sub-urban arrangements of dried flowers. Magazines and newspapers laid out on a table were mere patterns, unread. The cat wasn't allowed on the rug in front of the fire. It was a house in which you could only feel at ease on tiptoe, in which appearances mat-tered, not life.

Its air of oppressive contrivance had its effect on Wolf. He was subdued as Emily had never seen him – embarrassed, it appeared, by his stepmother who made a hollow fuss of him, and at the same time asked him questions which she then answered herself for fear he should contradict her. Contrary to Coral's predictions, the evening did not turn out to be a lively one. Side by side at the clinical kitchen table, Wolf and Emily had a supper of nicely balanced proteins, then escaped to Wolf's room as soon as they could. There, for the first time with Wolf, Emily felt shy. They had been told by Coral to undress and get into bed, but they sat on the floor, surrounded by a swirl of electric trains, ill at ease. Wolf fiddled with them: they made quiet, buzzing noises, darted forward in short spurts, then stopped.

'Coral gave them to me,' he said. 'I've often told her I wasn't interested in trains, but she just said all boys like trains. Silly old cow. If I don't pretend to play with them at least once a week she gets tears in her eyes. One day I shall kick the whole lot to pieces and let her really cry.' Emily smiled.

'She doesn't seem too bad,' she said, 'but I think she smells funny.'

'That's nothing to what she smells like when people are coming to lunch or dinner. Everywhere she goes she leaves this awful stink behind her. You can't go into any room she's been into for at least an hour afterwards without feeling sick. I stay up here. I don't know how Dad stands it.' He kicked at a large train, derailing it. 'Anyway, what's your mother gone to London for?'

'Just a party.'

'I wish Coral would go up to London to parties and leave me and Dad in peace. You're lucky having such a nice young-look-ing mother who gets asked to parties. You're lucky having a real mother at all, as a matter of fact.'

'I know,' said Emily.

'In fact,' said Wolf, 'I'll tell you a secret, if you like. Only swear on your heart not to tell anyone.'

'Swear on my heart not to tell anyone.'

'Well, I wouldn't at all mind if Coral and my father got a divorce.'

Emily gasped.

'But how would that make it any better?' she asked. 'Just you and your father on your own? You sort of need a mother person around to cook and things.'

'Well, Dad could find another one, easy as anything. I bet you he could. And anyhow if he couldn't we'd be fine. Whenever Coral has been away we've had a smashing time, cooking sausages on the fire at tea-time for lunch, and not having any baths. That sort of thing. He's quite different when she's not there.'

Emily pulled her knees up under her chin, warmed by Wolf's confidences. She supposed, really, compared with him, she was quite lucky, even though Papa did have to go away so often. She could afford to be generous.

'I see what you mean,' she said, 'but perhaps she'll get better.'

'Oh no, not likely,' replied Wolf. 'She's getting much worse.' His face was very solemn, his voice quiet. Emily felt a great urge to help him.

'We could make her an apple pie bed, one day,' she said. 'And serve her right.'

Wolf's face revived. He laughed. It was an appealing idea. Also, an idea which wouldn't affect his father, as they slept in single beds. Happily, they began to plot, kicking at the trains as they did so, gently bashing them up, but not quite badly enough for Coral to notice.

Later, when they were both in bunk beds, Mr Beasly came to say goodnight – a pale, shaggy man with tired sandy eyes and narrow shoulders. He was friendly to Emily, affectionate to Wolf.

'Well, don't talk quite all night long, will you, old man?' He ruffled his son's hair.

'Won't you tell us a story, Dad? – Dad tells smashing stories about when he was a Japanese prisoner of war, don't you, Dad?' Wolf was proud.

'Not tonight, he doesn't, Wolfie.' Coral had slipped into the room. 'Daddy's got to have his supper, hasn't he? He's had a long day.' She was all over the place, tweaking the curtains across the window, retucking immaculately tucked beds.

'Another night,' said Mr Beasly, quietly.

'My father tells marvellous stories, too,' said Emily.

'Does he, dear?' Coral kissed Emily on the forehead.

Emily tried to control her grimace at the smell of the repulsive scent. 'Well, sleep tight. Mind the fleas don't bite.' She gave a small laugh. 'Come along, Gavin, or your soup will be cold.'

When they had gone Emily curled down into the narrow bed. The sheets were stiff and smelt of the laundry. She had forgotten the two Patricks: the bed felt naked without them. She looked round the room, lit clearly by the moon. The curtains were covered with pictures of trees with their names printed underneath. She thought they were the nicest things in the room. She didn't like the pictures of racing cars and old aeroplanes on the walls, and it was cold.

'You all right?' Wolf's voice came from the top bunk.

'Yes,' said Emily. There was nothing precisely wrong. Nothing she could tell Wolf about.

'She never lets Dad tell me stories at night. You'd think she was jealous or something.' Emily could hear him turning over in bed. 'If Dad married your mother, that would be quite good,' he said.

Emily thought about it.

'But then what about my father?'

'That's a point,' said Wolf. 'I suppose they're best together. Perhaps your mother's got a friend a bit like her who could marry Dad.'

'I could ask her, if you like,' said Emily.

'Ask her tomorrow,' said Wolf. And fell silent.

Emily had so much to ask her mother tomorrow. She began to count the hours till she came out of school. But halfway through she changed to counting all the different necklaces that lived on the side of Fen's mirror. The jewels and beads blurred in her imagination till they were no longer hanging, lifeless things, but flung out from Fen's neck, bright coloured stars as she danced and danced on a foggy floor.

Eventually, Emily slept.

Fen came back from London effervescent, full of energy. She brought Emily a packet of her favourite caramel lollipops. She told about the party in vivid detail, making Emily laugh. She said London was all right, just for a day, but she'd never live there again. She was pleased to be back. Very pleased. For her part, Emily experienced that pervading warmth of return that obliterates the hollow chill of past absence. She forgave her mother as unconsciously today as yesterday she had condemned her.

And at the weekend Uncle Tom came to stay, bringing with him a lymphatic blonde called Janie, and Kevin McCloud. Wolf spent most of the time at the house and was naturally drawn to Kevin, in whom he found a common interest in traction engines. In fact, Emily admitted to herself, she couldn't help agreeing with Wolf. Kevin wasn't at all bad. He spent the whole of Saturday afternoon helping them make a very elaborate tower – more fanciful by far than anything *they* had envisaged – for their bird town. He then went out to buy special glue and helped them stick the whole thing together. Uncle Tom, meanwhile, on whom Emily relied for surprising adventures on Saturday afternoons, disappeared with Janie for a rest. Apparently they were both very tired, though in Emily's judgement Uncle Tom looked his usual lively self. When they returned at tea time, it seemed that Janie, at least, had received no benefits from the sleep. She lay limp in the armchair, her occasional twitter reduced to total silence. Emily was scornful. No girl would ever get Uncle Tom that way: what he liked was to laugh with a woman, as he did with Fen: to find a woman in whom wit, curiosity, and enthusiasm matched his own. If Fen hadn't been his sister she would have been his ideal wife. Strange how his girls – and they changed almost weekly – all seemed to be beautiful but unrewarding, with impressive breasts but lesser brains. He spent so much time on them, too. He would explain to them in his mellifluous voice the difference between Keats and Byron, only to be rewarded with a vacuous nod and a look of loving adoration. Still, Emily didn't really mind, because at this rate it looked as if he wouldn't be married for years, and she herself had plans to be his wife. Always had had, for as long as she could remember. She had proposed to him once, a few years ago, at the end of a chapter of *Peter Pan*, when he had done Captain Hook's voice so well she had laughed till she found herself crying with love. Uncle Tom, not a moment's hesitation, said of course he would have waited for her, had it not been for the law. But this hardly deterred Emily. With a stalwart optimism she felt the law, whatever that was, was sure to change by the time she was old enough to marry Uncle Tom. Consequently, there was no unhappiness in her waiting.

Saturday evening, Wolf still with them, was a lively one. In comparison with the fatigued Janie, Fen was refulgent. Emily could never remember her looking younger, happier. She supposed it must be to do with lots of things: bravery about Papa being away; Uncle Tom's jokes, the wine they had had for lunch, and the warmth of the fire that protected them from the dark frost outside. There was music and laughter. Wolf did his imitation of a pop star on the kitchen table, much encouraged by the enthusiastic response. Emily imitated him, wiggling her hips with astonishing rhythm and skill.

'Sexy!' shouted Uncle Tom from the armchair. Janie was lying all over him, limp, her head on his shoulder. For a moment Fen whirled about the room in Kevin's arms, her head on one side, his cheek close to hers.

'Sexy!' shouted Wolf, still stomping on the table. Laughing, Fen and Kevin parted at once. At the same time Emily stopped dancing, too. She liked it better when her mother danced alone, flinging out her arms, like she sometimes did for Papa. And her own mood of wild dancing was suddenly over. The light in the kitchen trembled, and she was glad when Uncle Tom removed Janie from his lap and she was able to take her place.

Sunday morning, as was her custom, Emily came down early to fetch her mother's breakfast. On the way she met Kevin in the passage, dressed in pyjamas. He picked her up, gave her rigid body a friendly hug, and kissed her lightly on the nose. He explained he had taken the papers in to Uncle Tom and was now going to fetch some coffee for Fen. When Emily explained that was exactly *her* purpose, Kevin was most reasonable. In that case, he said, he'd go back to bed. Perhaps Emily would even bring him something, too? She watched him go down the passage. When he opened the door of the small room in which Marcia Burrows had slept so tidily, she had an instant's view of clothes all over the floor, but a barely ruffled bed.

Then she noticed Kevin had dropped his handkerchief. She picked it up, screwing it up in her hand. She would return it to him with his breakfast.

But later in the morning the handkerchief was still a bulge in the sleeve of her jersey. She wondered if anyone would notice, giving her the chance to say sorry, she had forgotten. But they didn't. And as the sun shone, and Wolf wasn't due for a while, she went out into the garden. She walked down the hill, cold crackling grass, to the stream. The water gurgled along quite fast. She watched it for a while. Then, bending down, she put in a finger. Icy. The handkerchief, she thought, would sail down-stream a long way before becoming waterlogged. She could watch it out of sight, then run along the bank and rescue it.

70

Emily pulled the white handkerchief from her sleeve. It was warm. She shook, cold. But, determined now, she threw it quickly. It spread a little, floated. Faster than she had expected, it spun away. Soon it was out of sight, round a bend, the way the watercress had gone.

Emily tried to move, to chase it, to carry out the next part of her plan. But her legs remained motionless. Then, with a sudden, nefarious joy, she found herself running back up the hill. She would tell Mama, sometime, explaining first she had done a very wicked thing. Well, perhaps if Kevin didn't notice, it would be better to say nothing. Or would it? She couldn't decide. Not for the moment, anyhow.

Four

*T*he northern town in which Kevin lived was suffering from a particularly bleak winter. The sun, when it occasionally shone, was unkind in its revelations of blackened stone, blackened trees, blackened moors beyond hills and dales of mean houses. It was unusually cold. People bowed their heads as they went about, not bothering with greetings in this raw air, aiming only to return to some kind of warmth. In the large house where Kevin lived – once belonging to a mill owner, converted now to flats – something had gone wrong with the boiler. While they waited for it to be repaired, the inhabitants lit small gas and electric fires. But their thin warmth stood no chance against the force of this kind of cold, re-echoed through the stones of the old house. Impatiently, they suffered.

The night Fen told Emily they were going to spend the week-end with Kevin in the north, Emily cried. She cried rarely: on this occasion she was unable to understand why she was racked by tears, unable to explain to her mother her melancholy reaction. Ordinarily, she was receptive to almost any suggestion of travel or a visit. Her reluctance to go north was nameless, but acute. Fen tried to encourage her.

'You'll see a new bit of England. We'll go up on the moors. It's beautiful there.'

'Why can't we just stay here?'

'Because –'

'I like it here.'

'I know you do. Of course you do. But think of Kevin, how awful it must be for him, up there so much of the time.'

'If it's awful for him, why will it be nice for us?'

Fen smiled, wiping away Emily's tears.

'Now, come on,' she said. 'You wouldn't want me to leave you behind, would you?'

'I wouldn't mind.' Emily sniffed. In the face of such a disagreeable choice, she felt helpless. 'I don't see why we have to care about Kevin so much.'

Fen hesitated.

'Well, we just do,' she said. 'I mean, he's a friend, isn't he?'

Emily felt too weak to resist further. Sometimes, she was unable to make herself clear, perhaps because she was not quite clear within herself. And children who were not positive, she had discovered, always lost battles. The chances were loaded against them. It was pretty unfair.

They travelled by train. Emily slept most of the way, her head leaning against her mother's shoulder, her cheek tickled by the fox fur collar that sparkled with damp from the station. The fur smelt good and the carriage was warm.

In sleep, the rhythm of the train rumbled through Emily's bones and she dreamt she was on a merry-go-round. In front of her, on a painted wooden horse with a wild gold mane, Fen rode side-saddle. Beyond Fen, on an identical horse, galloped Idle. The only strange thing was that behind Emily rode a small boy with fair hair who kept calling out to her that he was her brother. She could hear his calls above the music. But when she turned to look at him, although his hair was quite clear, same colour as hers, his face was a blur. She couldn't tell if he was laughing or crying. She shouted to Fen to turn and look, too; but Fen couldn't hear and didn't turn. So Emily gave up worrying about the boy, whoever he was, and concentrated on the chase. Because it seemed that's what they were doing, chasing each other on these horses that moved in great bounds, but never progressed in catching each other up.

The merry-go-round came to a halt, the train stopped. Emily woke.

'I wish I had a brother,' she said.

'Oh, for heaven's sake.' Fen was getting down cases. 'We've been into all that before. You know I'm much too old to start having more children now.'

'I don't think you are. And anyhow, I would have liked to have had an older brother, like Wolf. So I suppose if you did get a baby now it would be too late.'

She knew she sounded accusing and that her timing for such observations was wrong. But then everything, on waking, was wrong. She would have liked to have gone on dreaming till one of the horses had caught up with another. The station was dank, freezing. Her suitcase was heavy. She felt rather sick. And Fen was impervious to her condition, maddeningly cheerful.

They lunched in the station hotel. A vast, almost deserted dining-room, with a high domed ceiling. It was painted with gold stars, some faded so pale they were near invisible, like real stars on a cloudy night. On a small stage an orchestra of three saddened gentlemen in maroon coats skimmed their way through a Viennese waltz. Fen said she thought they must be practising for some special occasion tonight. She herself, as Emily knew, liked running into any kind of band at any time of day. Her fingers played on the white tablecloth. She seemed very happy.

'Isn't this *fun*, Em?' she said.

'No,' said Emily.

She was worried by the amount of waiters who guarded two trolleys of silver domes, almost the same shape as the ceiling. They must be very bored, waiting for someone to ask them to raise these lids for a helping of roast beef. And even when the order came, it couldn't be all that interesting, just slicing away at meat, day after day. What would they tell their wives when they went home in the evenings? 'Six slices today'? Or, 'Someone wanted nothing but the crackly bits'? It would be awfully boring being married to a waiter, except on the days he spilt something and made a customer very cross. Then, of course, there would be a chance to sympathise, and he'd think you were a good wife interested in his work.

'You are a spoilsport, sometimes,' said Fen. 'What do you want to eat?'

Emily decided to have the roast beef in order to cheer up the waiters. There were so many of them, so bored, longing for something to do. She wondered if the thrill of her order would cause them actually to fight over who should do the carving. She supposed if they *did* fight it would be up to the head waiter to part them by squirting them with soda water. If all that happened, lunch would be much more full.

But it didn't. All the young waiters stepped back to let an old grandfather of a waiter glide up to her, pushing the trolley elegantly as if it were a dancing partner. His feet almost kept time with the waltz now being played. Emily felt a certain fairness had been achieved, but she couldn't help being disappointed.

As they began their lunch, a solitary new customer came into the dining room. A youngish man, well dressed, with a single curl on his forehead. He looked slowly around. Immediately the unemployed waiters scrambled about him and he flicked a hand in the air, as if he had suddenly decided to conduct the waltz. The gesture sent three of the waiters scurrying back to their waiting place by the huge table of untouched hors d'oeuvres. The one remaining privileged waiter led the man to a table far away from theirs, but directly opposite. He sat down and ordered very quickly, without looking at the menu, which sent the waiter into a pantomime of confusion. Then he looked across at Fen and Emily. Both returned his look.

'I'm so glad *he's* come,' Emily said. 'It'll give them all some more work.' She was feeling better now. Warm and less sick. Besides, it was hard to resist Fen's gaiety. Perhaps the north wouldn't be so bad after all.

As they ate, the man across the way from them continued to stare with some curiosity. Then, on finishing his soup, he whispered something to the devoted waiter. The waiter nodded, raising his eyebrows. The man stood up. He made a direct line across the dining room to the table, laid for one, next to Fen and Emily's. As he sat down, he bowed his head to them. Fen smiled a little.

The waiter pursued the man, carrying a bottle of red wine. This was followed with a plate of roast grouse. He began to eat, concentrating hard. Now he was near them, he stared no longer. Emily could see Fen was puzzled. And on looking round the room she noticed that the few other diners were glancing in their direction, and the band of waiters were suddenly happy, full of mysterious smiles.

Then, as Fen and Emily began their trifle, they heard above the music a soft whistling. Fen looked up at the man, from whom the sound came, and he looked back. Both smiled. Fen blushed. She talked quickly to Emily, trying to suppress a laugh. The man had finished his grouse. He stood up again, picked up his wine and glass in one hand, his chair in the other, and came across to their table. He sat down, easily, as if he'd been invited. Patted his bottle of wine.

'Much better than yours,' he said to Fen. 'I could tell that from a great distance. Will you share it with me?'

Fen hesitated only for a second. Then she nodded and the man poured her a glass. He did not explain why he had come to their table: merely said he was a businessman from Brussels, in Yorkshire for twenty-four hours. His name was Rubrick.

'And I never expected,' he said to Fen, 'to run into a beautiful woman like you in a place like this.'

'I'm not sure if your approach is ridiculous or bold.' Fen blushed again.

'Both, probably,' said Rubrick. 'Laughably corny, too. But sometimes events in real life are like that. I mean, there's a moon most nights, for a start. Quite a few lovers are going to benefit from it.'

'Well, you didn't exactly run into us,' went on Fen, in a spirited fashion. 'You approached us very determinedly across the dining room.'

'Quite. But then I had a purpose. I wanted to try my luck. I wanted to ask you if I might have the honour of taking you out to dinner tonight. With your daughter, of course.' He spoke like a man in a play, his voice stilted. This time, Fen couldn't refrain from laughing.

'I'm sorry. But of course not. We've come up here to stay with someone. Thank you, all the same.'

'I quite understand. It was an outside chance.' He sounded so sad Emily felt quite sorry for him. She was pleased when Fen called for the bill. They should leave at once, so that Rubrick would get over his disappointment quickly. But he and Fen had a prolonged argument about the bill. Emily couldn't follow what was going on, but it seemed he wanted to pay for their lunch as well as his own. Fen sounded firm, and eventually produced her own money. When they left, Rubrick bowed and shook hands with both of them, very polite.

'Such a small chance,' he said to Fen. 'But I'm a born loser.' Fen gave him a wonderful smile in return, as he squeezed her hand, and this seemed to make him happier.

The incident had added to Fen's elation.

'Kevin'll think it so funny when I tell him,' she said out in the hall.

'Will Papa think it's funny?'

'Of course.'

Emily remained puzzled by the humour of the situation. Grown-ups found the oddest things funny. She thought it had been rather sad. For Rubrick, anyway.

'Why did he come over to us? What did he want?'

'Like he said. He wanted to take us out for dinner. I expect he was lonely.'

'I think he was. But you've always said people shouldn't go out with strange men.'

'That's one of the reasons I said no.'

Outside, there was sleet on their faces. Emily thought about Rubrick again, the steady way he walked across the huge dining room, like a soldier on the march.

'Do you think perhaps he thought you were sexy?' She'd learnt the word from Wolf, and had been looking for a chance to use it.

'Sexy?' Fen laughed. 'Darling, really. I don't know. Perhaps.'

'I think,' said Emily, 'if you weren't married to Papa and didn't have me, you'd have a lot of boyfriends.'

'I don't suppose so.' She was hailing a taxi. 'I don't suppose so for a minute. And anyway, as I *am* married to Papa, we'll never know.' At that moment a new squall of sleety wind cut their faces, wiping away Fen's laughter that only a moment before had quickened Emily with the absurd happiness of a shared joke. She reached for her mother's hand.

They left the city by taxi and drove to the lugubrious small town some miles south where they were to meet Kevin at his factory. Emily was startled by the blackness of the place. She had never seen such dirty old buildings – the grime, you could see, was thick as lichen. No wonder so few people were about. They kept indoors so that they shouldn't be distressed by the gloom outside.

It had stopped raining. They passed a canal filled with a flat, unshining substance that bore no resemblance to live water. The reflection of a winter sun lay untrembling on its surface, the only bright thing in the townscape. A child in a long scarf played on the bank, dabbing at the water with a stick. But the stick made no ripples in its turbid skin. It remained dead. Emily thought of the stream at home, and she longed to be home, far from this place.

Kevin's factory, a nineteenth-century converted warehouse, was tall and gloomy as all the other buildings, its façade slit with a great number of small, prison-like windows. Some of them, with a tiny chip of gold light, sparked back at the flaring sun. Most of them were lifeless as the canal. A modern prefabricated wing had been added to the warehouse for offices. The inside reminded Emily of a hospital; the smell of heating, and soft linoleum on the floors so that your footsteps made no noise.

They were led along a corridor. On each side, in glass cubicles, Emily caught sight of girls bent over typewriters, their chubby knees parted, their stiff hair all different shades of yellow. All Kevin's girlfriends, she thought, perhaps. With all of them around, she didn't see why he should be lonely in the north. Although, admittedly, none of them was half so pretty as Mama. *She* pranced along, face excited by all she saw, damp hair curling about her fur collar, a foreigner in this strange place. Emily noticed the typing girls look up as she passed, nudge and whisper to each other, and she felt herself smile.

They were shown to a small office and asked to sit and wait. Mr McCloud wouldn't be long. Fen lowered herself cautiously on to a steel chair, as if afraid to make a noise. Emily fingered the cold metal of a filing cabinet, which reached to the ceiling. Then she, too, sat on a steel chair. The walls of the office were a nasty green, whitened by the light from a long neon bulb in the ceiling. They listened to the hiss of a gas fire.

'How long will he be?' Emily asked, eventually.

'I don't know. How could I know?' Fen's eyes flicked about, over the calendar of sepia nude women, the dead geranium in a plastic pot, the photograph of some unidentifiable bit of machinery.

'And what will we do when he *does* come?' Emily was kicking the leg of her chair with her heel.

'He'll take us round the factory, I expect.'

'I don't want to see the factory.'

'Oh, Emily. Shut up unless you can be a bit more enthusiastic.'

'Well, I don't.'

'And stop that kicking.'

'We've been waiting for ages. It's very boring.'

'We've been waiting five minutes.'

'Well, it's very boring.'

'Shut up and be patient.'

'It's all very well for you.' Emily sighed. The filing cabinet was tall as a chimney, grey as smoke. It looked as if it stopped at the ceiling, but probably it didn't. Probably it went on up through the next storey, and the one after that, a giant bean stalk gone mad – on through the roof and sticking up into the grey old sky like another chimney.

Kevin arrived. Boredom, impatience, silence all crumbled. He took Fen into his arms, their presence filled the small room. Emily kept her eyes on Fen's face, suddenly efflorescent in the appalling light. Then it was Emily's turn. Kevin picked her up, huge hands straddling her ribs, top of the filing cabinet level with her vision for a moment – no, it definitely didn't go on through the ceiling. Kevin kissed her forehead, some nasty kind of tobacco breath. He apologised for keeping them waiting.

She was on the ground again, too hot, opening her coat. Fen was right. The factory was to be inspected. Already they were hurrying along the corridors, just in front of her, eyes looking up in the glass cubicles again.

Kevin swung open a heavy door. The muffled corridor gave way to the vast warehouse of screaming machinery, raw cacophony doubly echoed in the dank air. Emily put her hands to her hurting ears. She trembled. Kevin, turning to her, smiled. He mouthed something to her, but she couldn't hear what, against the noise. He offered her his hand, but she shook her head.

They walked up and down the lines of machinery. Kevin stopped every now and then to point out something to Fen. She seemed to understand, or at any rate to be interested. The men working at the machines, faces scrubbed of any expression, glanced up at her as she passed them, registering no surprise. Their minds, while their hands worked mechanically, had winged off to other places, other times, so that their eyes were left blank, their mouths dead shapes of lips. One or two of them, at the sight of Emily, and thinking perhaps of some similar child at home, would give a small nod or a twitch of a frozen mouth. But she, in her discomfort, could only scowl back.

For the third time that day she was very cold. Now, too, she had a headache. The orchestra of jagged sound, intent on torturing her ears, brought tears to her eyes. She blinked, ashamed, not wanting people to see. She looked above her where in the high ceiling poles of blinding neon light crossed each other and far, far beyond them a small thread of orange sun puckered the gloom in the rafters. Dazzled, confused, hurting, Emily felt a cry escape her. She knew it came because of the constriction, then the release, in her throat. But she couldn't hear it. Nobody heard it. It was swallowed in the grander noise. Taking a cold hand from her ear, so that instantly one side of the pain in her head grew stronger, she clutched at her mother's arm. And Fen suddenly remembered her. She drew Emily towards her, ran a warm hand (how could it be warm in this place?) over her head and cheek. They stopped at yet another piece of machinery that flashed up and down, too fast to see clearly, and Emily shut her eyes against her mother's sleeve. For a moment she revelled in the familiar smell of flowers, private and frail, but still existing among the public smells of oil and metal. She was comforted by the warmth, the softness of the cloth coat. Then, very gently, Fen pushed her away, and touched Kevin's arm, pointing to something. Emily muffled her ears with her hands again, and followed them.

She had no idea how long they spent in the factory, or what the machines made, or why Kevin seemed so pleased by it all. It became to her a confusion of rasping sound, hurting lights, inhuman faces: a tide of icy sensations that she struggled to walk against, dreading that the wire within her would snap, and she would cry.

But she didn't cry, and suddenly it was over. They were outside, darkness now, a livelier fresher kind of cold. Kevin led them to a small car. Emily climbed into the back seat, half occupied by small lumps of strange machinery.

'That *was* interesting,' Fen was saying.

'You should see it in a year's time. There'll be twice the production. Two years' time there'll be a second plant.' Kevin turned to Emily. 'Afraid that was all a bit boring for you. I'm sorry.'

'That's all right.' Emily managed a smile, but he probably didn't see it. In the marvellous quiet her headache had become more visible: a white graph in her head, with peaks and dips of pain, regularly spaced. She wondered if the old waiter would be on his way home too, now, or if he had to stay till after dinner, till the last guest had gone. That would be lonely, in the huge dining room, the piano shut, the lights dim, crumbs and crumpled napkins on the few used tables. Emily shivered so violently that Fen turned round.

'All right?'

'Yes thank you, Mama.'

'It's been a long day.' She sounded far from tired.

'Still, I've got some crumpets for tea,' said Kevin, 'and I've arranged a small room for you all to yourself. It's not very grand, but it'll do for one night.' Kevin was pleased with himself, happy. Emily remained silent. There was no point in saying anything. Mama seemed far away, chatting on with Kevin about factories and boring things like that. It would be impossible to tell her that all she wanted was to go home now, immediately, by some magic way that avoided the journey, and get her into her own bed. It would be impossible to say: *I wish we'd never come.*

Kevin's flat was the master bedroom in the mill owner's house, divided recently into three. In its original state, with its high ceilings and elaborate cornices, it must once have had a certain magnificence. Now, partitioned, the rooms were quite out of proportion. Their decoration revealed the landlord had more sense of economy than taste. A geometrically patterned wallpaper in the sitting room made an incongruous base to the plaster curlicues that lapped round the ceiling, and threadbare curtains strained but never quite met across the window. In Kevin's bedroom the landlord had, perhaps, given way to his private fantasies: black walls were enlivened with gold and silver snakes and stars. Only Emily's bedroom, not much more than a cupboard, junk piled high round the camp bed, was left with its old grand wallpaper of Regency stripes, much the worse for wear. The boiler still had not been mended, and every room was very cold.

Emily sat on the divan, which Kevin had tried to brighten with a scrum of gay cushions, in the sitting room. She was dazed, tired. Her ankles slumped, so that her feet turned in on the floor. Kevin and Fen, meanwhile, full of energy, lit electric fires, made tea in the minute kitchen (out of which came an icy draught) and grilled crumpets. Then they brought them to Emily, saying she looked pale. They sat on the floor at her feet, eating and smoking and laughing, Fen with her overcoat still round her shoulders, the silvery fur brushing her cheeks. They were kind and friendly, but still talked about boring things. Plans. Something about Scotland. Something about the South of France – Emily hardly listened. The crumpet was burnt and hard, the butter scarcely melted upon it. Her head still ached.

'Where's Mama going to sleep?' she asked, suddenly.

Kevin patted the divan.

'Here. I've slept here myself. Often. It's very comfortable.' He patted Emily's knee. 'Don't worry about her. She'll be fine.' Emily saw a smile go between them. And as for your bed: it'd win a prize for the most comfortable camp bed ever, any day. Now. What would you like to do? Are you warmer?'

'Yes thank you.'

'How about a game of Monopoly? There's an old set round somewhere, I'm sure.'

'Don't bother,' Emily said. 'I don't really like Monopoly as much as I did.'

'Or Scrabble. I'm better at Scrabble. Or vingt-et-un?' Emily could see he was trying hard. She hesitated, not knowing what to say.

'I don't feel like playing any games, actually.'

'Then what *would* you like to do?' An almost imperceptible impatience in his voice.

'Yes, what would you like to do, Em?' Fen was gentler.

'To go to bed.'

Fen looked at her face. At such moments she was good, quick, unquestioning.

'Come on, then. I'll help you. You'll soon be warm.'

In the tiny room they shut the door on Kevin. Fen unpacked Emily's case, laying the things on the end of the bed as there was nowhere else for them to go. Emily, still shivering, kept on her vest and pants under her nightdress.

The bed, as Kevin had said, was surprisingly comfortable. But she didn't like the tall piles of books and records and boxes all round her.

'What a lot of junk,' she said.

'Kevin's tidied it up best as he can,' said Fen. 'It's only for one night. You are an old grumbler, sometimes.' She kissed her daughter. 'Come on, Em. Cheer up. We'll have a nice lunch on the moors somewhere tomorrow, then we'll go home.'

'Good,' said Emily, and saw Fen sigh. At that moment, Kevin came in, and sat on the end of the bed, making it creak.

'Tell you what,' he said quietly, feeling her ankle through the blankets, 'I thought now might be just the time for the story about the hippopotamus. What d'you think?'

Emily shut her eyes. She couldn't look at him. She spoke to him with them still shut.

'Not tonight, thank you very much,' she said. 'I don't think I'm awake enough to listen properly tonight.' When she looked at him a moment later she saw he had understood. She also saw that one of his hands was on Fen's shoulder, rubbing it beneath the coat. Emily wanted them both to go away, quickly, quickly. She didn't want to see them any more. She shut her eyes again. They kissed her – flowers, tobacco, tea – and left. She slept. When Emily woke it was completely dark, absolutely quiet. She felt, immediately, very awake. The bed was warm now, but her head still ached.

She lay on her back, unmoving, eyes open. As they grew accustomed to the darkness she began to make out the tall shapes of the piles of things all round her, trees in a night jungle. Trees that might come crashing down on her. The skin under her left eye twitched, tickling, irritating. In the gap between the curtains she could see a star. Where was she?

She knelt up on the bed, drew back one of the curtains. They must be up a hill, somewhere, because far below she could see the lights of a town. Then she remembered. She remembered the whole of yesterday in a single flash, and the memory of the noise in the factory jarred her head. She would get up and ask her mother for an aspirin. It would be impossible to sleep again, like this. And she was thirsty.

She climbed off the bed. The linoleum was cold under her feet but she hadn't the will to search for her slippers. She crept to the door, pulled it ajar. In the sitting room, by the light of the moon, she could see that the cover of the divan was pulled back. Fen's clothes were scattered at the end of it, but she wasn't there.

Strange. They had definitely said they weren't going out. They wouldn't have gone out and left her, would they?

Emily felt her heart begin to beat more quickly. She opened her door wide and crept into the sitting room. There she paused, standing in a patch of moonlight that blanched her hands and feet. An icy draught still came from the kitchen.

The door that led to Kevin's room was not quite closed. Suddenly, from his room, Emily heard muffled voices. Her heart, already racing, now leapt in irregular bounds. She strained to hear the words. All that came to her ears was a dim laugh: Mama. Why would Mama be talking and laughing in the dark?

Emily made no conscious decision, but found herself tiptoeing towards Kevin's door. On reaching it, she pushed it, fractionally, with a trembling hand. It made no noise, but opened an inch further. Then she thought: *Why don't I just knock and go in? Why don't I just say Mama, can I have an aspirin? They wouldn't have any reason to be cross with me.* But some instinct forced Emily to keep her silence. She inclined her head towards the door, and put her eye to the gap.

Kevin's room was the only one with thick curtains. No shafts of moonlight penetrated here: the furniture was reduced to almost indistinguishable shapes. But as she stared, holding her breath, the darkness diluted a little. Emily could make out a shape too big for one person in the bed. Under the covers, it seemed. A sort of relief released her taut body: *of course, it was so cold. Mama must have been cold. Maybe Kevin was rubbing her back, to warm her before she went back to her own bed.*

Even as such thoughts flicked through Emily's mind, there came a cry from the bed: Mama. And then a stirring movement and the shape rose, higher. Fen cried again. Kevin's dark head was thrown back, distinct, wild, just for a second, before it plunged back on to the murky shape of the pillow.

He was hurting Mama . . .

Emily felt her own cold fingers over her mouth as she suppressed a scream. *Kevin was hurting Mama . . .* The floor, ice, glass, under her feet, burning cold as she fled from the small patch she had warmed – what could she do?

In her bed again, the warmth of the sheets all gone, she sat, hunched, arms round her knees, head buried in her hands. Her body shook, arrows cluttered her head, a live wire of pain stretched from her throat down through her chest and into her stomach.

And then she heard a laugh. Yes, a laugh. Her mother's laugh. She lifted her head, slowly, to make sure. The noise came to her again. The familiar, warm ripple of her mother's happiest laugh. How could she laugh, when Kevin had been hurting her?

Mama, how can you laugh when Kevin has been hurting you?

Rigid with cold now, Emily wriggled back under the bedclothes. The various pains in her body and head contracted, blotting out even the confusion. She pulled the sheets right over her head, drew her knees up under her chin till her forehead rested on their bones. Having made herself this foetal world, she found in it no light, no warmth, no comfort, no explanation. And Emily had no notion she was crying until she felt the warm damp of tears upon her knees. She fought for control, something she liked to exercise even in private. But although she bit her knuckles to stop herself, a strange, fearful cry escaped her. She knew she was going to die.

The horror and despair that feed on darkness, inextinguishable at the time, are granted strange mercy when daylight comes. Perhaps this is due to the eternal optimism in the workings of nature, a persistence in the supplying of renewed energy, however, brief, with a new day.

That Sunday morning in the north was, for Emily, less terrible than she had envisaged in her shell of blackness the night before. She was light-headed, drained, but not unhappy. Hungry, even, and warm. There must have been some mistake, last night: but she didn't ponder upon it. The boiler had been mysteriously mended at dawn. The new warmth was cheering, and there were only six or seven hours till the train back to London. Emily ate eggs and bacon and read her comic.

Later, they drove up on to the moors, sullen with mist. Fen's spirits seemed to be undaunted by the weather. She was very gay, laughing at grown-up jokes that Kevin kept making and Emily couldn't understand. They stopped at an inn with lights in its windows even though it was midday. Kevin helped Fen out of the car with great care, as if she was an invalid or an old woman, and took her arm as they ran through the rain to the door. Even inside, he kept his hand on her arm.

They lunched in a busy room full of loud-voiced people, smoke, smells of roast beef and Yorkshire pudding. Emily, sitting opposite Fen and Kevin, could only just hear what they were talking about. Something to do with the Prime Minister, which made them smile. All the same, they looked fidgety, like people running out of time: Fen's fingers strummed the striped tablecloth. Emily counted the beams in the ceiling: thirteen down, fourteen across. That must be wrong. She counted again. No, she was right. She felt inclined to point this out to Kevin – he would be able to explain. But his head was bent towards Fen's, listening to her. He didn't look as if he wanted to be interrupted. So Emily turned her attention to the knives and forks.

They had wooden handles, nice to feel, black as the beams. She wondered if they had a life of their own, in the darkness of their drawer, which we could know nothing about. Her fork, for instance? Was it married to her knife? Or merely a friend? Or perhaps an enemy, furious at having been laid opposite this knife? Emily picked them both up, wondering.

'Put those down,' said Fen. 'What on earth are you doing?'

Emily spent most of lunch in silence, working out a story about a runaway spoon who was adopted by a kind old knife and fork. The reason the spoon ran away was because it hated its unkind stepfather, who was a sharp carving knife. On the train, if she wasn't too sleepy, she might tell the story to Fen to see if she thought it was a good idea.

The pudding arrived. Orange banana jelly. Emily pushed her plate away.

'What's the matter with it?' asked Fen. Her cheeks were unusually pink.

'I don't want it.'

'But you ordered it.'

'I don't like the look of it, though. Please need I eat it?'

'Half of it,' said Fen, finally. 'There's nothing more boring than children who are fussy about food.'

Emily pursed her lips, dug her spoon into the glossy jelly. She looked up at Kevin, who was watching her.

'I was the one who stole your handkerchief,' she said. Kevin looked surprised, glanced at Fen.

'What handkerchief?'

'Didn't you miss it? You dropped it at our house that morning.'

'No, I didn't miss it,' said Kevin. 'What did you do with it? Can I have it back?'

'Afraid not. I let it float down the stream. I suppose I could have rescued it, but I decided not to.' Emily felt her mother's eyes unflinchingly upon her. She dare not meet them. She ate a spoonful of the jelly.

'Why did you do that, Em?' Fen's voice was puzzled but

gentle. Emily shrugged, still not looking at her mother. Fen bent towards her, not noticing Kevin now.

'Dunno.'

'You've never done anything like that before, have you?'

'Course not.'

'You know about stealing. I mean –'

'I know it's wrong,' Emily interrupted, 'but I just felt like doing it.'

'Well, just so long as you don't feel like doing it again,' said Kevin. He smiled at her. She felt the burning of tears behind her eyes, but controlled them. She swung the melted jelly about in her mouth from cheek to cheek. All this understanding was confusing. 'We'll have to be leaving in half an hour if we want to catch that train,' Kevin was saying.

'And leave that revolting looking stuff, darling. If you want to get down . . .' Fen's eyes were sad. Emily ran from them.

She ran outside into the grey squalls of rain, where the cold instantly quenched the fire in her cheeks, and spat out the jelly in the car park. For a moment she wondered where to go, then she saw a grey stone outhouse with a notice nailed near its door: *Pottery for Sale*. Emily made her way through the huddle of cars to the door of this building – a stable door, the top half open. Tiptoeing, she looked inside.

An old man sat at a potter's wheel, his fingers fluid in the spinning wet clay beneath them, the only sound the soft rasping of stone as the wheel revolved. Emily opened the door. She went in. The potter looked up, his hands fluttering over his lump of clay in absolute harmony, like a pair of wings, as he did so.

'Nasty out,' he said.

'Yes,' said Emily. She stepped nearer the wheel. A dark hollow was now forming in the clay, and its sides bulged a little, just for a moment, till the potter decided to press them back again. In a faraway corner of the roughly converted room the yellow-green flame of an oil stove flickered behind its small windows, suggesting warmth within itself, but jealously forbidding that warmth to escape.

'Why are you working on a Sunday?' asked Emily.

'Like it. Like working every day of the week. If you like your work you don't care which day it is, do you?'

'Like my father,' said Emily.

'Besides,' the potter went on, not appearing to have heard her, 'my hands are seizing up. Cold like this, they aren't much good. Not many more years.'

'Till you die, you mean?'

'That's right.' The potter lifted one hand from the clay and curled up his fingers, testing them. 'Then all that's left of me is these few pots.' He nodded towards a table behind him, scattered with an assortment of jars, mugs and plates. Simple things, their ridged sides glazed peaty brown or terra cotta. Emily went to the table and picked up a shallow ashtray. Its bottom was marked with white, twig-like strokes. Wintry.

'You can have that if you like,' said the potter.

'Oh no, really. My mother will give me some money.'

'You take it, luv. There's not many that comes in of a Sunday, and if they do they disturb me. You haven't disturbed me. I'd like you to have it.'

Emily thanked him and left. Outside she met her mother and Kevin making for the car. She ran to them, excited, and handed the ashtray to Kevin.

'Look what the old man in the pottery shop has given me! He said I could have it for no money.'

Kevin examined it, Fen close to him. The rain dimmed its glaze.

'Beautiful,' he said.

'Would you like it?' Emily asked.

'Thank you, Em. But I think you ought to give it to your father.'

'*That's a* good idea. I hadn't got a present for him.' She took it back at once and wiped the rain from its surface.

At the station the truculence that had afflicted her for two days – a disagreeable feeling that rose within her but she felt unable to combat – came upon her again. Fen stood at the window waving at Kevin – silly little nervous waves – while Emily refused to move from her seat.

'Kevin's an old fat pig,' she said, and then remembered about the ashtray. Fen didn't seem to have heard – noise of the train starting. Emily was glad. She opened her book, and shortly fell asleep.

Five

There was no news of Idle's return from Africa. As the Nativity Play drew nearer Emily began to fret. Fen's promises that somehow he would manage to be there were no consolation. She needed positive assurance. As it was, the anxiety began to detract from the pleasure of rehearsals, the excitement.

It wasn't till the morning of the play itself that a telegram arrived: all being well, Idle planned to arrive at the airport just in time for Fen to drive him straight to the school. Emily's relief and delight were boundless. She ran off through the snowy garden singing to herself, shaking branches of the trees as she went. Some of their snow fell around her in small showers, but laughing out loud, she scarcely felt their wet or cold on her cheeks.

At school, everything was wonderfully abnormal. In the Hall, the Christmas tree was lit with blue and green bulbs, giving the place an unfamiliar and mysterious glow. Miss Curtis played the morning hymn with trembling fingers and great nicety of feeling, while on the bosom of her crochet cardigan bobbed a posy of plastic holly and tinsel fern. Miss Neal, a character less swayed into celebration of annual events, in spite of her dedication of the spirit of the Nativity, made only one concession to the importance of the day: a hairnet sprinkled with tiny diamonds. While the headmistress asked in her confident voice that God should bring peace into the hearts of parents and children, Emily, screwing up her eyes in the black cup of her hands, prayed that she wouldn't stumble over her lines: and by the time the many requests to the Lord were over fresh snow was flowering against the glass of the grey windows.

The seniors were allowed to change first – lucky things, as Emily said to Sandra – almost directly after lunch. From the door of her classroom Emily watched with some envy as they went by: first, the troupe of Dancing Angels, in one-shouldered white tunics. They had gleaming pink lips and haloes of small lacquered stars, whose wire structure, carefully hidden in their hair, could just be observed from behind. They carried their huge gold wings, ready to put them on at the last moment. Meantime, wingless, they were trusted to spend a quiet hour in the library, reading, still as possible so as to cause no creases.

Then came the kings and shepherds, in rough and bright Eastern clothes. Their faces had been made up by the art teacher, whose talent and experience had taught her what looked impressive from a distance. Close to, their livid brown skins and wild black brows were almost clownish, though their eyes remained solemn. Finally, Mary. Jennifer Plomber, ace of the netball field, transformed to an unimaginable gentleness of bearing. She came up the steps, navy school mackintosh flung carelessly over her long, blue cloak, twinkling with snow. As she lifted her long skirts, showing a flash of wet gumboot, she smiled at Emily. Emily returned a sighing smile, and counted the years.

Finally, the Children by the Manger were allowed to exchange their uniforms for their simple dancing tunics, garlanded only with strands of real ivy over their shoulders. They pinned these sprays on to each other, fingers unusually clumsy, and squealed as the cold leaves touched their bare arms. The room in which they gathered behind the stage smelt of sweat. The floor beneath their feet was ice. The first carol, muffled by the curtains, began.

When the time came for Emily's solo, she was calm and untrembling. Alone on the steps leading to the stage, a spotlight in her eyes, she listened to her voice funnelling into the quiet blackness of the audience. At the end of her verse they applauded. (Miss Neal had said they would do no such thing until the very end: it would spoil the atmosphere.) As Emily stepped down to the side of the stage, containing her pleasure in the slightest flicker of a smile, a booming voice from the back of Hall quickly came to the rescue of that atmosphere, cutting short the applause.

'. . . And suddenly, there were with the shepherds, the angels of the Lord, praising God and saying . . .'

The stage curtains snapped back. There they were, the dazzling bank of Dancing Angels, piled up on their hidden chairs and step ladders, paper trumpets to the ready at their mouths, wings and haloes a-glitter: the results of all their rehearsals triumphant now, as they kept their tableau of uncanny stillness. Before them, on the ground, the shepherds were twisted into ingenious positions of fear, equally frozen.

'Holy, Holy, Holy,' shouted the angels, breaking the dramatic tension, and the smallest shepherd, overcome, dropped his crook with a great thud. Under cover of all this activity Emily glanced quickly at the dim faces of the audience. Unable to see her parents, she hastily lowered her eyes again. This was an occasion when make-believe worked for her. The Angels, ordinary school girls any other day of the year, conjured a strange wonder on the stage. And as the next carol filled the Hall an old and private world of clear midnights and snowbound stars, which flames the dullest soul at Christmas, dazed Emily, until cramp struck her leg, God's holiness receded a little, and she came back to reality.

One of the few advantages of being a Child by the Manger was that, not being required for the final tableau, they were able to change first, and thus find their parents first when the performance was over. The great surge of parental pride that burst forth with the final curtain applause and tears in almost equal measure, therefore went unheeded by the Children. They were already in the basement cloakroom, ripping off their ivyed tunics and leaving them in blue pools on the stone floor, as they clamoured with excitement, impatient for anticipated praise. Emily was one of the first to race back to the Hall. Brightly lit by the tree and other lights, the awe of so short a while ago quite scattered now, jabbering parents stood thickly together, united in their feelings. Almost at once Emily saw Fen. She stood by the piano in a long, mustard velvet cloak, a black scarf swathed over her head, rather in the fashion of the shepherds. Emily quickly pushed towards her. Fen smiled at once, and bent down to kiss her.

'Darling, you were absolutely marvellous.'

'Where's Papa?' asked Emily, looking round.

'I'll tell you. Let's go.'

Fen took Emily's hand. They made their way out of the Hall and into the drive. There, small gusts of snow blew into their faces.

'What happened to him?'

'No one could help it,' said Fen, 'but his aeroplane was delayed. He rang me from the airport in Capetown. He was dreadfully upset.'

Emily stopped. For a moment she watched the snow pile up on the toes of her boots. Then she said:

'But I wanted him to come,' and buried her head in her mother's shoulder.

'I know, I know. But there was nothing he could do. He'll be back very late tonight. He'll be there when you wake up in the morning.'

Emily felt a shudder go right through her body. She detached herself from the warmth of her mother. She could think of nothing to say.

They walked a few paces up the slight incline of the drive till they came to the windows of the Hall. There, at Emily's instigation, they paused again. They looked in. Mothers and fathers greeted their children with shouts and gestures of congratulation, laughing and smiling.

'It was so good, too,' said Fen. The circle of snow in which she stood was grapefruit coloured from the lights inside. Emily, turning from the scene in the Hall and looking up at her, saw that her black scarf merged into the night sky, its long ends billowing among the clouds, and her face was pale but distinct. 'Marcia Burrows is waiting for us in the car,' Fen added.

'Marcia Burrows? Why's she come?'

'She was going to be all ready for Papa's return so that she could get on with whatever he wanted done right away.' Fen paused. 'Kevin's there too. He didn't think you'd mind. He so wanted to see you . . .'

Emily let her eyes fall from her mother's face to her cloak. It was the ugliest colour she had ever seen. A sickly, hideous colour against the snow.

'I didn't want Kevin to come,' she said.

'He thought you were—'

'I didn't want him or Miss Burrows. I didn't want anyone but you and Papa.'

'Oh, Em.' Fen shifted her feet, cold. 'There was nothing anyone could do, you know. I thought –'

'Whatever you thought, you thought wrong,' Emily shouted. Snow blew into her mouth. 'But anyhow, it doesn't matter because it was an awful play and I was terrible and I wish I hadn't been in it.' She swung back to the windows of the Hall, hunching her shoulders. 'Look in *there*!'

Fen stepped towards her.

'It doesn't look to me as if there are many fathers, in fact, darling.'

'I don't care. I wanted Papa to come.' Suddenly she pressed her head against the glass pane and felt the snow that had lodged there crowd against her forehead. 'All I wanted in the whole world was for you and Papa to come.'

Fen tugged at her arm.

'Come on, Em. It's so cold. Please.'

Emily didn't resist. She no longer cared what she did,

whether the snow covered her completely, or she died of cold, anything.

'I was praying not to forget my words,' she said. 'I didn't even think I should be praying for the aeroplane to get here on time, or for Marcia Burrows and Kevin McCloud not to come.'

'Don't go on,' said Fen, a little desperate, 'there are so many other years.'

Emily hadn't seen Kevin since the weekend in the north. He sat in the back seat of the car, Marcia Burrows beside him.

'Congratulations,' she said at once. 'You were quite a little star, dear.' She wore an angora beret pulled down over one eye, angora gloves to match.

'Well done,' said Kevin. 'We enjoyed it.' Emily said nothing.

Fen drove cautiously to the station – it was still snowing, and settling quite deeply. Kevin left for London with a final tribute to Emily's performance, but still she did not respond.

Her spirits remained dulled for the rest of the evening. Silently, she noticed that on this visit Marcia Burrows seemed a little easier, more at home. She took out her knitting, after a glass of sherry, without asking Fen's permission, and chattered on about how comparatively lucky were the birds of Holland Park during a hard winter. So many people seemed keen to feed them. She herself went there most Saturday mornings, with a small bag of special bird food, though of course priority was for the few sparrows, almost tame now, who came to her house in Olympia.

Soon after supper Fen left for the airport, telling Emily to go to bed. She doubted whether she would be back much before midnight in this weather. She wrapped herself up in her cloak and scarf again, and took a torch to the door. Emily knelt at the window and watched the timeless shape of her mother, guided by the thin beam, bent against the flurrying snow. She felt a moment's anxiety. But the feeling, settling as it did on the surface of the baser sadnesses of the last few hours, was lightweight. By the time she sat at the fire once more, it had gone, to be replaced by a great longing for tomorrow.

She watched the fire. Marcia Burrows' needles clicked with a definite rhythm. Her ankles were crossed on the floor. The green sage stuff of her skirt just covered her knees. She had straight, thinnish, dull legs, the kind that look easiest in walking shoes. Her fingers had beautifully polished nails – short but shining. There was something reassuring about her appearance: a firmness, a sense of constancy, and responsibility, not immediately apparent when you first encountered her slight frame, and were impressed only by its neatness. Looking at her now, Emily understood why the sparrows kept on going back to her house: she would see to it they always found crumbs. Also, decided Emily, she had rather a nice face. Especially when she thought no one was looking at her. It was only when people questioned her, paid her attention, that her features recoiled almost imperceptibly, leaving her with an expression of anticipated disapproval, or perhaps it was caution. At least she wasn't bossy and interfering. She said nothing about bed. Instead, after a while, she remarked how good she thought the play.

'It must have taken months of rehearsal to get it up to that standard. That girl, whoever she was, who played Mary. She was especially good. And yet I couldn't help thinking . . . in fact I said to myself, I said: my, I'm sure that girl isn't at all a Mary character. I'm sure she's good at *netball*, or something like that.'

Emily sat up, respect increased.

'How did you know that?'

'What?'

'That she's netball captain?'

'I didn't know, of course.' Marcia Burrows smiled. 'I was only guessing. But there was something about her, the way she sat over the crib. It seemed to me her natural inclination was to pounce, jump high. Her cloak and halo couldn't hide her sportswoman's body. She must be the first Mary I've ever seen whose problem was to contain, not her body, but her mind. I felt, should a whistle suddenly blow, she'd be the first to leap up, and damn the baby in the cradle!' Emily smiled. 'That's why she was so good, you see. All those spirits, contained, made her calm much more effective. Some genuinely dull girl with a placid face wouldn't have been the same thing at all.'

Marcia Burrows was quite animated. Emily watched as two pink spots, at first quite small, spread rapidly over the entire plains of her cheeks. Her sudden warmth made Emily bold.

'Do you *disapprove* of anything ?' she asked.

'Well, of course. Why do you ask?'

'I don't know. Sometimes you look very disapproving, like at supper when Mama stubbed out her cigarette on her plate. Then just a little while later you say all those nice things about the play, and you guess right about Jennifer Plomber which I don't suppose even Uncle Tom would have done.' Marcia Burrows smiled but didn't reply. 'So what *do* you disapprove of?'

Marcia thought for a while.

'Obvious big things,' she said finally. 'And then, on an everyday level, the things they spring from. Unkindness, for instance.' She paused again. 'And some methods of kindness.' Her mouth shortened.

'What do you mean?'

'Do you really want to know? Well, simply, when there's a choice in a way of doing things, I believe in absolute honesty from the start. Of concealing nothing. It saves so much . . .'

Suddenly her ball of wool fell from her lap and skittered across the floor. She reacted with a look of sadness out of all proportion to the happening. Emily returned the ball to her lap, not quite understanding, nor indeed wanting Marcia Burrows to go on. She tried a new subject.

'Are you going to get married ?'

'Oh yes, I hope so. One day.' Marcia Burrows managed a real smile.

'My mother married Papa when she was very young, you know.

'Your mother is a very beautiful woman. Gay and clever, too.'

'I know.'

'We don't all have that good fortune.'

'Oh, I think you're quite clever. Mama can't knit like you.'

'Thank you.'

'Anyhow, I think you'd be a good wife to someone.' Again Marcia Burrows smiled. 'Has no one ever asked you?'

After a pause Miss Burrows replied, quite brusquely. 'Do you want to know proper grown-up answers to all these questions, Emily?'

'Of course.'

'Well, then, if you really want to know, a man did propose to me once. He was called Derek and he had one leg longer than the other.' Emily giggled. 'But I didn't want to marry him – nothing to do with the leg, of course. He just wasn't very – prepossessing, if you know what I mean. There was nothing you could put your finger on and say: *that's* Derek.'

'So what about the man you did want to marry?'

Marcia looked up, startled.

'How did you know about him?'

'How did you know about Jennifer Plomber?'

'There's not very much to say about him.' Marcia had found a new; resigned voice. 'We spent some happy times. He was good to me. But he didn't know how to tell me he loved someone else more. He tried not to hurt me, but of course I found out. By that time there wasn't much left for me . . . I don't attract friends,' she added. 'There wasn't a crowd of supporting people to turn to, was there? Just the knowledge that all the time he'd been someone else's, not mine.' A tear suddenly ran from one eye down her cheek. Emily was startled.

'Miss Burrows!'

'Forgive me, child. I don't know what came over me. I don't know what made me talk like that.'

'Do you want me to fetch you a handkerchief?'

Miss Burrows shook her head. 'Really, thank you. I usually have one. Now, it's time you went to bed. Your mother said. I shall do just a couple more rows and go myself.'

Emily got up.

'I'm awfully sorry,' she said, 'if I made you cry.'

'It was nothing to do with you, dear. As my mother always said, the quickest way to self-pity is a glass of sherry. Now, up you go.'

Emily bent down and kissed her, carefully choosing the cheek without the tear.

'Papa'll be back in the morning,' she said.

'That's good,' said Miss Burrows. 'You're lucky to have such a nice father, you know.'

'I know,' said Emily.

She couldn't sleep. She lay, eyes open, thinking of Marcia Burrows and her odd-legged admirer. Perhaps he had run after her shouting his proposal behind her, only of course he wouldn't have stood a chance of catching her up if she had been going fast. So after a while he would have had to have given up, sit on a bench and get his breath, and wonder what to do next. If he had decided to go along to her house and knock on her door, would she have slammed it in his face? Or would she have asked him in to tea and called him 'dear' as if nothing had happened, as if he had never chased her round the park, people laughing, people shouting? That chase he was bound to lose. Perhaps it was a bit mean of Marcia Burrows to say no to Derek if she really didn't mind about his leg. Surely she would have been better off with a man with a limp than no man at all? She didn't look particularly happy on her own. And she ought to be happy because she *was* a nice woman. Kind. Gentle. She wouldn't frighten any sort of man, as perhaps Mama would. No one could imagine a man with a limp chasing after *her*. Wouldn't dare. Well, it would be silly. All her boyfriends before she married Papa, she once said, were young Lochinvars who swept her off her feet to exciting places before she had time to say no. She had liked that, and she had probably been good to be with once they were at the places. Whereas Marcia Burrows, it had to be admitted, wouldn't be the most lively person anywhere, however exciting.

The church clock struck twelve. The square of night sky in Emily's window was filmy still with snow. It was absolutely quiet. Then, immeasurable time later, the noise of the car's engine.

Emily sat up. She strained her ears. Voices downstairs, but no words. She heard a laugh, Papa's laugh. He was back, back. The moonlight shapes about her began marvellously to flower: now her room was a ship in a stormy sea pitching towards him – she swayed back and forth. Certainly they wouldn't capsize. Now it was Aladdin's cave: she had only to rub her tooth-mug and magically he'd spring up out of the floor. Actually, why wasn't he coming up to say goodnight to her?

Suddenly impatient, Emily jumped out of bed, crept down the attic stairs and along the passage. She peered over the banisters that led directly into the kitchen. Thus she could see her parents, but they could not see her.

They sat at the kitchen table, Idle at his own place at the end, Fen at one side. They had plates of very hot soup. Emily could see the steam and smell the onions. Idle looked tanned, his hair unusually white against his dark skin. His glasses, which he sometimes wore when he was tired, had slipped down over his nose. Fen wore an apricot coloured jersey with a high neck. It colour, in the candlelight, reflected up into her face, making it a summer gold. It was as if she had never experienced etiolation. Her cheeks, pale as they had appeared earlier in the snow, must have been an illusion.

'So now tell me what you've been doing,' Idle was saying. Fen hesitated.

'We've been mostly here,' she said. 'Tom came one weekend. I told you in my letter. He brought Kevin McCloud with him, and some new bird of his called Janie.'

'You didn't tell me that.'

'Didn't I? Well, it wouldn't have been your kind of weekend. God knows how Tom'll end up. Each of his blondes is stupider than the last. This one was the epitome.'

'He doesn't need any of them, so it doesn't matter for a while.'

'No,' said Fen. She sipped her soup from the bowl.

'And you. Have you been all right?' Idle touched her hair.

'Of course.'

'It's the longest I've ever been away.'

'I've great reserves of activity,' Fen smiled. 'No trouble in filling my days.'

'I think after all these years I've begun to believe you. You really are good at being on your own.' Fen nodded, hands cupped round her bowl, blowing softly. 'More than I would be,' Idle added.

Emily shifted her position on the stair. She was getting cold. She decided soon to go down and surprise them. They couldn't be cross, not tonight. Idle was pushing his soup away, unhungry, lighting a cigarette.

'It's strange,' he said, 'what contortions of the mind distance brings about. Terrible fantasies, quite unreal. Nightmares. Wracked nerves. I'd wake up shaking every morning, for no reason. Quite ridiculous.' He smiled to himself. Fen raised her eyebrows a little. She sounded concerned.

'You work so much too hard. You just push yourself and push yourself. One day you'll go too far. You'll get an ulcer or have a nervous breakdown.'

'No, no. Of course I won't. But I suppose I was overtired. Distress is tiring, and it was distressing. The conditions in the compounds, the feeling of defeat, of utter weariness, the hope almost gone. Then the endless official justification for the way of things. The refusal to have any kind of open mind: the stubborn persistence that within the closed mind lay good reason.' He rubbed his eyes. 'But those were the living nightmares. The worse ones were about you.'

'About me?'

'Perhaps if I tell you about them that'll do the trick of exorcism.'

'Go on.'

'Well, I had a funny instinct that this time I was away too long. That some kind of pressure would be put on you, or you'd be lonely down here, whatever you say – it's not like when we were in London – or perhaps you wouldn't miss me. I don't know.' He put his hand over Fen's.

'Of course I missed you,' said Fen. 'So did Emily. Terribly.'

'Good,' said Idle quietly. 'But I shall try never to be away again for so long.' He paused. 'I suppose I can never believe, even after ten years' absolute trust, that you'll still be there. Every time I come back I gear myself to thinking that my time must surely be up, and you're off at last with some younger Lochinvar.' Fen smiled briefly.

'You *are* in a bad way,' she said. 'Tonight you must take a sleeping pill, and tomorrow I'll see no one disturbs you.' She seemed a little brusque, as if she wanted to shake off his mood. Emily, on her stair, stood up. At the same time so did Fen, taking a soup bowl in each hand. Idle looked up at her.

'Darling love,' he said. 'You're thinner, aren't you? You haven't been looking after yourself.' Fen bent down to him. They kissed lightly.

'*Me* not looking after myself,' she said. 'I like that.'

Idle, too, got up. He wandered quietly round the room touching things, letting his hands curve over the mound of eggs in a basket: he rubbed an apple on his trousers then returned it to the pile of autumn fruit, he tested the weight of a log then threw it on the fire, and smiled at the instant flames. There was a kind of tired pleasure in his journey. He came to rest at the sink, beside Fen, and put his arm round her shoulders.

'It's all the same,' he said. 'I must have been quite mad.'

Fen didn't answer and Idle, hearing a creak on the stairs, looked up. He cried out with surprise, rushed to the bottom of the stairs. Emily threw herself into his arms, speechless. He smelt of faraway sun and familiar blue shirts. He hugged her till laughingly she had to shout to him to stop. Fen turned round quite slowly and smiled at them. Idle at last put Emily down on the rug by the fire.

'Papa!'

'You're awake!'

'I was waiting for you. You're a funny colour.'

'Here, shall I get you your present now?'

'Ooh, yes please.'

From a dark corner of the room Idle brought forth a wooden giraffe – brown spots on pale wood, as tall as Emily herself.

'An old man in Kenya carved it. They let it sit on the seat beside me on the aeroplane.'

'It's lovely,' said Emily. She touched its nose. 'Isn't it, Mama?'

'Lovely.' Fen was putting away plates.

'I'm so sorry about the play, Em,' said Idle. 'The wretched aeroplane.'

'Oh, that's all right. I wasn't very good, and anyhow.'

'Nonsense,' said Fen.

The giraffe was admired for many moments. They all sat on the same armchair and sometimes one of them would stretch out a hand to touch its smooth wooden skin. The room smelt of smoke and onions, and burning apple boughs. Outside, the snow turned to rain and smattered against the windows.

'Good thing Marcia Burrows is asleep,' said Emily. 'Do you know what she told me? She told me that a man called Derek with one leg miles longer than the other wanted to marry her.' For some reason this made her parents laugh. She saw them looking at each other, and joined in. When it seemed the laughter might stop Emily sprang from the chair and ran round the room in imitation of someone with a limp and it flared up again. All the time they could hear the rain

'Hope it turns back to snow for Christmas.' Finally exhausted, Emily flung her arms round the neck of her giraffe. 'God,' said Fen quietly, 'Christmas.' Suddenly all the gold left her face. She went and knelt by the fire.

'Your best time of the year,' said Idle.

'Maybe.'

'Only six days. And do you know it's one o'clock and I'm not at all tired?' Emily had heard the church clock strike.

'Well, I most certainly am,' said Idle. 'Bed. Come on.' He picked her up and carried her protesting up the stairs. From the place on his shoulder where she had lain her head she saw the picture of her mother flicker through the banisters, flame shadows on her flame jersey, her face turned up towards them, all smiling again.

Six

*E*mily's wish was granted: there was snow at Christmas.

Down on the south coast there was snow on the ground and thin icy rain in the air which, when it fell, needled through the whiteness and turned it to slush. Wind blew through the skeleton trees and gloomy laurels in the gardens of the large houses whose plainness was only dimmed by high summer. They had expensive wreaths of holly and scarlet ribbon hanging on their front doors, these houses, funereal rather than festive: and out at sea a red flag snarled its warning above the vicious waves.

Mrs Whicker, Emily's grandmother, lived in one of the largest of the ugly houses. With some triumph she had bought it after the death of her fourth husband: for all their goodness to her – and each one of them had been generous in his own way – none of her husbands had been persuaded that an English seaside town was the Mecca Mrs Whicker believed it to be. Thus only in widowhood she had achieved what in marriage she had always missed – a stiff breeze the year round, when she opened the window last thing at night, to give her courage. (In fact her room was a good mile from the shore: noses less keen than Mrs Whicker's had been known to miss the salty fumes that her nostrils alone were able to detect.) However, the move to the south coast was on the whole a failure. As Mrs Whicker was the first to admit, the timing was wrong. The need for the particular courage she required was long over. So, with a common sense she was not much renowned for, she transferred in her mind the benefits of the sea breezes – they gave her strength to face her old age. But they were poor compensation for lack of entertainment.

Having had sixty lively years of heterogeneous marriages, Mrs Whicker was little skilled in tolerating dull widowhood. Rich enough to buy pleasure, she lacked imagination about what to purchase, and scoffed at all advice. The days bored her. Her neighbours she considered a dying breed and made no attempt to associate with them. Her few friends (also a dying breed) lived in Kensington and had many excuses for not being able to visit outer Bournemouth. Her only son, Idle, was dutiful, but abroad much of the time. She had no desire to renew uneasy acquaintance with her dead husbands' relations – they had been bad enough at the time they *had* to be endured. And so she was left with an uneventful life. Her grumbles about the present were rare, but coruscating memories of the past fell upon the ears of one person alone – Marble, her companion of thirty years.

Marble had started her days as housekeeper to Mrs Whicker, a considerable position when she first took it. She was in charge of nine indoor servants and a cupboard of linen that contained no less than sixty pairs of double sheets. (Mrs Whicker had been Lady Warren at the time: the house – a Georgian mansion near Crewe.) But such are the perversities of English domestic economics that Marble, by remaining faithful to her employer, found her status diminishing rather than ascending. Now, the permissive society took its toll. On Tuesdays and Thursdays, the charwoman's days off, Marble herself was forced to use the electric floor polisher. She also had to serve afternoon tea, in the unlikely event of a visitor, and cook Sunday lunch. Thirty years ago, in her heyday, such activities on her part would not, of course, have been tolerated. The very idea of the housekeeper lowering herself in such a manner would have been risible. But Marble was something of a sport about keeping up with the times, and went about her new and alien duties with a stony face. Besides, there were rewards. Her relationship with Mrs Whicker, for instance, had grown undeniably closer. With all husbands gone, some barriers between mistress and servant were relaxed. Mrs Whicker would sometimes come into the kitchen for her elevenses and, sitting at the high old-fashioned table, give way to sweet memories of her husbands. As far as Marble could remember, they hardly tallied with the truth as she recalled it. But to be made recipient of the reminiscences at all was an honour Marble appreciated, and it wasn't her place to disagree. From her part, she could return little to Mrs Whicker's other than a sympathetic ear. Her own philosophies, she knew in her heart, bored her employer. They were based on a complicated version of the powers of the solar system. On a rainy morning she would observe, 'Well, what can you expect? It's Tuesday, after all. The sun's conspiring.' Details of her theories, such as the difference between conspiring and aspiring, may have confused Marble: nothing would shake her faith in the broad principles of the idea, and the idea from any angle failed to arouse Mrs Whicker's interest.

Christmas shook a little life into the house each year. It was an event Mrs Whicker looked forward to, and prepared for well in advance. April was the month in which she chose her Christmas cards – a process which annually enraged her as she found the shops full of Easter cards at that time, and went so far as to write to *The Times* about the matter. By October, all presents had been sent for from the Army and Navy Stores catalogue – Mrs Whicker chose this store in deference to her third husband, Felix, who used to buy his ties there. By November the presents were all wrapped, so one of Marble's extra autumnal duties was to flick at them twice a week with a feather duster. By December 24th when Fen, Idle and Emily were traditionally expected, everything had been ready for so long that the acute observer might light upon a certain air of fatigue about the decorations. The tree had begun to moult, the holly to die, the paper chains to sag and the presents themselves, piled on the floor, Marble had dusted in vain Badger, the half-blind Airedale, stumbled daily among them and the fact that he had mistaken most of the large parcels for lamp posts was evident from the blurred colours of the wrapping papers. They sat like half-ravaged islands in a sea of stained carpet, and it occurred to no one to re-wrap them. Badger, however, remained unreprimanded.

The Harris family always arrived at tea time. Soon after lunch, very severe in order to conceal her excitement, Mrs Whicker would give Marble orders to come upstairs and help her dress. When people came to the house, or were about to come, their relationship reverted to its old formality for the sake of appearances. If this arrangement hurt Marble, she kept the fact to herself, and gallantly referred to Mrs Whicker as 'M'Lady' left over from the day of Lady Warren – and which appealed to her more than 'Madam'. She kept up this term of address until they were on their own again.

This year, Mrs Whicker rose from her chair with unusual agitation as the hall clock struck two. She had a feeling – stronger than other years – that this would be her last Christmas, and she wanted to savour the best moments. So, waiving coffee, at a minute past two, with Marble and Badger behind her, she made her way up the grand staircase, a Tudoresque fantasy of 1930s' oak, to change for dinner. A few moments later, as she trembled into the dark tunnel of her cold silk dress, miles away in Oxfordshire Idle switched on the wipers of the snow-encrusted car.

'I'd do anything to stay at home,' said Fen, beside him.

'Me too,' said Emily. She looked back at their house, roof and window ledges thick with snow, no lights, sad at their departure. 'Why do we always have to go to Grannie?'

'There won't be many more years,' said Idle. 'She's going downhill fast. I wouldn't be surprised if this wasn't her—'

'You say that every year,' interrupted Fen, petulant. In response, a slight frown drew together Idle's grey brows. He started the car.

*

Fen and Idle, Emily behind them, followed Marble (in pleated cap and apron) through the gloomy hall. They waited for her to undo the heavy double doors into the morning room. They knew what they should see. Mrs Whicker had a special pose, same every year, for their arrival. It hadn't changed.

She sat very upright in a throne-like Tudor chair, shrunken but regal, ebony stick in hand, Badger at her feet. Her hair, which she kept a brave burnt-umber, was a skinny pile on top of her head, and two diamond brooches flashed on her flat bosom. From where Emily stood, far across the room, Mrs Whicker's eyes seemed to have receded far back into her head, into the shade of two deep hollows. Perhaps that's what Papa meant when he had said she was going downhill fast. Her eyes were rolling away.

'My dear Idle. Frances, Emily. You've arrived,' Mrs Whicker's voice rapped out at them, surprisingly vigorous. She tapped her cane on the floor. They all went towards her.

The journey over the rich red carpet towards her grand-mother's throne Emily had been making for as many Christmases as she could remember. It was a journey she found both fearful and sickening, stepping as they did through the droppings of light that fell from the deep silk shades, into shadows cast by large pieces of furniture. This furniture was dark in sunlight, quite black in the evening, only highlighted by the glow of an occasional red cushion – a cushion which, Emily knew from experience, was a hard and solid thing built for ornament rather than comfort. The room smelt of musk, sweet potpourri and sickly joss sticks, burning in their brass holders. Emily felt her stomach lurch, her step falter. The dread with which she approached her grandmother made her dizzy. She tried to reason with herself: she felt sorry for the old woman, so frail, so lonely. She wished to be kind and polite to her. But, since the incident of the false teeth, the act of touching her was something that required great self-control. Emily could think of nothing she hated more.

But she had to go through with it. It was already over for Fen and Idle, the little ceremony of kisses and welcomes. Now it was her turn. Closing her eyes, she briefly rubbed cheeks with Mrs Whicker, smelling in that instant, beneath the superficial zephyr or powders and scents, the unbidden smell of old, crimped skin.

She stepped back. It was over. This near, at the back of the hollows, she could see clearly the red orbs of her grandmother's eyes. Mrs Whicker surveyed her, moving them slowly. They were dull rubies, lustreless.

'Obvious to say you've grown, Emily. But you've grown *much*.' She waved her stick round the room. 'You can see what I've been up to no doubt? Frances, Idle? I've been acquiring things from the attics. Those bowls, over there. They belonged to dear Felix. That tapestry chair, Idle: your father bought me that in Quimper. On his way to Dunkirk. Turned out some wounded soldier sat on it on the deck of a fishing boat all the way over. It has a blood stain down one side, still, I believe. Now, a glass of sherry before dinner? I presume Emily will eat dinner with us this year, will she not?'

She rose from her chair, straight backed, hardly taller than Emily. Taking Idle's arm, she led them back to the door. It seemed to Emily, now her eyes were more used to the light, that a kind of dawn had stolen into the room, making everything a little paler, less frightening. But still the smell was sickening. She was glad when they reached the cool of the hall, and the brighter aspect of the drawing room.

If the morning room was a shrine to Lord Warren, stuffed as it was with the lugubrious furniture he had enjoyed owning, and had bestowed upon his wife upon the occasion of their divorce, the drawing room was a tribute to the other three husbands. The mixture of memorabilia – a tiger carpet shot by Bruce (the Colonel), the mother-of-pearl sewing box (Felix), the Jean Harlow chaise-longue from Maples (Robert, the poorest but sexiest) added up to a wonderfully strange taste. But at least it was cheerful. In here, much to Emily's relief, the Christmas tree and presents stood in the bow window, and most of life went on. The morning room was only for receiving. 'Keeps the damp out, receiving people there,' as Mrs Whicker explained. 'Rooms should be used or they die. So I keep dear Warren's spirit alive in the red room, just by visiting it on special occasions. It never needed much to keep *his* spirit alive,' she would add mysteriously. 'He was a master of indiscrimination.'

While Emily eyed the presents from a distance – she had learnt in previous years that to be too inquisitive too soon was bound to cause displeasure – Mrs Whicker dealt with the decanter of sherry. She poured Fen a small glass.

'You're looking marvellous as ever,' Fen said to her, uncertainly. It wasn't easy to guess whether Mrs Whicker would react better to a compliment or no kind of observation. Tonight, it seemed, Fen had judged rightly. Mrs Whicker was in a mood for compliments. She tossed her head.

'Thank you, Frances. Well, four husbands, you know, and still looking around.' She spoke more with the relish of a divorcée (which she was) than a widow (which of course she was also, but the husbands had all died after the divorces). 'Not doing badly, either.' She clutched the decanter to the diamonds on her breast. The gold liquid inside swayed about making her, too, sway a little on her feet, and cast about for her stick. Sometimes, time confused her. Tonight, perhaps, she was thinking the brooches were a new acquisition. 'Dear Felix,' she murmured. 'So kind, Felix. So kind, Idle.' She remembered the present, suddenly, as she felt Idle take her arm, take the sherry and lead her to a chair.

Later, Emily remembered that Christmas as a series of impressions, sleety, sloping a little: vivid, but not entirely clear. The thing that most perplexed her was that the dullness of the two days, the dullness she was used to, was spiked this time with small darts of an incomprehensible unease. Something, somehow had changed in Mrs Whicker's house. Thinking about it the first night, Emily put it down to her grandmother's predicted death. Maybe the approach of death made grown-ups uneasy. She didn't see why, in her grandmother's case. It was quite time she died, after all. Well past eighty, and not enjoying her life. And making poor Marble work so hard, too.

But at dinner MFS Whicker gave little impression of a dying woman. In the dining room, lit only by red candles on the table, she sparkled. It was Fen Emily worried about more actively. Her face was very pale. And surely thinner than usual? Noticing this, suddenly, Emily looked again. Yes: she was positive she was right. It was beautiful, in the semi-darkness, but thinner. When had that happened? Which morning had she woken up with those huge purple shadows under her eyes? Emily noticed then that her mother ate little, and was unusually quiet. She felt a moment's concern – until she remembered. Mama didn't like this house, didn't like coming here for Christmas, either. Of course. That was it. She was sad at leaving home. When you did things for the sake of other people it often showed on your face, even if you didn't say anything Emily knew that.

She returned to the ordeal of her turtle soup. Then she looked up to find her grandmother's hand, a small withered turtle itself, shuffling across the table towards her.

'Leave it, Emily. I can see you're not liking it. It's the sherry.'

'Really—'

'Go on. Leave it. Knew whichever I ordered it would be a mistake.' She gave a wicked sigh and snatched back her wandering hand to touch her brooches. A pat for each one. Reassurance. She looked up at her son and daughter-in-law. 'Oh! Such peace in here tonight. I never eat in here when I'm alone, you know. I find it restless. Now there's a contradiction for you, isn't there? The place is peaceful when you're here, restless without you.' Emily looked into the depths of her brown soup. She felt vaguely they were being accused, all three of them. 'But then perhaps it's just my weakness, restlessness. Would you say, Idle? Houses, husbands, places. I always thrived on change. Awful for you, Idle, come to think of it. I was only thinking the other day. Can't think why I never thought of it before, as a matter of fact. How awful it must have been for you.'

'It had its compensations. It was an exciting life.' Idle spoke

114

kindly. Emily often loved him for tolerating so nobly his mother's foibles, for supporting her when others criticised.

'Exciting it may have been. Not all twelve-year-olds ride elephants in India, I daresay. But the psychologists these days claim what children need is security, not ups and downs. They disagree with Shakespeare. "Mortal's chiefest enemy," *he* said it was, didn't he? Well, Emily here is the product of security. And look at her.' Mrs Whicker alone cast her eyes upon Emily, who felt herself blushing. 'Perhaps there's something in it. I shall be quite pleased to go to my grave thinking that my grand-daughter, at least, will never suffer what her father suffered. That's a good thought, isn't it, child?'

Emily, confused, shook then nodded her head. Across the table Idle winked at her, a private sign no one else saw. The top half of his body, rising as it did from the darkness of the table, and set against the darkness of the walls, was magnificent: green velvet jacket, silver hair, twinkling eyes. Emily wanted to run to him, to hug him, to say: *this is all grown-up talk, Papa. What does it mean? I don't understand.* She sat silently, fingering a silver salt cellar. When at last she looked up again she saw that her mother, in the act of taking a sip of wine, had lowered her eyes. Her cheeks, previously so pale, were now quite flushed.

'Mama?' said Emily.

'Yes?' The violet eyes right upon her, innocent, enquiring. Emily's mind raced for a question. Any question.

'Tomorrow, can we? Tomorrow . . .'

'You shall all take a walk on the shore, tomorrow.' Somehow Mrs Whicker had picked up Emily's lost thread. 'You shall gather me a handful of winter shells, if you will, Emily. And when you come back, you shall tell me all about it. I shall look forward to that.' Her hand scurried for the silver bell. She rang for Marble to clear away the soup.

Emily had a plan which she hoped would materialise after her grandmother died. There would be no more Christmases by the sea. She and Wolf would be together.

She had put the idea to Wolf and he had thought it a good one. His Christmases, too, were bleak: no other children, just Coral and his father in the stuffy house, Coral starting to drink brandy soon after breakfast so that by the time lunch was ready, very late, Wolf said her eyes looked funny. Somewhere in the future, though, Emily and Wolf both imagined another world of Christmas in which the early morning routine, stocking opening, would be more fun: in which it wouldn't matter if grown-ups were tired by mid-afternoon because there would be somebody else to play with.

But this year, physically, it was much the same as every other year for Emily. She woke early to find a stringy daylight in her room, making opaline veils over the cumbersome furniture. Emily fingered the lumpy shape of her stocking, impatient to open it. She crept to her parents' room and pushed the door softly. Their room was darker than hers, but she could see they lay at opposite sides of the bed, back to back, asleep. After a moment's hesitation she decided not to disturb them – though she had done so other years, and they hadn't minded – and went on downstairs to the kitchen. There she found Marble busying about, in the navy dress she had worn last night, her fringe dampened into four curls that all turned to the left. Perhaps she had never been to bed: Emily wouldn't have put it past her grandmother to make Marble stay up all night working, and to insist she looked immaculate the next morning.

'Oh, Miss Emily. Just the person I need. Here, come and help me with these legs. I'm blowed if I can catch them.'

A vast turkey lay in a roasting dish on the table. (Mrs Whicker could make it last, by careful planning of many disguises, for nearly three weeks. The smallest January croquette would bring back vividly to her mind the happy day on which Idle had raised his knife to carve the first slice from the whole bird.) Its sawn-off legs rose wide and recalcitrant, refusing to be drawn together by the string Marble wound hopelessly round them.

'Here. You hold the thighs, will you? Push them together, so.' She slapped at a thigh with each hand, making a dull noise.

Emily approached the naked bird. There were lumps of dripping on its breast bone, soon to turn its cold white skin to crackling brown. Its thighs, mottled mauve, were plump and soft under her palms. As she squeezed them, forcing the scaly shins together so that Marble was easily able to catch them in her wild loops of string, Emily felt something of a traitor. Marble, close beside her, smelt of dough and lavender. Then, as she secured the final knot in the string, a more pungent odour filled the air – the high-pitched, sweaty smell of triumph. Smiling to herself, Marble clenched her fist and rammed a lump of chestnut stuffing back into the cavern between the turkey's thighs. Emily moved away, suddenly cold.

'There. That's got him. I don't know what she expects, getting me to see to the bird. Anyone would think I was a chef on top of everything else, wouldn't they?' Marble made a clucking noise with her lips, moving her top teeth, and lifted up the roasting dish. The effort caused her arm muscles to strain, and her skin roughened into a rash of white pimples, so that for the precarious journey to the oven the flesh of the dead turkey and its captor were strangely similar.

'When d'you think Grannie's going to die?' asked Emily.

'Not yet awhiles. Or could be tomorrow.' Marble slammed shut the oven door. 'If you ask me, she'll give us all a surprise. Typical Gemini she'll be, if you're asking my opinion, when it comes to dying.'

Emily helped herself to cereal. Her stocking, still full, lay on the table beside her.

'Won't you be afraid, being alone in this house with her when she dies?'

'Not me,' said Marble. 'I'm one of those who can cock a snook at death. I've seen so many. My mother, she laid out everyone in the village that got taken, didn't she? For nothing, mind. For no reward.'

'Goodness,' said Emily. 'The part I wouldn't like would be putting false teeth into a dead mouth.'

'That's no bother.' Marble, sipping steaming tea, was all

courage. 'Teeth, when they're out of a mouth, are dead things anyway. You get used to them. You don't think of them as talking things when they're lying in their glass at night.' Tentatively, her tongue tripped round the edges of her own fair set, causing them to dance a little, *allegro non troppo*. 'But I don't know what's got into your head, really I don't, Miss Emily. This isn't what I'd call Christmas talk.' She appeared quite shocked, suddenly. A moment ago, Emily could have sworn, Marble was just as interested in the conversation as she had been. Now, she urged Emily to hurry; she had a lot to do before it was time for Mrs Whicker's breakfast.

Emily picked up her stocking and left the kitchen. Perhaps, she thought, her parents would be awake now, and she could open it with them.

The hall was gloomy. Marble hadn't yet swept up the ash in the grate. Glancing at the upstairs landing Emily saw a subdued light hovering there, too frail still to fall to the ground and cheer the place where she stood. She heard a creak, a step. Then she saw her mother gliding along the passage, her hand skimming the intricacies of the oak banister. She wore her mustard cloak. It billowed behind her as she hurried down the stairs.

'Em! Happy Christmas! You didn't come and wake us.' They were hugging, whirling about. The velvet of the cloak had caught Fen's smell of stephanotis.

'Where are you going?' Emily asked, when they stood apart again.

'Out for a moment.'

'Why? Can I come with you?'

'No. I won't be long.'

'Oh please, Mama.'

'I said no.' Fen pulled the hood of her cloak over her head. 'You go and get dressed and take your stocking into our room. I'll be back by that time and we can all open it together.' She moved to the door. Emily followed her.

'But what are you going out *for*?'

Fen laughed.

'You are an inquisitive thing. Maybe it's something to do with Christmas surprises, so you'd better not say anything to anyone. Promise?'

Let in on the secret, Emily understood.

'Promise,' she said.

Fen hurried through the front door, causing a draught of air that chilled Emily, standing in her pyjamas. When her mother had gone she stayed where she was for a moment, listening. A muffled clatter from the kitchen was the only sound. She tiptoed to the cloakroom and pulled down from a hook an old raincoat belonging to her grandmother. She put it on, and slipped her feet into a pair of fur boots. Then she, too, crept through the front door, shutting it quietly behind her.

Out in the drive there was a strong cold wind. Emily ran against it, stooped, to the front gate. There, she hid behind an icy laurel bush and peered down the road. Her mother was running towards a telephone box at the end of the road. When she reached it, Fen opened the door and went in. Shivering, Emily turned back towards the house. She tried to imagine what the surprise must be: something that Fen couldn't talk about on the telephone in the hall. Well, she'd soon know.

On her way she looked up to see her father standing at the window of his room. He waved at her, a surprised expression on his face. Emily increased her speed. No doubt he'd ask her what she had been doing. She'd think of something. Not for anything would she break her mother's trust, especially when a telephone call was most probably something to do with a present for Papa. That's what it definitely must be. Something to do with a present for Papa. A flicker of excitement burnt out the cold in her body. She threw off the raincoat and boots and hurried upstairs, dragging her stocking behind her. Strangely, her father asked her no questions.

In the afternoon Emily went with her parents to the beach. In spite of the cold she was glad to leave the house, relieved to get away from her grandmother for a while, who seemed to be possessed by some demon of a Christmas spirit. In church she had

119

sung out of tune with such gusto that each member of the congregation had taken upon himself the charitable act of giving her a staring frown, trying to make her take heed of her vocal antics. Mrs Whicker realised both the attention she was causing and the vagrancies of her voice at the same time. In reaction, she tipped back her head and laughed out loud. Then, worse, she shouted her apologies in a shrill voice that soared above the organ. People hid their smiles, but not well enough. The vicar himself was forced to clap a hymn book over his mouth to hide his own grimace. Idle alone was unconcerned. He bent over his mother, and whispered something, pointing with his finger to the right place in her carol book. Emily, filled with shame, had marvelled at his compassion.

The beach was quite deserted, the sky and sea an interchangeable grey. A long range of beach huts, padlocked and shuttered, were brightened by a crust of pure white on their roofs, while snow that had fallen among piles of seaweed was of a more sullied kind: the iron in the weed had stained it ugly yellow. Same colour, Emily thought, as her mother's cloak.

She walked in silence over the ribby sand between her parents. They kept in step, their breath three balloons in the air before them. The brush of the outgoing tide was a distant sound. Nearer, harsher, a couple of seagulls made ragged cries above their heads. Other years, when she was small – even last year – Idle had carried Emily part of the way on his shoulders. The gulls had dipped and swayed about her, almost near enough to touch. Now, she was too old to suggest such a thing. She sighed quietly to herself, thinking of the distance to the far breakwater.

'Extremely cold,' muttered Idle. His hands were deep in the pockets of his London coat, his shoulders hunched.

'Don't know why we always come,' answered Fen. 'It's never a pleasure.'

'Sometimes you've enjoyed it, darling, haven't you?'

'Never.'

They continued in silence some way. A charged silence. Emily felt compelled to break it. She put on her most cheerful voice.

'Oh, Mama, don't you remember that year I was awfully young and I fell in a pool and got soaking? That was funny.'

'Yes – *that* was funny.' Idle was eager. 'That made us laugh. We had to run all the way back.'

Fen sniffed. Gulls' screams tore at the air.

'Horrible birds,' she said.

Idle stopped and looked out to sea, his eyes concentrated on the horizon.

'Look, Em. That huge ship. Perhaps it's coming from France.'

A few yards beyond them Fen stopped, too, searching out the ship in the indeterminate greys of sky and sea.

'Oh yes! Look, Mama!' She bounded from her father to her mother. She clung to Fen's arm, shouting – unsure why she was shouting. The sight of a boat on the horizon didn't interest her in the slightest. 'Look, Mama. It might be coming from France.'

Fen glanced down, hair blowing about her face, eyes filled with tears. Emily was sure they were tears, though a second later, when Fen looked back to the sea again, they seemed to have gone.

'What's the matter?' Emily asked quietly.

'The matter?' Fen began walking again. 'Nothing's the matter except the wind hurts my eyes.' She wiped them with the back of her hand. Emily imitated the gesture.

'Mine too,' she lied.

Idle caught up with them. This time he went to Fens other side and took her arm.

'Let's go back,' Fen said.

'But we're not halfway there.' Idle sounded surprised.

'So? You were complaining about the cold.'

'But we always get as far as the breakwater . . . Every year.'

Fen gave a sarcastic laugh.

'Then why not let's take our chance and break the great tradition? We're not *enjoying* it – are we, Em?'

Emily kept her silence for a while, until she was prodded by Idle.

121

'You decide then, Em. Which do we do? Go on like we usually do? Or turn back?'

Still Emily remained silent, contemplating.

'*Which*?' snapped Fen.

'I don't mind, really.' Emily could barely hear her own voice against the gulls. 'Perhaps as it's *specially* cold this year . . .'

'Very well,' said Idle.

They turned and began walking back. Emily concentrated on stepping into her old imprints in the sand. She came across a cluster of shells, and remembered her grandmother. She bent to pick them up. Fen and Idle, separated again, paused to watch her.

'For goodness sake hurry up, Em.' Fen was stamping her feet. 'It's freezing. We can't wait around while you collect shells. Grannie never *does* anything with them, anyway.'

Emily looked up.

'Hurry up,' said Idle, gently. 'Just a few will do.'

Emily quickly stuffed a handful into her pocket. They walked on, not speaking.

Then in a rare moment of quiet from the gulls, Fen suddenly turned to Idle and burst out:

'Your mother may not be dead by this time next year, but it's absolutely the last time I come here!' She startled Idle and Emily with her vehemence.

'Darling! What's the matter?'

'I hate this bloody place,' Fen went on. 'It's the gloomiest place for Christmas I know. And anyway, what sort of fun do you think it is for Emily?'

Cautiously, Emily took her mother's arm. It was rigid. Idle remained calm.

'It's not much fun for Emily, is it, Em? We all know that. It's not much fun for any of us. But we always make up for that when we get home, don't we? And the poor old girl. She'd never come to us. Imagine what it would be like for her alone. She looks forward to our coming the whole year. You know that.'

'The poor old girl,' Fen scoffed. 'She's an evil old woman.'

'Darling, please.'

'Well, she is.'

'*Fen.*'

'You can do what you like, next year.'

'We'll talk about it later.'

'You won't change my mind.'

Emily was aware that her father sighed. She stretched out her hand towards him. He took it and drew closer to her.

'What a silly old argument,' Emily said.

'Quite,' said Idle.

'Mama, isn't it?'

'I suppose so.' Fen smiled out to sea. Her arm relaxed a little. 'I suppose I just can't bear the thought of three-handed bridge this evening when we could be at home with Tom and people. I can't bear the thought of cold turkey and Marble's disgusting salad for dinner –'

'I helped tie up the turkey this morning, by the way,' Emily interrupted.

'You didn't! What did you have to do?' Idle seemed particularly interested.

'Oh, I just squished its legs together while Marble tied the string.'

Fen looked down at Emily and laughed.

'Race you,' she said.

'Right. Race you.' But a surge of relief had weakened Emily's knees. As they both broke away from Idle she had to cling to her mother, needing to be pulled. They remained side by side, their footsteps chipping into the hard sand. Then they heard Idle pounding up behind them.

'Caught you ! You're hopelessly slow.'

They all stopped, panting, laughing, warm now. Idle put an arm round each of them. Emily could smell the nearby seaweed. A tomato sun had appeared from its day behind cloud and hung low in the sky, its reflection a small scattering of confetti in the sea. Squares of light were appearing in the dusky buildings of the town above them, and a solitary church bell began to ring.

They climbed the steep steps to the promenade, holding hands, helping each other, and returned to Mrs Whicker for an evening of annual festivities peculiar to the house – bridge, ginger cake, and records of Chopin played by Paderewski, with whom the ubiquitous Lord Warren had once shaken hands, many Christmases ago.

When they arrived back Emily felt a peculiar tiredness. It was as if she had exerted herself in some way – what way, she could not fathom – and the effort had left her drained. She curled up in a satin armchair, her limbs heavy, relieved that for the moment no one required her attention.

Her grandmother and parents were playing cards in front of the fire. The only one to whom the game gave any real pleasure was Mrs Whicker. Bolt upright in her chair, which she shared with Badger, her mouth was set in an unmoving smile. She wore a silvery dress with a ruffle of red and green parrot feathers sewn round the collar. These she had plucked herself from the dead body of Matilda, a parrot Robert (the most romantic husband) had given her during their engagement, and who had died, sensitive bird that it was, a few days after their decree absolute. Robert had kept the parrot, to the horror of his secretary, in his room at the Foreign Office for three months before giving it to his future wife. The purpose of this period of isolation was to teach it to say 'I love you'. It learnt the words but not the discrimination that should go with them, and shrieked that it loved everyone who came into the house. Its endless amatory proclamations affected Mrs Whicker with a new neurosis – she confused the parrot's words with her husband's feelings, and the foundations of their romantic marriage were shaken. However, after their divorce Mrs Whicker's feelings (as they always did) reverted to ones of unblemished love, such as they had been for Robert in the beginning, and as the parrot was the only one who declared its love for her at the time, she loved it in return. It was her habit to wear mementoes of her husbands as well as to furnish her house with them: thus, when Matilda died, the idea of the feather collar seemed to Mrs Whicker an inspiration. Robert had been in no position to give her jewellery: the feathers were soft, glorious colours, and reassuring to the touch as diamonds. She stroked them from time to time, with great gentleness, and continued to smile at the fan of cards she held in her other hand.

Emily slept. She dreamed she and her parents were back on the beach, a crowd of gulls above their heads so thickly massed together the sky was invisible behind them. The birds didn't make ordinary gull cries, but laughed human, scoffing laughs. When she tried to ask her parents why, only a croak could come from her own mouth. Fen and Idle began to run. Low in the air the gulls pursued them. Emily, too, tried to follow them, but her legs would not move. She saw her mother stretch out her arms and rise into the air, joining the birds. Then, a long way from Emily, her father flapped his arms to follow Fen. But he remained on the sand, immobile. Emily couldn't reach him, he couldn't fly away. The gulls' laugh grew fainter as the birds flew higher. Emily, waking, saw her grandmother's smile.

The following morning Fen complained of a headache, and stayed in bed. Idle seemed unusually concerned about her and looked, Emily noticed, as if he himself had had a bad night. Fen, lying back on her pillows in the giant bed, was pale and lethargic. She stared dully at a shower of sleet that swept against the windows, her eyelids swollen, her hair tangled. Emily, who had climbed on to the end of the bed, felt at a loss as how to entertain her. It was so unlike her mother to be without energy. This lack of spirit unnerved her, made her afraid.

'How do you actually feel, Mama?'

Fen gave the faintest smile.

'As if a block of concrete was pressing down on my head.'

'How horrid.' Emily tried to imagine it. They listened to the sleet in the wind. 'Well, anyway, we're going home in about four hours, aren't we?'

'Yes.'

'Mama? What was that secret you were going to telephone about yesterday morning? Was it something to do with a present?'

Fen moved her head a little.

'It was all something to do with a very complicated plan, too complicated to explain, really.' She shut her eyes. Emily was hardly satisfied with the explanation, but saw that this was a bad time to pursue the subject further. She debated whether to suggest telling her mother a story, or whether to leave her to sleep.

At that moment her father came in. Fen opened her eyes. Idle sat on the end of the bed, beside Emily. He and Fen exchanged a look which Emily didn't miss – the kind of look, she knew by experience, that was the harbinger of bad news.

Idle began gently.

'Em, there's something that Mama and I need very badly: that is, a holiday. I've been working terribly hard for months and months, and Mama – well, this weather seems to have bitten into her. She doesn't look very well, does she?'

Emily fiddled with the elastic top of one of her socks. Now she considered it, Mama didn't look all that bad.

'I suppose not,' she said.

'So. Now is the only time I can get a few days off. I think we really ought to take our chance. I'd like to take Mama away to the sun.'

Emily looked at her mother. Fen's eyes were worried, enquiring.

'What would I do?' Emily asked.

'Well, we thought you might like to go to Aunt Tab. Just for a few days.' Tabitha Wylie was a distant relation of Idle's. Emily hadn't seen her for a couple of years. She recalled a woman with a loud voice, a lot of dogs, and gigantic cedar trees in the garden. She had enjoyed herself there, once, because Aunt Tab had given her limitless sweets. 'How would that be?'

'But you've only just come back.' Emily turned to Idle. 'I've only seen you for a few days.'

'I know, I know. It's bad luck all this should happen in your holidays. But it really will be for such a short time. We thought you'd understand. All right?' Emily climbed down from the bed.

'I suppose so,' she said.

'Here.' Fen stretched out her arm. Emily went to her. 'We wouldn't be doing this, Em, unless we really needed to. You know that, don't you?' There was an urgency in her voice. Emily nodded, not trusting herself to speak.

She left the room and went downstairs, trailing her feet, trailing a hand down the banisters. Marble was crossing the hall. She seemed deflated now Christmas was over. Her navy dress, no longer pristine, reflected her melancholy, and the curls of her fringe went every which way. She looked up at Emily.

'You look like a wet week of Sundays,' she observed. 'Just like I feel.' She went through the kitchen door, slamming it behind her.

Emily made for the drawing room. There, to her dismay, she found Mrs Whicker. Usually her grandmother stayed in bed late every morning. Now she sat on the chair she shared with Badger, reading a paper. It was too late for Emily to retreat. She had been seen.

'What a dreary face,' said Mrs Wicker. 'When I was a child we were taught to have pleasant faces all the time. Come on in and tell me about it.'

Emily walked silently across the room. Mrs Whicker's eyes, scarlet veined, followed her closely. She sat on the floor by the fire.

'What's the matter, child?' Mrs Whicker persisted. 'You're going home. You should be pleased.'

Emily couldn't help smiling at her grandmother's perspicacity.

'Mama and Papa are going away for a holiday,' she said.

'Quite right, too,' snapped Mrs Whicker, folding her paper with great care. 'They look as if they could do with a holiday. Parents need to get away, you're old enough to realise that.' She paused, then added, 'Especially from their children.' There was a cruelty in her tone that made Emily look up. Her grandmother, backlit by the sleety window, was a rigid, hideous figure. An ivory frame, large as a saucer, hung from a gold chain round her neck. In it was a sepia photograph of herself and Lord Warren on their wedding day, two blurred smiling figures, their arms locked as if for life. In the photograph Mrs Whicker's young mouth tilted up with great beauty: now, it was a downward arch, bitter, ugly. As Emily made no response Mrs Whicker went on,

'Due to circumstances your father spent much of his child-hood away from me. It may have been a little hard for him at the time, but it had its excitements, it was never boring. And look at the man he's turned out to be.'

Emily, who was afraid of her grandmother in such moods, felt a sudden boldness.

'I'd like to have a really boring life with Mama and Papa just there all the time,' she said.

'Stuff and nonsense, child.' Mrs Whicker's scorn made her draw herself up even higher in her chair. 'And what a dull child you'd turn out to be if that was the case.' She stood up and walked over to the Christmas tree, whose coloured balls had lost all their sparkle in this bruised morning light. 'When it comes to you, Emily, my dying wish will be that you may never have a boring childhood, or a boring life. Pain, yes. We all need a little of that. Incomprehensible happiness, yes. Ups and downs. Excitements and disappointments, but never boredom.' She tapped at the lower branches of the tree with her cane. A small shower of fir needles dropped to the carpet. This seemed to please her. She turned on Emily. 'I don't think, as a matter of fact, my wishes will be necessary to you.'

She smiled. Her mouth became a caricature of her younger smile caught in the photograph in the ivory frame on her breast. Then, she might have been an ordinary woman. Now, Emily saw, she was a witch. A mad, evil witch, and in spite of the fire a shiver went down her spine.

Arrangements were made with shocking swiftness. A day after the pleasure of returning home Emily found herself being trans-ported again, this time to the care of her Aunt Tabitha Wylie.

Aunt Tab had fallen on hard times. The fall had not been a very steep one, in fact: her parents had been comfortably off but not rich. They had left everything to their unmarried daughter, who was also comfortably off but, due to the high taxation of private incomes, and a certain consumption of gin, was a little less rich. But it wasn't with her own background Aunt Tab liked to compare herself. It was her great-grandparents, illustrious landowners, from whose grandiose life she felt herself to have fallen. The fact that she had never met these ancestors, or indeed so much as visited their estates, made no difference to her standpoint. Telling the story of her tribulations so often, she had come to believe it herself, many years ago. Now, one of the pleasures left to her was to grumble about the necessity of her humble circumstances – an expensive country club – and as the grumble wasn't a very real one, it was easy enough for her to assume a brave face. Her courage was considerably fortified by a secret supply of alcohol, though in the public bar she made a point of drinking nothing stronger than tomato juice.

The country club in which Aunt Tab had stoically lived for seventeen years was a large Regency house set among undulating lawns – a constant worry to its owners, who weekly threatened to pull it down and sell the land for building plots. Aunt Tab, who felt after all these years that the place was almost her – unsuitably humble though it was – had volunteered to mow the lawns herself once a week. This served as a placatory measure for some time, though at any hint of a new threat Aunt Tab found herself offering yet more responsibility for the garden. 'Let me weed the herbaceous border,' she would cry. 'That shall be my job . . . no need to worry.' They accepted her offer, and she was the only one who worried: the gardening depressed her more than she would admit. Mud forever under her nails, the mower heavier every week, pains in her back and arms. But not for anything would she give in, having taken on these duties.

The black cedar trees Emily remembered stood at intervals on the lawns, vast keepers of the doomed grounds. (When the time came for building plots, they would have to go first. This thought, above all others, brought tears to Aunt Tab's eyes, and re-spurred her to tackle the endless yards of neglected shrubs and flowers.) She loved the protection of the trees. The domed spaces under the lower boughs were the only unseasonable parts of the garden. There, neither snow nor sun were able to penetrate. The green gloom, the rotting foliage underfoot, the almost undiscernible wind in the great branches filled Aunt Tab with perpetual awe. Daily, she encouraged her pack of dogs from one tree to the other, hurrying across the tiresome stretches of lawn between them. Daily they disobeyed her and ran amok in the herbaceous border, tearing down plants she had so carefully tied up. But Aunt Tab's tolerance towards her dogs was without limit: they were the gaiety in her life. They could do anything they liked, so far as she was concerned, except die. That alone was betrayal.

Emily arrived at the country club on a cheerless afternoon. Snow lay in spines along the branches of the cedar trees, but was shrinking from the edges of the lawn. Aunt Tab, hearing Emily's taxi, wrenched herself from a confused reverie from under one of the trees, and banged her way over the lawn. She had a strident voice and a strident walk: all parts of her moved out of rhythm, the arms of her khaki anorak swinging against her thick sides.

'Yo ho, Emily my dear. Glad to see you.' Her voice echoed across the snow. 'Seen the boys anywhere, have you? Hope one of them isn't off down the road. Lads!' She stopped, legs apart, and whistled. From all parts of the garden her loyal pack came bounding, each in his own fashion. Whippets and bulldogs, many of them so old their leaps were reduced to stumbles. Seeing Emily through their half-blind eyes, they jumped upon her as best as they were able, sending up clouds of revolting breath. Her hands were clutched at by decaying teeth, and made slimy by mauve tongues. The trembling nails of a geriatric whippet scratched at her legs. She hadn't remembered so many dogs. Hating them, she backed away.

'Aunt Tab . . .'

'Down, boys.' The dogs were deaf to Aunt Tab's command. She lunged at them, boxing some of their ragged ears, kicking softly at their swollen bellies with her gumboots. They slouched away, then, the excitement over. 'They like to see a new face. What can you expect?' Aunt Tab pinched Emily's cheek and pulled her hair with the same mixture of authority and love she had bestowed upon the dogs. 'Good to see you. You haven't heard the news, have you? Being away for Christmas. Phoebe's died. Christmas Eve. I never thought she would, somehow. Come and see her grave before we go in.'

They approached one of the mountainous trees. Aunt Tab lifted a lower branch, as if she was opening a front door, for Emily to duck beneath. A black-green cathedral of boughs rose above them. They had kept out the snow, but not the snow silence. The earth was soft and dry, the light mottled uncooked turkey – blotchy purple. She ran a hand, matching colour, through her grizzled hair.

'There it is. The headstone,' she said.

Emily looked down. The stone, a simple cross, was inscribed with the words *Beloved Phoebe. Jan 14th 1948–Dec 24th 1974.*

'She must have been quite old,' ventured Emily.

'Game to the last,' replied Aunt Tab. 'Full of spirit. Fought for her life to the end. They filled her full of drugs and fixed her back legs on wheels. But she managed all right. Oh, she managed. And with dignity, too. You weren't really *aware* of the wheels, with Phoebe . . .'

She felt in the pocket of her anorak and brought out a Mars Bar.

'Here.' Breaking it, she handed one half to Emily. That was the strange thing about Aunt Tab. Just as she had plunged you into the deep end of her own concerns she rescued you with something practical like chocolate. Aunt Tab held up her own half of the bar as if she were about to propose a toast.

'No disrespect to the dead, Phoebe,' she said quietly. Emily saw her grey lashes flutter quickly about her eyes, disturbed.

They stood looking at the grave, eating their chocolate. A

funny old grown-up world, this one, thought Emily. This would make Wolf laugh if he was here. If he was here we could have quite a good time in this house and garden. Without him, there was not much point in exploring.

'There'll be snowdrops on Phoebe's grave,' said Aunt Tab, 'when the snowdrops come.'

What a strange place, Aunt Tab's world. You could visit it, of course, but it wouldn't change, not for one moment, just because of your visit. Grown-ups were so often like that. So absorbed in their own lives that they just didn't notice you at all, and you couldn't get through to them, no matter how hard you tried. A grown-up's preoccupation was something almost not worth fighting. But children – luckily they weren't like that. Wolfe and she, for instance. They could be very absorbed making their bird town. It interested them, they concentrated hard. But if someone came into the room, they would at once inquire whether that person had any ideas. And if they had, they'd be prepared to abandon their bird town. Immediately. They wouldn't just carry on as if a visiting person made no difference . . . which it didn't to Aunt Tab. She was pleased to see Emily. But if Emily hadn't come she would still have gone to Phoebe's grave, eaten half a Mars Bar, gone on to feed the other dogs. Beyond this small space of quiet under the tree, the dead Phoebe and the rest of the pack who just clung to life, nothing else seemed to exist for Aunt Tab. As she gazed at this woman who kicked gently at the grave with her foot, Emily suddenly realised this. She realised the sadness of the condition in which a visit can make no difference to you any longer. Aunt Tab's absolute aloneness made her afraid.

'That will be nice,' she said, meaning about the snowdrops, though it was a long time ago since Aunt Tab had spoken. 'And later you can put other flowers.'

'Oh yes. I shall do that.' Aunt Tab bent down and touched the gravestone with her hand. 'I can't believe she's turning to dust down there, you know. Not that I can ever imagine her like that, dead. In my mind's eye she will always be the young pup I bought in Farnham Common on a winter's day, much like this.'

She paused, made her voice bright. 'When they go, you see, they leave a hole that happy memories are just no good at filling. No good at all.'

In reaction to the force of Aunt Tab's melancholy Emily felt a brief desire to giggle. But then an idea struck her – an idea which might even console.

'You could always get a puppy, couldn't you? I mean one of the same kind as . . .' Seeing the sudden horror on Aunt Tab's face, she trailed off. Somehow, she had made a mistake.

'A *puppy*, Emily? To replace Phoebe?' Her voice rose. 'How could any puppy . . .?' Her eyes were hard with the impossibility of the thought. 'You should never have suggested such a thing. You should know some things are irreplaceable. What would be their worth if they weren't? But I'm sorry. You couldn't know, could you?'

She took Emily's arm and led her back through the branches to the brightness of the snow lawn. Having felt sorry for her, Emily's sympathy had now quite vanished. Suggest a puppy and the woman had gone all peculiar, a quivery voice as if she was going to cry. She had been angry, too. Why had she been angry? Suddenly Emily didn't care, or even want to know. She had had enough of Aunt Tab's gloomy life. She wanted no more of it. It was a weight she didn't care to understand.

Emily spent four days with Aunt Tabitha. They passed with a slowness she had never experienced before. She made charts, dividing the time down to minutes and seconds, but nothing hurried the hours. They seemed interminable.

She spent much of her time in her aunt's private sitting room, which had long ago been given over to the considerations of the dogs. Their bowls of food cluttered the floor, never quite finished. Their upset water made damp patches on the carpet, and their moulting hairs had given the sofa and armchairs an impermanent furriness: patches of hair stuck to any human – second-class occupant of this room – who ventured to sit down.

Then there was the smell. While Aunt Tab seemed oblivious

to the stench of canine life, Emily was unable to get used to it. Mornings, she would sit at the oil-cloth covered table, clear herself a space between the tins of minced rabbit, and set herself to painting. She concentrated hard, trying to take her mind off her surroundings. But it was impossible. The background hum of catarrhal snufflings aggravated her ears. The occasional high-pitched yelp, from whichever dog Aunt Tab happened to be brushing – and thereby reducing its threadbare coat nearer to a dull glow of hairless skin – sent shudders of displeasure through her body. Did her parents, she wondered, know the decayed state of Aunt Tabitha's life? Had they really supposed they would enjoy her stay here? (As she indeed had when she was much younger, when the dogs were younger, and the pleasure of sweets a tireless one.) Probably they didn't know. Well, they soon would. She'd tell them all right. She'd also tell them she was never coming here again. Never ever. That was quite definite. And what were *they* doing? She drew them, water-colour people with huge smiles, jumping about in the sea. She added herself to the picture. By rights she should have been there too. Why hadn't they wanted her to go? After all, it was her holidays. She wouldn't have been any trouble. She'd just have sat in the shade, reading or something. Not a bother to anyone.

Here, rain fell against the windows. It was cold in spite of the gas fire. Any moment Aunt Tab would ask her to come on the morning walk. It wasn't fair.

'Time for a breath of fresh air,' Aunt Tab was indeed saying.

'What, in this?' Despondency, the kind so acute that you can watch the skin shrinking to goose-flesh, penetrated Emily. 'Hadn't we better wait till it lays off a little?'

'It may never lay off.' Aunt Tabitha was squeezing the dogs, one by one, into wool-lined mackintosh coats. 'Come along, now, Emily. On with your boots. You can be responsible for Solange.'

Solange was a particularly noxious whippet. Emily had been put in charge of her each morning, and had always had the same trouble. This morning was no exception. As the rain battened down with increasing force, so grew Solange's determination to stand – all four quivering legs astride – in a puddle. She refused to move. Emily pulled at the chain leash, until the collar cut into the skinny neck. She shouted words of encouragement, pushed the trembling buttocks with a frustrated hand – all to no avail. Solange stood her ground, her muzzle darkening as it grew wetter. Emily, cold, despairing, watched Aunt Tab's boxy figure become smaller in the distance, the rest of the pack snuckering about her, apparently enjoying themselves. To avoid being left in her miserable position until Aunt Tab's return (an hour, at least) there was only one thing left to do. Emily bent down and picked up the dog. Its ribs rattled under her hands; its skinny legs scrabbled against her and it raised its top lip in a delicate snarl. Such loathing Emily had never felt for any living creature. Revulsion almost blinded her. She waded through the puddles, rain meeting with tears on her cheeks, and started running to catch up with Aunt Tab. Never again would she touch Solange, or any of them, no matter how angry it made Aunt Tab. She'd tell Mama and Papa. She would. They'd understand and never make her come here again. Then she remembered: no, they wouldn't understand. How could they? At home, it would be impossible to describe how this morning had been. It would simply sound like a funny story.

'The funny thing about Solange,' Aunt Tab was saying, when Emily at last reached her, 'is that she shouldn't have been a dog at all, but an otter. That's what I often think.'

It rained for four days, decaying the snow, drenching Emily and Aunt Tab and the dogs both morning and afternoon. Between walks much time was spent fitting wet clothes – dogs' and humans' – on to the one lukewarm radiator. They were never quite dry in time for the next walk.

Apart from going out, the only time they left Aunt Tab's private apartment was for meals. In spite of relief from the dogs, Emily dreaded these intervals. For in the public dining room Aunt Tab gave vent to her most outrageous feelings about her fellow country club guests. In a voice well suited to bellowing across open spaces, she would indulge in observations that would cause Emily to blush throughout the meal. (The heat of her face made an uncomfortable contrast to the chill that had settled over the rest of her body.)

'Of course, these people aren't anybody,' Aunt Tab would say, netting in her glance the dozen or so middle-aged people who ate in the compromise silence brought upon them by years of compromise marriage. 'Anybody who's anybody knows that dogs are allowed into the grandest dining rooms in England. They're absurd, the sort of rules they make in these places.' A few diners would look up, scarcely interested. They'd heard it all before, were apparently impervious to insults. But their indifference only served further to enrage Aunt Tab – particularly at dinner, when the three glasses of iced water upstairs 'to cool me off' had failed to do so. Her voice would increase in volume, easily rising above Brahms' Ten Greatest Hits which the muzak played over and over again. 'If one of the lads should have a heart attack during dinner, and I arrived too late, we know who we should blame.' She bent towards Emily. '*We know who we should blame, don't we*?' As Emily made no reply she added, 'In my grandfather's house one of the labradors died in Queen Elizabeth I's bed. No one minded, naturally. But then the upper classes understand about style, always have. Whereas these people . . .' She flicked a contemptuous hand over her plate, knocking a row of prune stones on to the tablecloth.

A short time later Emily followed her aunt out of the room with a feeling of great wretchedness. She hated at any time to be stared at, and the other diners now openly watched their exit. Aunt Tabitha seemed strangely unsure of her step. Though the tables were set wide apart she managed to bump into them, provoking sharp looks from their occupants. Embarrassment – an almost permanent emotion since she had been here – made Emily quite stern.

'Come *on*, Aunt Tab,' she said.

Upstairs, as was her habit every night, Aunt Tab poured

136

herself a glass of brandy 'to warm me up'. She slumped into an armchair. Her legs were slung apart, bulbous, against the old dog rug that covered the chair. Emily, opposite, averted her eyes from the wadge of thigh, also visible, that puffed out from knicker elastic. Hands cupped over her nose, she watched instead the bloated face. Once, it might have been handsome. Now, swollen lids shut, ragged mouth turned down, it was all askew, too revealing. It was difficult to feel sorry for Aunt Tab, looking as she did.

'Game of snakes and ladders, Emily?'

'No thank you.'

'Good. Chocolate?'

'No thank you.'

Various dogs breathed uneasily in the silence. The gas fire hissed. To think, this, every night. Emily rubbed cold hands on her cold knees.

'It's the evenings I can't abide so well, you know.' Aunt Tabitha had opened her eyes. She had said the same thing every night. Next, there would be the bit about the Common. 'In the old days we would spend every afternoon walking over the Common. All of them, racing about, loving it. But they've aged since the war. Some of them died, whenever it was.' She gulped at the brandy. 'You have to consider your dogs. Have to judge when to cut down their exercise. But those walks tired us out nicely, you know. After dinner we'd sit by the fire, all of us, each one in his special place, and feel wonderfully sleepy.' She smiled, and added, 'Some of the older boys would nod off before bedtime and I'd have to wake them up to get them upstairs. "Wake up, Rudolph", I'd say. "Wake up, Rudolph, or you'll be cold down here all night".' She kicked one feeble foot in the air, dislodging a loose shoe. 'He'd wake up and smile at me.'

Emily stood up. She would go to bed now, count the final hours till morning on the chart hidden under her pillow. She wanted to hear no more. Aunt Tab still kicked at an invisible Rudolph.

'Angus handed over the whole pack to me before he went to the war. The whole pack before he went to the war . . .'

'Good night, Aunt Tab.'

'He put the whole responsibility in my hands. Are you going to bed now? Well. If he'd come back and we'd . . . He'd have found them all in good shape.'

'I'll see you in the morning.'

'I don't think he would have thought I'd let him down.'

Aunt Tab didn't notice Emily leave the room. Her glass was raised in her hands, her eyes smeary with pink liquid.

'Angus . . .' she was saying.

Emily's camp bed had been put up beside Aunt Tab's single bed. The room was chaotic, but at least no dogs slept there. Only Phoebe's basket, left as she had died in it, stood in one corner. Emily, lying down, listened for a while to Aunt Tab stumbling about in the next room, filling water bowls, talking to the dogs. In contrast to her firm stride by day, her unsure evening step was unnerving. What exactly was the matter with Aunt Tab? Was she just very tired? Whatever it was, Emily wanted to see no more of it, ever again. She prayed to sleep quickly, because she dreaded to see the struggle Aunt Tab must surely have undressing. Her hand trembling, partly with cold, she put out the light.

Brightness suddenly behind her lids. She woke, surprised. It wasn't morning. Her back was to Aunt Tab's bed. She heard a groan. She spun round, fearful.

Aunt Tab, quite naked, was clambering with some difficulty on to the end of her own bed. Her loose breasts lolled over the mound of her stomach, the nipples shockingly brown: a curled up foot, out of control, kept slipping off the blanket.

'Aunt Tab! Whatever . . .?' Emily heard the scream in her own voice. Aunt Tab grunted. Her face seemed very dark. Heart attack . . . purple face. Wolf said something about a man in the street he'd seen with a purple face having a heart attack. The realisation blazed through Emily's head. Her own fingers were claws over her eyes, but she could still see.

Aunt Tab had mounted the bed now. She stood upright, for

perhaps a second, back to Emily, poised like a diver. A black line thin as wire split the obscene expanse of her bottom. Pulp flesh. If she fell, the whole thing would break apart, rotten fruit.

She fell. As she crashed to the floor, Emily screamed again. Next door a dog whimpered. Then silence.

Emily ran to her aunt. Her whole body, now, was askew, a slack old cushion flung on the worn carpet.

'Aunt Tab . . .?' Emily's hand touched the head. It was warm. The rough grey hair had fallen into a maze of white partings. 'Aunt Tab, are you all right ?'

No sound. Eyes shut, oozing tears. Mouth half open, oozing saliva.

Emily ran, blindly. She was aware of the stairs, the sudden warmth of red carpet under her feet. Lights, dressed people round the bar. Talking, laughing. They didn't notice her at first. Then one of them gave a shout.

'The child's sleepwalking!'

'Please. Aunt Tab's ill.' Her hands and legs shook. 'Quickly.'

The owner of the country club, a nice pale woman, was beside her.

'I'm coming at once. Reg, give me a hand.' Her husband's mouth fell open, making a black hole under his wide moustache. They ran back up the stairs, after Emily. At the sitting room door Emily stopped.

'Wait a minute, please.'

'Why? We'll come with you.'

'*Please.*'

They let her go back to the bedroom alone. Quickly she pulled down from behind the door Aunt Tab's old plaid dressing gown, misty with dogs' hair. She threw this over the body. It hadn't moved. She ran back to the sitting room.

'Please help her quickly,' she said. 'I think she's had a heart attack.'

They left her and she went to sit on the stairs. The carpet pricked her skin through her pyjamas. She looked down at the lights in the hall, and listened to the laughing people in the bar.

139

Gradually, her shivering stopped. And later, when they gave her something hot to drink in a strange warm room, they told her Aunt Tab hadn't had a heart attack. She had merely eaten something that hadn't agreed with her.

'The prunes, perhaps.' The moustache gave a sort of laugh. 'She wasn't at all herself, but she'll be all right in the morning.'

They took her back to bed. Aunt Tab snored in the dark, the same shaped hump, under the bedclothes, as she had been on the floor. Emily's own bed was cold. Her head on her pillow was crowded with the white grain of jumbled words. *Mama and Papa, why did you send me here? Why did you leave me?*

The questions pounded but the answers lay beyond some unreachable horizon. She didn't cry – she'd tell them she didn't cry – and eventually a winter dawn paled the curtains.

Emily was watching when Aunt Tab woke at seven. The relief, at the sight of her open eyes, made her very tired.

'Lads!' cried Aunt Tab, heartily, as all the other mornings. The dogs came snortling in from the next room. 'Morning all,' she said, shifting under the bedclothes. 'I had the strangest dream.'

At the sound of her voice the dogs lapped more eagerly round her bed, some rising stiffly on their back legs, trying to jump upon it. Aunt Tab smiled, a grey mouth. She slipped one hand from under the sheets, let it hang down. The dogs scrabbled to lick it, tongues with ghostly shadows of visible breath.

'There, lads,' said Aunt Tab, softly.

Seven

'Coral got stinking drunk while you were away,' said Wolf. 'She fell down the back stairs and twisted her ankle. It was quite funny, really.'

'Well, Aunt Tab had a heart attack. She went purple in the face just like that man you told me about in the street. They told me it wasn't a heart attack – she was just ill or something. But of course, I knew.'

'Course. They can't fool you about a heart attack.'

'What does Coral do when she's drunk?'

'She's absolutely revolting. She sways about and drops things and nobody can understand what she's saying very well, though it seems to be the same thing over and over again. Then she's inclined to take her clothes off. She starts tugging at her scarf and undoing the buttons of her shirt. That drives my father really mad. He starts to pull her from the room so that I shan't see, so she hits him and they have a real old ding-dong.' Wolf paused. 'In a way it's quite funny, except that my father usually comes off worse. He's not as strong as Coral.'

'Poor him,' said Emily.

They sat on a bale of old hay in the barn loft. In the last few months they had tidied it up a bit, and stored a collection of secret things on the one shelf: a tin of biscuits, a knife, a pen that wrote with invisible ink, and Emily's spasmodic diary, which she sometimes let Wolf see. They had left the carpet of chaff and

141

straw: it dulled their footsteps and hid the rotting floorboards. They had tried but failed to open the small window in the sloping roof. Its glass was matted with cobwebs and dirt, and through it a shaft of dun light speared the brown gloom. The place smelt of must and old apples – a persistent smell that didn't, like more sophisticated scents, fade with familiarity. No one ever disturbed them in the loft, and they revelled in the warmth of its privacy.

'I once saw Coral in the bath by mistake,' said Wolf.

'Did you?'

'She was lying back with these two sort of mountains sticking out of the soapy water.' He giggled. 'She was absolutely revolting. As a matter of fact, I don't think even my father goes for her that much without any clothes on. Sometimes, when she comes in, I've seen him turn his head away when she just takes off her hat.'

'Aunt Tab hadn't got any clothes on when she fell off the bed,' said Emily. 'She was pretty revolting, too.' They both giggled again, quietly, not looking at each other. Then Wolf caught Emily's eye.

'I suppose we'll all become like that in the end,' he said.

'What, you mean all fat and squidgy?'

'Yuh.'

'We won't. Not if we're careful.'

'You bet we will.'

Emily glanced at Wolf's bony knees straining against his jeans.

'I can't imagine you fat and disgusting,' she said, 'ever.' More boldly, Wolf let his eyes run over Emily.

'Can't really imagine you, either,' he said.

They heard someone moving about in the barn beneath them. Wolf leaned over to look through the trap door, which they had fastened back. Usually, fearing no disturbances here, they only shut it on ill-defined but special occasions.

'It's your mother,' said Wolf, and leant back against the wooden wall again.

They listened as she climbed, hesitantly, the ladder: watched as her head emerged through the hole in the floor, the edges of her hair shifting with quiet colours in the winter loft-light. Then her neck, muffled in a long woollen scarf of multicoloured stripes, and finally her bosom, taut under a sloppy dark satin shirt that flickered like her hair. When her waist was floor level she stopped, lifted her hand and buried her face in a bunch of snowdrops she held. In the poor light they were a solid lump of white crystal. *My mother is a mermaid,* said Emily to herself, *she's come up from the bottom of the sea, white rock in her hand.*

'Just the first,' said Fen. 'There are going to be masses and masses in the orchard. It's going to be absolutely white.' She waved the bunch in an arc through the gloom, and guided them to swoop down, together, a clutch of falling stars, on to the floor once more. Through the permanent hay and apple smell they had cut a small trail of some lighter scent, which vanished in a moment.

'Hope you didn't mind my coming up without asking permission,' Fen was saying. 'I just wanted to show you.'

'That's all right,' said Wolf. 'You can come any time.' From the tone of his voice Emily knew that he meant what he said, and what he had left out was that Coral could never come. 'Why don't you get right in?' he added. 'It's not terribly warm or comfortable, but we like it.'

Fen appreciated the compliment, but shook her head, smiling. Her skin was still brown from the French sun, her teeth as white as the snowdrops.

'Heavens, no. I won't disturb you any more. I'm just going in to put these in water. Then I'm going to cook you an amazing tea. Sweet corn with poached eggs and sausages.'

'Fantastic,' said Wolf.

'Aunt Tab'll be putting snowdrops on Phoebe's grave,' said Emily.

'What?' said Fen. She was already slipping away from them, head only left now, a final smile that conveyed some uncontainable happiness.

'She's a smasher, your mother,' Wolf said, when she had gone.

'I know,' said Emily.

'Where's your father this weekend?'

'Working in Brussels. He's always working.'

'That's men,' said Wolf. 'It's bad luck they have to work so hard. I wish your mother'd stayed for a bit.'

Emily lay back more comfortably on the bale of hay. Now that Fen had gone the loft seemed darker than it had done before her arrival.

'Perhaps in the summer,' she said, 'we could make a kind of restaurant up here and invite the grown-ups. They'd have to pay of course, but we'd make them menus and things.'

'There wouldn't have to be any candles,' said Wolf, 'or the whole place'd go straight up in flames.'

'Course not, stupid.'

'Well, they have candles in real restaurants.'

'You wouldn't think it a soppy idea, though?'

'Not really. Men work in restaurants.' Wolf was chewing a piece of hay. 'We'd have to ask my father but not Coral. We couldn't have her falling about in here spoiling it all. How could we manage that?'

There was a long silence between them.

'We'll think of a way,' said Emily. They fell back into easy silence, each thinking of a way. They listened to the purr of a couple of pigeons in the barn beneath them, a lulling accompaniment to their concentrated thoughts, dissipating them almost immediately. Then, abruptly, they heard the noise of a car swinging into the drive. At once they were both alert, craning their heads through the hole in the floor. Emily began to climb down the ladder.

'Perhaps it's Papa home early for a surprise,' she said.

Wolf followed her. At the bottom of the ladder they saw instantly that the car was a strange one. Kevin's.

'Oh, him,' said Emily, quietly. 'He hasn't been around for ages.'

They stayed where they were, in the shadows of the barn, without moving. Kevin hooted the horn, an ugly blare in the shrill quiet of the afternoon. He got out of the car and looked about, much as he had the first time he came. Almost at once Fen came running from the house, the ends of her long scarf flailing behind her, laughing, shouting something they could not hear. Kevin caught her in his arms and lifted her up so that for a moment she was raised right off the ground. She was standing again, but they still clung to each other. Kevin's face was buried in her hair, her scarf: his hands pried about her shoulders.

'Whew!' Wolf breathed quietly to Emily. She sensed his body, close to hers, was stiff. 'Everyone seems to love your mother so much,' he said.

'Oh, they do.' For her part, Emily felt a sudden ache behind her eyes. She watched, unblinking, as her mother and Kevin went up the path to the house, arm in arm. 'We might as well go in too.'

'You'd never see Coral hugging anyone like that, she'd be afraid of untidying her hair, silly old bag,' said Wolf.

They followed the grown-ups into the house. In the kitchen Fen and Kevin still had not separated. They leant against the Aga, Kevin's arm around Fen's waist, laughing at some private joke. They were unaware for a moment that the children watched them silently from the door.

'Hello, Kevin,' Emily said eventually. Kevin immediately moved away from her mother. His apparent pleasure in seeing Emily and Wolf was not reflected in Fen's face. In fact, she looked suddenly annoyed. But she made an effort.

'Look who's here,' she said, 'after all this time. Isn't that a lovely surprise?'

'We need you to help finish our bird town,' Emily said to Kevin. 'We got a bit bored of it.'

'Of course. Where is it?' Kevin seemed enthusiastic.

'Not *now*,' said Fen. 'Later. For heaven's sake. Kevin's only just arrived.'

'After tea, then,' said Wolf. 'I'm ravenous.'

'So'm I. You said you'd make us an amazing tea today, Mama.'

'Oh, darling.'

'You said in the loft.'

'I know I did. But we didn't know Kevin was coming then, did we?'

'What difference does that make? He'd probably like some too.'

'*Emily!*' Fen's voice was sharp, her head high, her satin shirt a solid sheen over her breasts. 'Sometimes, you're the most selfish child. You never think of anyone else. You only think of what *you* want.'

'Don't.'

'And don't argue.' Fen sighed, restraining herself. 'Listen, why don't you two go –?'

'– why don't you two go off and play?' chorused Wolf and Emily together, interrupting.

'Just for a while,' continued Fen. 'I haven't seen Kevin for such ages.'

'Just before Christmas, not all that long.'

'Oh, *Em*. Go on, please. And then you can have sausages, whatever you want. Promise.'

'Are you staying the weekend?' Emily asked Kevin.

'Heavens no. Back to the north.'

'Poor you,' said Emily.

She started upstairs, Wolf following her, their footsteps heavy with protest.

'Can't think what grown-ups have to say that's so *private*,' Wolf grumbled, when they were out of earshot. 'It seems to me their conversations are so boring.'

'Terribly boring,' agreed Emily, 'but I suppose they don't want to be interrupted.'

'I'd have thought they'd have been *grateful* to have some of their boring conversations interrupted.' They sat on Emily's bed, kicking its sides with their heels, disconsolate. 'I mean Coral, on the telephone, she's awful.' He put on a squeaky voice. '"Oh, darling, and do you know what she said to me and I said to her and she *didn't*? Honestly? Bla bla bla . . ." I can't think. Hours of rubbish on the telephone. I'd rather listen to the guinea pigs chattering.' Emily giggled. Wolf stood up. 'Anyhow, let's go and listen to their boring talk,' he said. 'There's nothing else to do.'

'Better not, had we?'

'Why not? Come on, cissy. They'll never know. If it's too boring we'll come back.'

'Oh, all right.' Emily was reluctant. But not wanting to appear unwilling in Wolf's eyes and lose his respect, she followed him back to the top of the stairs. There they stopped, rigid with quietness, certain they could not be seen. They could hear easily enough.

'It was *torment*,' Fen was saying.

Emily raised her eyebrows questioningly to Wolf. He ignored her. She leant over to him, and whispered in his ear.

'What's torment?'

'Torment's torment, silly. Shut up.'

Abashed, Emily rejoined him in listening.

'Absolute.' Fen's voice was quieter.

'Aren't you being over-dramatic?' Kevin.

'Probably.'

'At least you look better.'

'There was *sun*!' Fen was scornful. 'There was plenty of sun. But what did we do? He spent most of the time on the telephone, long distance calls to Africa. In his mind, he never stopped working for a moment. He can't ever stop working. He's afraid to.' There was the noise of some heavy china thing being dumped on the table. 'We can't talk to each other any more. Well, only domestic things. He has no idea, *no idea* what's going on in my mind, these days. Perhaps he doesn't care. He used to.'

'Perhaps it's just a bad patch.' Kevin's voice was louder than Fen's. 'Don't marriages have cycles?'

'It's a bad patch all right, for me. I don't suppose he's had time to notice anything's wrong. And it's not really helped by you.' Her voice was smiling.

'Shall I be off?'

'Silly. All I mean is, my energy to make things work is no longer directed towards him, is it?'

'I don't know what exactly you want. I seemed to drop into your life by accident, and felt compelled to entertain you a little, to take your mind off things. If I can be of some help, that would be good. But you won't ever bank on me for guaranteed assurance, will you? Or, I don't know, positive things. I'm no good at all that.'

'Kevin!' Fen's voice full of alarm. 'You're miles away! Where are you? Why are we talking like this? Here. Come here, please.' In the long pause that followed Emily could hear Wolf's distinct, regular breathing. Then her mother's voice resumed more softly. 'Of course you're a help, in one way. I don't know what I was saying. It's all this waiting business, the guilt, the expectation, moment to moment. It – ungrounds me so.'

'You got that from *The Dark is Light Enough*.'

'Of course I did.' Pause. Laugh. 'Quite right, entertainer. Why aren't you still just an entertainer? That was how we meant it to be, wasn't it? But somehow it isn't like that any more.'

'How is it, now?'

'How do you think?' Fen's voice was scarcely audible. Then, the swish of her skirt, the small shuffle of shoes on the floor, and more silence. Wolf stepped a cautious pace forward. Emily followed him. They peered down the stairs. They saw Fen clasped to Kevin, her arms thrown high round his shoulders, her head on his chest. He was kissing her hair, her eyes.

Emily stepped back, pulling at Wolf's shirt.

'I'm going,' she said. Her mouth was a downward line. There was a chill over her skin, a fine dew of sweat down her back. Wolf followed her back to the bedroom. He flung himself on to the bed, all-knowing, impervious to her distress.

'So he's your mother's *boyfriend*.'

'He's not.' Emily stood by the window looking out at the church, her face away from Wolf.

'What were they on about, then?'

Emily shrugged. She thought fast.

'Kevin's still an actor,' she said at last.

'So?'

148

'They were rehearsing part of a play. All those things they were saying – they were just their lines.'

'Don't believe you.'

'Really. It's true. Mama often helps him with his lines . . .' Emily turned slowly towards Wolf, her face a mask of honesty.

'And does she often have to kiss him to help him with his plays?'

'Sometimes. Not *often*, actually.'

'Well, she's a pretty good actress is all I can say.' Wolf seemed almost convinced.

'I told you, she's good at almost everything, Mama.'

They stayed silent for a while. Then Wolf said:

'I hope they've finished rehearsing by now because I'm hungry. I'm going down.' Mischief in his eyes.

'You don't still believe me,' Emily said.

'Oh, I do, if you want me to.'

'You should, because it's true.' Behind her back, she crossed her fingers.

'I'll ask them about the play.'

'Don't do that.' New panic stirred within Emily. 'Because it's a secret about their rehearsals. I shouldn't have told you. Mama'd be *furious* with me.' Emily looked directly at Wolf's doubtful expression. She made one final effort to quell his suspicion and to suppress his curiosity. 'I tell you what, when the play comes on, I'll get you tickets. We'll go, even though it's a grown-up play and probably very boring Then you'll see if I'm not right. You'll hear the bit about torment, or whatever the word was. Promise.'

Wolf got up.

'What's the play called?' he asked.

Some months before, Emily had written a play herself. Its title now did her a great service.

'It's called *Will You Fall in Love?*' she said.

'All right.' Wolf rubbed his hand all over his face, a gesture which Emily had learned was his sign of agreement. 'Let's go,' he said.

*

149

Fen kept her promise and cooked them a good tea, but her spirit seemed to have gone out of its production. Her shoulders slouched, her head was bowed. It seemed difficult to believe that the enthusiasm that inspired her so short a time ago, her wonderful smile and laughter in the barn, had existed. Her body was sad, the cheerfulness in her voice a hollow thing. Emily, realising something was wrong but not knowing what to do, sat silently at the table. Wolf, less sensitive to atmosphere, made patterns with matches by his plate.

Kevin, too, was subdued. Maybe because he had to go back to his horrible flat in the north, Emily thought. Anybody would be depressed if they had to return there. It was understandable, really, that he should sit in a corner, reading a paper, legs crossed, mouth bent downwards. One of his huge feet twitched regularly – up down up, every few seconds. He said no more about the bird town.

As soon as they had finished eating, Emily suggested to Wolf they should go out again. But he was in an unresponsive mood.

'Whatever for? It's freezing.'

'I want to see the stream.'

'It's almost dark. You won't see much.'

'I'll take a torch. Can we go, Mama?'

'If you put on coats.' Fen didn't seem to care.

'Come *on*, Wolf.'

'Oh, all right.' Wolf rose to follow her. '*What* an adventure.' Emily winced at his sarcasm, but reached for her coat with determination.

Outside they stood on the garden path a few yards from the house.

'What do you want us to do now?' Wolf asked.

Emily wondered. What should they do in the winter dusk? She suggested looking at the stream again, not that she had any real desire to see the stream. The only thing she knew, quite positively, was that it was essential to be out of the house for a while. She led the way to the field. Wolf, muttering complaints, followed her.

They stood on the banks of the stream in the long grass, wet with a cold evening dew. They looked down into the dusky waters.

'Very interesting, listening to stream water, I'll say.' Wolf had his hands in his pockets and his shoulders hunched up. He was frowning.

'Oh, Wolf. Shut up. What's the matter with you?'

'What's the matter with me? What's the matter with you, more like?' He turned to her. His face glowed damply, the freckles all blurred. 'Ever since Kevin what's-his-name arrived you've been mooning about. Couldn't get a thing out of you. At one moment I thought you were going to cry.'

Emily paused.

'Well, I wasn't,' she said. 'Don't be so silly.'

'Anyhow, I'm bored out here. And cold.' He stamped one of his feet, desultory thuds in the grass. 'I'm going.'

Emily knew she couldn't ask him to stay. She shrugged.

'All right. If that's how you feel. I don't mind.'

Wolf moved away. She watched him. He only went a few paces, then stopped and turned back to her.

'And anyhow I don't believe that silly story about them rehearsing a play,' he shouted, and turned away again. Above the mist that crouched on the ground his words spun in a solid ball, dropped, split the mist, disappeared, leaving a hole in the grey vapours. Leaving holes, threads, everywhere. Emily kicked at the greyness. Wolf was running up the hill, now. She wasn't looking but she knew he was running. He'd probably go home and tell his father she was a soppy date and he didn't want to play with her any more. He'd probably find another friend in the village – perhaps a whole gang. All because of this. All because of Kevin coming. It was all his fault. All Kevin's fault. He was an interfering old nuisance, Kevin, coming to things he wasn't asked to, turning up when he wasn't expected, sitting in Papa's chair, making Mama either laugh too wildly or almost cry. Emily stamped the ground, wishing it was Kevin she had trod upon. He should stay in the north in the future, or she wouldn't speak to him any more. She would tell Mama and Papa and Tom to keep him out of the house, because it was his fault Wolf had run away.

Emily climbed the hill to the orchard. There she stopped again, very cold, undecided. The trees were indistinct shapes in the thickening gloom. Under the hedge the first snowdrops were a thin scum of white, shining in the darkness of the ground cautiously as the first stars in the premature night sky. Lights were on in the kitchen: two squares of golden light in the black mass of the house. Comforting blocks of warmth and brightness, they were, in all this damp and cold and increasing darkness. Emily moved slowly towards them. When she came level with the first window she stopped and looked in. Kevin had not moved from his chair by the fire. Fen sat on the floor by his feet, her head thrown back on to his knees. There were flames in the dark satin of her shirt, and she was smiling, sleepily. Kevin was stroking her hair. He always seemed to be stroking her hair, or kissing it.

Emily stood watching them for a while. Once, Fen lifted her hand to Kevin's face, and rubbed his nose. This must have tickled him, because he laughed, and pushed it away. Fen laughed too, then, opening her mouth wide and showing all her teeth. But the laughs, from where Emily watched, were noiseless. She could hear no sound, and the silence of the laughter made her shiver. She realised that her hands and feet were very cold, and the hair round her face hung wetly from the damp. *I must go in*, she said to herself. *I must go in, I must go in, I must go in. Perhaps they won't notice me. I can slip up to bed and when I wake up in the morning Kevin will have gone for ever and Wolf running away from me will all have been a dream.* She turned to go into the house, her feet horribly sluggish. Perhaps it was the cold.

'You look like a ghost, Em,' said Fen, in the kitchen. 'What on earth have you been doing outside?'

'Nothing much.'

'Where's Wolf?'

'Gone.'

152

Kevin's hand was still rummaging gently through Fen's hair. Emily stared at it, but it didn't stop.

'Had a row, you and Wolf?' he asked in a laughing voice. Kevin had a funny way of guessing things accurately. Emily drew herself up.

'Not exactly. He was cold, that's all, so he went home.'

Fen stood up, slowly, sleepily, as if the act of rising was in itself a luxurious gesture. She went next door and put on some music. Chopin. The notes very fragile, very precise, winging into a frail melody that inspired Kevin's twitching foot to move with some kind of rhythm. Emily flung off her coat and sat in her own place at the kitchen table.

'When are you going?' she asked.

'Why? Am I bothering you?' Kevin stopped twitching his foot and kicked at the logs on the fire.

'Not particularly.'

'I won't be long.' He didn't look at her. He drank from his glass of wine and shifted nearer the fire, as if he owned it. Fen came back and resumed her old seat beside him on the floor. He put his free hand on her shoulder.

'Don't you want to watch television, darling?'

'No.' Emily looked her mother straight in the eye.

'Done your prep?'

'Yes.'

'Are you just going to sit there looking cross?'

'I'll go up to bed when Kevin goes. Will you read me a story tonight?'

Fen sighed.

'Tell you what, I'll read you the story. I'm the actor. I'll read to you both.' Kevin was being very friendly, considering. For a moment Emily felt guilty about her hostility. She said nothing.

They sat there, the three of them, almost without moving, listening to the music. Watching the fire. The flames split and flickered like sun through the branches of the apple tree. Last summer. Mama stood under the lower branches calling to Emily. Emily ran to her. Looked up, like Fen. Sunbeams dazzled the leaves, burning out their edges. Mama, head tilted back like it was now on Kevin's knee, had screwed up eyes to search among the greenery for a bullfinch. Where was it? Had it flown away? She hadn't seen a bullfinch since she was a child. Would Emily climb the tree, try to see it? *Oh yes.* Eagerly. She hoisted herself up, branches warm and scratchy under her hands. She thrust her head into a cloud of sparkling green. No bullfinch. She turned, looked down. There was Papa, suddenly, close to Mama, looking too. Very seriously.

'Jump, Em.'

She jumped. He caught her with a huge safe grasp. She slid to the ground, aware again of the smell of warm grass. Papa's arm went round Mama's waist now, and a couple of white butterflies flirted about her head. Then, a simultaneous shout from them both.

'*The bullfinch!*'

The bird spun away above their heads, his breast the briefest flash of scarlet, like sun on a cluster of falling rain, before he disappeared into the blue. Mama laughing, so pleased. Saying she knew she'd been right. Papa murmuring: 'I like you excited by such funny things.' Fen wasn't really listening. She held Emily's hand. Her eyes still followed the speck of bullfinch.

Papa was looking down at her, amazement in his eyes. Then he began to shout.

'My God, Kevin, what are you doing here? What the bloody hell are you doing in my house?'

In a split second Emily fought to realise that her father was no longer the man in her daydream, but here in reality, unexpected, shocking them all with the surprise of his return, and very angry. Never had she heard his voice so fierce. Never had she seen his face so contorted, almost to ugliness. While he shouted, Kevin and Fen leapt up simultaneously, startled as new flames on the fire.

'Idle . . .' Kevin held up his hands.

'Oh, Idle . . .' Fen clutched at the neck of her shirt, surreptitiously doing up the top button. Emily was forgotten. She remained quite still, watching. Her father, in the doorway, seemed to sag. He ran a hand through his troubled grey hair. With reluctant eyes he looked at his wife and Kevin.

'I'm sorry, forgive me. I thought the arrangement, though . . . I thought the arrangement?'

'It was,' said Fen, quietly. 'It was.' She walked over to Idle, her back very straight, her face flaming. She stopped a couple of feet short of him. The music had come to an end. There was a moment's absolute silence. Then Fen said:

'I'm sorry, Idle. We broke the arrangement this afternoon.'

Idle gave a kind of smile.

'Well, arrangements get broken. I'm sorry I shouted. It was the shock . . . I wasn't expecting.'

'I'll be on my way,' said Kevin, moving towards the door. But the door was blocked by Fen and Idle.

'It was the first time, honestly,' Fen was saying. 'Just tea . . . He was passing by. It's a pity he has to be in Oxford so often.'

'Quite,' said Idle. 'I can quite see the temptation.'

'All the same, we've broken our word and I apologise.' Kevin sounded more confident now Idle had calmed down. Idle straightened himself. His face had resumed its normal calm.

'Well, that's all right, old man. That's all right, really. Might as well stay now you're here – mightn't he, darling? Dinner or something. Perhaps we better talk it all over a bit further.'

'Really, Idle, there's no need for you to behave so bloody well . . . I can go.' Kevin shifted himself unconvincingly.

'No, no, get me a drink. Get me a drink, if you will.'

The three grown-ups scattered. Fen ran upstairs without looking at Emily, her hand over her face. Kevin left the room, taking with him a glass. Idle came up to the kitchen table. He bent down to kiss Emily. The kiss turned into a prolonged hug.

'Darling Emily girl.'

'Papa . . .'

'I got away early to give you a surprise. I thought . . .' He seemed to have to stop. His blue eyes were far away,

155

concentrating just as they'd been when they followed the bullfinch into the sky.

'It's lovely you're back. Why did you shout at Kevin?'

'I was jumpy, tired. You know how grown-ups get. I was expecting just you and Mama. The sight of Kevin gave me quite a fright. Silly, really. I'm sorry.' He ruffled her hair, attempted a smile.

'That's all right. Everyone's been bad tempered today.' Emily paused. 'Wolf ran away from me in the field. I've never seen him cross before.'

'I expect he'll come back.'

'Do you? Why?'

'People come back. They get used to people. Even if you get quite cross with someone, you know, it's hard to leave for good.'

'Is it really? Perhaps he'll come back, then. If he does, tomorrow, will you play something with us?'

'Of course.'

Emily led her father to the chair by the fire so recently occupied by Kevin. He sat down, leant back, let his hands lie dead on the arms, the fingers spread a little, blue veins running through the white skin. They were smaller, older hands than Kevin's. His face was far more handsome, though: his hair silver in this light, his eyes deeply hooded and his face a cobweb of lines that turned into surprising crinkles when he smiled. Emily sat on his knee and swung her foot against his leg. Although her heart was still pounding fast, she felt more cheerful. She tried to recall the angry words Papa had shouted at Kevin, and the quiet things they had all said to each other. But her memory of them had gone. She could only recall how they had looked: her mother wild and confused, Kevin foolish, her father bowed and sad. But he seemed to be all right now. The good thing about grown-ups was that they often recovered quickly.

'You go away too much, Papa,' she said. 'I wish you were here more often.'

'I know, my love, I know. Perhaps I will be, one day. When I'm old and retired.'

'You'll never be old!'

'Oh yes I will.' He closed his eyes. 'But next week I'll be here for a few days. I'll get Marcia Burrows to come down and help me, then I won't have to go to London. How about that?'

'Really? Do you really mean that?'

'I really do.'

Emily gave a whoop of delight.

'Shall I go up and tell Mama?'

'She'll be down in a moment. You can tell her then.'

'She'll be terribly pleased, I bet. Every night, Papa, you know, we try to imagine what you're doing. We talk about it before I go to sleep. Mama says you're doing awfully dull things, but I imagine you making speeches in your coat with the tails and people clapping you and giving you all the wine you want and things like that.'

Idle smiled.

'You're both right. I usually am doing dull things, like making dull speeches. I had to make one last night, as a matter of fact. At the Russian Embassy. They gave me a lot of vodka – that white stuff that makes your ribs feel on fire. In fact they gave me so much I made rather a good speech.'

'Were you all by yourself there? I mean, did you know anyone?'

'I took Marcia Burrows. She'd been working very hard all day for me, and I thought it might amuse her. She doesn't have a very gay life.' Emily giggled. 'What's the matter?'

'I can't imagine Marcia Burrows at a party, that's all. She'd wear such old woman's clothes.'

'She didn't look too bad, as a matter of fact. She'd had her hair puffed up in some way. I took her to dinner afterwards at a Japanese place. We ate raw fish. They served it up very prettily with its tail in its mouth.'

'How disgusting, raw fish, I mean.'

'Marcia wasn't at all squeamish. It made her laugh.'

'I'd never eat raw fish. I don't think Marcia Burrows is too bad except she looks so sort of stiff next to Mama.'

'She's a good secretary. Now, why don't you go and take a torch down to the cellar – to Kevin? He's been ages. Probably can't find the light.'

Emily got up. Her heart was back to normal.

'Oh, all right. Was the raw fish alive? Mama'll laugh when she hears about it.'

Idle looked suddenly tired.

'I shouldn't say anything about it, actually,' he said. 'Because the funny thing about Mama is that she can't bear even the *thought* of raw fish.'

'All right, then.'

'You're a sensible one, sometimes, Em. Hurry up and get my drink, will you, my love?'

Emily marvelled at the cleverness of grown-ups. On occasions when it was necessary, they were very good at hiding things. Much better than children. At school, if any of them had a row, they were inclined to sulk for several hours after it was over, or continue to be quietly nasty to each other, or simply to ignore each other. Grown-ups, or at least the grown-ups Emily knew, took care to disguise their feelings, and she admired that because it made things easier for everyone.

There was no doubt in Emily's mind that her parents and Kevin had had some kind of bad row, a serious row, by the looks on all their faces, though what exactly it was about Emily was at a loss to know. They had all appeared shocked: equally, they had all masked their shock, and returned to their customary faces and voices with impressive swiftness. And in fact the evening had gone very smoothly. Only a couple of things confused Emily. When she and Kevin had come back from the cellar with a bottle of whisky, Papa had stood up and shaken him by the hand before taking the bottle. The shake had gone on for a long time and then Papa had given a kind of rough pat, almost a shake to Kevin's shoulder. Kevin had looked surprised, and poured himself a neat whisky – normally, he only drank wine. Then Fen reappeared, and Kevin, whose eyes usually followed her everywhere, didn't look at her for a while. She had changed into a dress Emily had never seen before. Its dullness surprised her – some kind of grey wool stuff with a high neck. She smiled a lot, tossed her head about, and joined the others in drinking whisky. Then she set about cooking spaghetti with unusual concentration: every time she picked up a saucepan or cut a slice of butter or emptied a packet, the gesture seemed to be curiously important. If Papa and Kevin noticed anything strange about her, they didn't show it. Papa, still in his own chair, told the best of his safari stories, spinning them out, adding bits that Emily, who knew them all by heart, hadn't heard before. But he was much interrupted by Fen, who asked a lot of the kind of questions she would never normally ask: where was the tomato ketchup? Did Idle know whether there were any more peppercorns? She addressed each question specifically to Idle, who seemed confused by them, but politely made himself out to be an ignorant old fool for not being acquainted with the contents of the larder. At one moment, when Fen had complained three times that she couldn't find the rock salt, Kevin quietly got up – Papa continued with his story – went to the dresser and took it down from behind one of Emily's paintings. Fen snatched it quickly from him, laughing at her own stupidity, her hand shaking a little.

At dinner, everybody seemed suddenly and curiously interested in Emily. Papa asked her a lot of questions about Berlioz, whom she was studying in Musical Appreciation, and Papa had never been a musical man. They all listened seriously to her answers: their concentration upon her was almost unnerving. Then Mama went on to talk about poetry at school, what a bore it was, how it might put off anyone for life. In her day, she said, the entire school had been made to chant *Ode to Autumn* every Saturday morning, till each one of them had every inflection quite perfect according to the histrionic ear of the drama teacher. Pushing back her plate of spaghetti, Mama had then quoted the whole of the first verse in the extraordinary fashion she had been taught to recite the poem, and Kevin and Papa laughed properly for the first time. The poetry conversation over, Kevin began to ask Emily about Wolf. But on that subject Emily wasn't prepared to be drawn, and suggested she might go to bed. She was still hungry, but the spaghetti had stuck in her throat: like Mama and Kevin she had not been able to eat it. Also, she was suddenly very tired, the kind of tiredness after a hard race, as if a long skein of energy had been drawn out of her. All she wanted was to sleep.

But in bed wakefulness came to her again. Eyes open in the dark, she reflected quite clearly on the events of the afternoon and evening. It seemed to her strange that such happiness (the hour in the barn, Mama beautiful and gay with snowdrops) and such sadness (Wolf being cross and leaving her, the grown-ups' row) could come so close together. Change was constantly, confusingly fast, sometimes. Mama's moods, Papa's sudden departures and returns, even the weather. You couldn't rely on anything, really, or anyone. Not even a friend like Wolf. In the end even he couldn't understand things you were unable to explain. So he wouldn't think twice about leaving, just when he was most needed, because he'd probably no idea what he was doing. Would he ever come back?

Emily alarmed herself by the question. She sat up, pulling the two Patricks towards her. What should she do to make him come back? The adrenalin of urgency breeds swift ideas, positive in their comfort if not always brilliant. Desperate, Emily became inspired. That penknife, the one in the village shop with lots of gadgets and a picture of the Tower of London on its side – for ages Wolf had been wanting that. Coral wouldn't give it to him because she thought that penknives, even for boys, were dangerous – silly old bag. His father said he had to save his pocket money – 10p a week. The penknife cost £1. Emily knew Wolf had at least eight weeks to go – for ever. She knew, too, that if she explained the situation in the right way to Papa, he would lend her a pound. Delighted by the skill of her idea, Emily was now impatient for the next day to put it into practice. She went to the window to look for the dawn. But the sky was still densely black except for a scattering of lemony clouds that netted the moon. The church clock struck midnight.

She had heard Kevin's car drive away some time ago: now, she heard her parents coming upstairs. Not knowing exactly why, she crept to her own door and down the few stairs that led from the landing to her attic room. Hidden by the darkness, she sat down. It was just possible to see, through her parents' half-open door, that Idle was lying back on the bed, feet up. He hadn't bothered to take off the cover.

Despising herself as she did so, Emily prepared herself to listen. Eavesdropping was something she had never contemplated apart from the one occasion with Wolf. At school, it earned wrath and scorn. But now, she reasoned to herself, she would not be hearing anything important or private. Simply a few words of innocent talk which would mean the row was all over, forgotten, and they were happy again.

'I don't know. I just don't know.' Fen's voice was muffled. She was hanging things in a cupboard, perhaps.

'Well, there's still time for us to do something.' Idle, flat.

'Oh! We could *do* something. We could put on a good face for Emily's sake, lead our own lives and be horribly civilised.'

'If we did that, for my part, there wouldn't be any women. Don't you see, darling? Don't you see I don't want any other woman, ever? Only you.'

'You haven't been with me much, in that case.'

'I know, I know, I know.' An audible sigh from Idle. 'Yet what can I do till I retire? I can't change the nature of my work. You don't want to come with me on trips. I've offered to take you often enough. But you're quite right. They'd bore you dreadfully.' A long silence. Then: 'What's happened, exactly, do you think?'

'Simple. Kevin. You were away and I . . .'

'But I thought . . . At Christmas you admitted it was just an infatuation. A passing thing, you said, soon over if you didn't see him any more. I quite understood, didn't I? Wasn't I understanding? I meant to be. I *did* understand how it was, after all.

161

My being away so much. You lonely, in spite of all your protests. Kevin attractive, gay. And you so responsive. You've always been so damn responsive. No wonder people fall in love with you. I don't think you've ever known how dangerous you are. You sit there responding – I've seen you at it, a million times – wonderfully innocent, never knowing what you're doing to some wretched man's heart. But until Kevin, it was always something we could laugh about. Heavens, I could tease you. It was never a worry, really. Till Kevin.'

'I'm sorry.' Fen sat on the bed too. On the edge beside Idle. Emily couldn't see her face, just the skirt of her brown dressing gown. 'I can't lie to you. It's got out of hand. We missed each other. Much more than we foresaw. I suppose we love each other. Irresponsible, I know. But it's happened. What can we do?'

'Things only happen if you want them to. Things can only have happened because of some lack, here. Well, we know the lack. For my part,' Idle coughed, 'there are two alternatives.'

'Yes.'

'Can't we try again? Harder? Please. I'll cancel my next trip. I won't go on any more trips for six months, and damn the government.'

'We could go back to the old arrangement.'

'What arrangement? We never really discussed it. Do you mean that I should accept Kevin as your lover and in return you won't leave me?'

'Perhaps we could try that.'

'I don't think I could bear it, darling.' Idle's voice was so low Emily had to strain to hear it. 'I'm not a very sophisticated man that way. I could even be a jealous man.'

'If only you could! If only you could explode at me sometimes, be outrageously angry instead of so bloody tolerant all the time! That might clear the air. Your reasonableness is a terrible incentive to my destructive whims. How far can I go, I think, before you show you positively care?'

'But we all either show or disguise our caring in different

ways. You've always known I was a mild man. I love you, which means I must give you freedom to do whatever makes you happy. I cannot rage at you because I love you. I'm not a raging man.'

'Please! Don't look like that.' At the frightened note in Fen's voice Emily dug her fingernails harder into her knees. 'It's not that I don't love you. You know that. I'll always love you in a way. It's all my fault –' Her voice seemed to be breaking.

'It's both our faults. Don't, please darling. Don't cry. I hate to see you . . . You never cry, Fen. Listen, we've just got ourselves into a muddle. We're lucky not to have done so before, in twelve years.'

'And Em! What would she do? This house, everything. I've been driving myself crazy thinking what to do. Then I get so *weakly* nostalgic for the past, knowing it can't ever be like that – unsullied, I suppose – again. All those heavenly years we had. And you the best husband in the world, in a way . . .'

Idle gave a small, comforting laugh.

'Couldn't we be a little nostalgic for the future? Wouldn't we do better that way?'

A pause, then a sob.

'Why do I have to destroy the things I love best? Why do I sit watching myself doing things I have no wish to do? Caught up in a sort of terrible compulsion. And there's a nice bit of self-pity for you . . .'

'Don't . . . let's talk any more about it tonight. Please. Here. Blow your nose.' His voice quiet and kind, the voice he used to Emily if she fell down and hurt herself when she was younger.

'And all the time *you're* so reasonable, so good, so understanding, so uncondemning.'

'How could I possibly condemn the thing I love most on earth? Love isn't about condemnation, silly thing. Oh my darling love. Please stop crying.'

A silence. Emily saw Idle's legs swing off the bed. He crossed the room and shut the door. The landing and Emily's stairway were now in total darkness. For a while Emily didn't move. She rested her head on her knees, shut her eyes. Any moment she expected that she, too, would cry. She waited, but the tears didn't come. Only a picture in her mind, curiously bright in all the darkness: the day they had made the bonfire. Mama and Papa laughing at her apples that had fallen to pieces in the hot ash. Marcia Burrows looking puzzled. There had been nothing to be puzzled about: just Mama and Papa laughing, laughing, laughing.

Eight

*T*he next morning Emily borrowed a pound from Idle and went down to the village shop. In spite of her lack of sleep she felt no tiredness, but a sense of tremulous exhilaration that comes some mornings in early spring, shaking the spirits into the happy awareness that the seasons, for all their reliability, are always surprising. The bare trees and hedgerows were ruffled with the beginnings of green: a cool sun was high in a cloudless sky. Omens, perhaps.

She bought the penknife and set off down the road to Wolf's house. Halfway there she met him coming towards her. They stopped, both cautious, a few yards from each other. Wolf rubbed the whole of his face with his hand.

'I was just coming up to your house to see if I could have lunch with you,' he said. 'My father and Coral are going out. They said I could come too if you couldn't have me, but it'll be awfully boring.'

'Of course,' said Emily. Her heart, for some reason, was pounding. She took a step towards him, but there still seemed to be great distance between them. She held out the paper bag. 'I've bought you this,' she said.

'What's that?' Gruffly, Wolf took the bag. Took out the penknife. Lay it on his hand, turned it over and examined each side. Incredulous. 'I've been wanting that like anything,' he said.

'I know.'

'Where'd you get the money ?'

'My father.'

'He must be richer than my father. I'll pay you back, gradually.'

'No, it's a present.'

'Oh. Thanks. Look, here.' They stepped nearer the hedge to avoid a passing car. Wolf began to take out the various blades, examining each one slowly with his finger. They flashed in the sun. Emily, close to him, resisted touching them. Then he snapped all the blades back and put the knife in his pocket. He kept his hand in his pocket to cover the knife: Emily could see by the shape of the bulge.

'I was going to go up the church tower. Thought if I could get up there before they start ringing the church bells, I could measure the vibrations.'

'Measure the vibrations?'

'Well, see if the tower shook, anyway. Coming?'

Emily nodded. They walked through the churchyard. Emily noticed bald patches in the moss on some of the gravestones – Wolf's doing. It reminded her of the day they had met, and she couldn't contain a kind of bounce in her walk: *it's all right, he hasn't gone, he hasn't gone.*

Wolf gently opened the studded oak door. Inside, the church smelt of old prayer books, old prayers. Hundreds of years of praying under the same roof were bound to cause a dusty smell. Maybe all the thousands of words of saying please and thank you had filtered up to the arched beams, and clung there, invisible, eating into them like woodworm. On the altar there were two copper urns of evergreen, unlit by flowers. The verger, with the trance-like movements of one who believes he is alone, was placing song sheets on the choir stalls.

Unobserved, Wolf and Emily crept to the small door that led to the spiral stone staircase. They ran up the stairs without panting, used to the climb, the merest bit dizzy when they reached the trap door. The top of the tower was a square fortress with a slatted wooden floor. Its walls, chest-high, were level with the

166

tree tops. Among lower branches of these trees they could see the broken lines of village roofs.

Wolf sat on the floor, leaning against one of the stone walls. He took out his penknife again and began to re-examine the blades. Emily sat beside him. It was uncomfortable, but they were sheltered from the breeze. As the stiffness of the various blades became familiar to Wolf, so his absorption in the knife grew. Emily sighed.

'What would you say,' she said, 'if I told you my mother and father were going to get divorced?'

Wolf tested the corkscrew in the palm of his hand, turning it just hard enough to dent the skin.

'Why? Are they?'

'They might.'

'What makes you think that ?'

'I heard them talking about it last night.'

'About divorce?'

'Not really divorce. Just jabbering on about love and all that sort of thing. They both sounded sad.'

'I bloody well wish my father would divorce Coral. He's been with her quite enough.' Wolf speared the largest blade into a soft wooden slat in the floor.

'Perhaps we could make a plan to get your father to divorce Coral, and my parents to stay together.'

'Those sort of plans never work. Coral'd never let him go. Do you really think your parents'll bust up?'

'Don't know.'

'They'd easily find other husbands and wives if they did,

'I wouldn't want them to.'

'It might be all right.'

'Sandra Buckle, a girl at school, she's got masses of step-parents and step-brothers and sisters and things. She says it's very muddling. She never knows who to call her family.'

'It must be a bit muddling, but I don't suppose it matters all that much. People marry and divorce, marry and divorce. You know.'

'Well, I wouldn't mind so much if once they'd had their new husbands and wives they got divorced from *them* and married each other again. So they were still married when they died.'

'Then they could all be in the same grave.'

'That's what I mean.' In truth, she hadn't thought of that.

'Coral says she wants to be in the same grave as my father, but my mother's already in there. I hope there won't be any room. But she keeps on saying it. She nags on in case my father might forget. '"When we're laid to rest,"' she keeps saying, when she's drunk. I hope she dies first then my father can put her where he likes. Miles away, I hope.'

Emily giggled.

'In R.K. at school –'

'– What's R.K.?'

'Religious Knowledge.'

'We call it Scripture.'

'Well, in R.K. at school they said something about being married in heaven. So your father could remarry your mother in heaven, and not ask Coral to the wedding.'

'Fat lot of good that would do.'

They were both quiet for a while, imagining the heavenly weddings. Wolf, with the smallest blade of the knife, began to dig at a scab on his ankle.

'What I think you ought to do,' he said, 'is to ask your mother what's going on.'

'What would I ask her?'

'Just if she's going to get divorced.'

'What if I'd got it all wrong?'

'Then at least you'd know. Once you know for positive, we could make a plan.' Wolf was so wise, sometimes. Emily could have bought him a hundred penknives.

'What sort of plan could we make?'

Wolf thought.

'Simple, really. Tell your mother your father said she looked smashing behind her back. If they start to have a row, do something to take their minds off it – spill the pudding or find a dog to chase the bantams or something. Things like that.'

'Do you think that'd really work? Where could I find a dog?'

'I could lend you Stover.'

'He'd have to be there all the time, waiting for the row.'

'Well, anyway, I could think up lots of other things if you wanted.'

'That'd be good, just in case.'

'Okay. Leave it to me.'

Wolf got up and at that moment the first bell began to ring. Up here, it was a deep, resonant sound, very close. Three other bells joined it, four different notes. They pealed out their monotonous scale, the first two notes full of cheer, always to be followed by two more dispirited sounds. Wolf was standing at the edge of the tower, leaning over the wall. He called to Emily to join him. They watched the first few members of what would be inevitably a scanty congregation walk up the church path. Old people mostly, wearing velour hats in dusky shades, some moulded into ridges and pleats, blancmange-like. They still wore winter coats, and carried Prayer Books in their gloved hands.

Suddenly Wolf gave a shout. Emily looked to where he pointed. Coral and Wolf's father were walking up the path. Coral's suit was a colour of green that Nature had wisely rejected, and she wore a hat of pink feathers that waved around her blob of hair. She clung to her husband's arm, in step with him. Although side by side, she gave the impression of being the guide. For his part, Wolf's father moved with the appropriate solemnity of one whose next duty is to read the lesson.

'Wish I had my water pistol,' said Wolf. 'Those bloody feathers could do with a drenching.'

'What on earth's she come for?' Emily shouted against the uproarious bells.

'Communion wine, course.' Emily laughed.

The crashing of the four notes beneath them, persistent, remorseless as they were, gave her a perilous feeling. It was as if she and Wolf were abandoned in a square sky-boat, battered by waves of noise, churning in the sea of sky. The nearby trees, heaving in the breeze, gave her the illusion that it was the tower, not the leaves, that moved. She found herself gripping the stone wall, excited, her head and ears almost numb from the huge bell sounds.

Gradually, they slowed, decreased. Three notes evaporated. The deepest and most solemn was left tolling by itself. When that, too, stopped, for a moment the silence was almost over-whelming. Then, with the renewed rustle of leaves, the day settled back into a tranquil Sunday. From far below them came a thin chant, irregular in its progress.

> *Glorious things of thee are spoken*
> *Zion, City of our God . . .*

'Better be getting back,' said Wolf. But he seemed reluctant to move, and to put off the moment he pulled out all the blades of his penknife once again and brandished it, starlike, above his head.

'There's one person we know who's never going to get her hands on this,' he said. 'On the other hand, *you* can borrow it when you like.'

They descended the spiral stairs and waited for the hymn to end. Wolf pushed the door a little, and peered through. Members of the congregation had heads safely hidden in praying hands. Wolf and Emily crept out, unobserved, once more.

In the orchard, Idle, in a silk London shirt, sleeves rolled up, was pulling viperous ivy from the trunk of an apple tree. Fen made motions of helping him, but her arms, as she raised and lowered them, seemed without vitality. Her hands were slow. She wore an old pair of jeans and as she stood, pelvis thrust forward, leg apart, Emily noticed how suddenly thin she was. Beneath the denim her hip bones made two sharp points. Under the long voluminous skirts she usually wore her loss of weight had not been so apparent.

Even from some way off, the length of the garden, Emily was aware of an apartness between her parents, for all their physical closeness. She recognised at once this intangible distance: she had felt it herself, earlier this morning, when she first met Wolf. It was confirmed by their faces – set, unspeaking faces, concentrating on the tree. Between them on the ground, dividing them, was a rising pile of ivy, dark starry leaves against the pale orchard grass.

Wolf and Emily walked towards them. Idle, glad for an excuse to rest, wiped his brow with the back of his arm. His whole face glistened with sweat, as if he had been working very hard. He smiled at Wolf.

'Hello, old man. You all right?'

'Thank you, Mr Harris.'

'Mama, can Wolf stay all day ?'

'Course. Anything you like.'

Fen, too, stopped pulling at the ivy. Idle looked at his watch.

'I'd better go and fetch Marcia.'

'Is *she* coming?' asked Emily, who had forgotten the plan.

'For a few days. So that I don't have to go to London.' Idle smiled.

'Oh, honestly.' Emily couldn't understand her own irritation. When she thought about it, she quite liked Marcia. Felt sorry for her.

'*Incredible* train fever,' said Fen.

'I don't want to be late.' Idle began to roll down his sleeves. 'You and Wolf want to come with me, Em?' Emily nodded.

'I don't mind, if you want to sit at the station for ten minutes.' Fen was scathing, twisting two strands of ivy in her hands. 'Do what you like.'

That was, as Emily came to learn, to be the pattern of things. Idle was encouraged to do what he liked. Fen seemed not to care. She was to do the same.

Marcia Burrows asked permission to abandon her typing to go to Evensong. As Wolf had gone home, Emily walked with her to the church. The one bell was ringing again, forlorn, less stern. Marcia Burrows wore a hat of canvas marigolds. They were packed so closely together that, had they been real, the life would have been quite squeezed out of them.

'When I was a girl,' ventured Miss Burrows, who feared silences and wanted to take her mind off the bells, 'I was taught that God was all about us.' She glanced around at the parked cars, the box of empty milk bottles by the gate, a sweet paper that blew close to her feet. Then she let her eyes rise to the trees, swaying against the nebulous sky. In looking up she tripped on a stone and stumbled. Emily caught her arm. 'Thank you, dear. I suppose He probably is, if you think about it.'

Emily was not much interested in God, and was little aware of Him about her. He wasn't often referred to by her parents, excepts when they swore, and on the occasions she did go to church she found the reciting bits and the sermon very boring. Sometimes, when things were difficult or went wrong, she tried to pray, but on the whole she had found prayer to be ineffectual. *Please God, help me with this sum*, and no help came. She supposed that, quite reasonably, He gave priority to those who called upon Him more often. Meantime, she had considerable belief in her mascot, a china ladybird. Last year in exams she had put him on her desk and come top in English and Picture Study. All the same, those people who talked about God as if He were a friend, or a dog even, temporarily out of the room, interested her. They all seemed to have a characteristic in common: when they mentioned Him, something funny happened to their eyes. They filmed over with a far-off glaze, indicating they could focus on some greater vision to which more ordinary people, who didn't belong to the God club, were denied access. At this moment Marcia Burrows had near-to-God eyes. They cast about high in the trees, as if perhaps He was playing a private game of hide-and-seek with her, and any moment she would spy Him.

'Oh dear, I should have my eyes on the ground, shouldn't I? All these rough stones.'

'What I don't understand,' answered Emily, who was willing to talk about God for the last hundred yards to the church if that would please Marcia Burrows, 'is that in R.K. they told us something about being *married* to God. I don't see what they mean. I asked the vicar, actually, and all he said was that *he* was married to God. We all thought he might marry Miss Curtis, but I suppose he can't if he's already got a husband. That seems funny, doesn't it? A vicar having a husband. Anyway, Miss Curtis is so deaf she wouldn't be able to hear his sermons.'

'Ah,' said Miss Burrows, confused.

'But what I think is, if *you're* not married to God already, you should look around for a proper man. Derek can't have been the only man to want you,' she added.

'Perhaps not, dear. It's hard to tell sometimes, just who wants what, when it comes to men.'

They had arrived at the gate of the churchyard – a Victorian gate sheltered by a Gothic arch. Miss Burrows paused, took off a glove, and touched its dark wood with her hand.

'One of my sisters was married in a church much like this,' she said, 'a little country church with a porch over the gate. It was a lovely wedding, but a terrible thing happened. They were just coming through the gate, Janet and Jack, towards the car, in a cloud of confetti. Everybody throwing it for all their worth. Well, one of those paper petals got stuck in Janet's eye. She tried to get it out – Jack tried to get it out, but it was no good. There was a terrible confusion. She began to cry, she was in awful pain. In the end the wedding car had to go via the hospital. I went with them – sat there in Casualties for half an hour, we did, before anyone attended to us, Janet trying to keep her train off the floor, feeling an awful fool, knowing everybody at the reception was waiting for her . . . Terrible way to start a marriage. Particularly when you've waited so long. She got him by waiting, you know. Not a bad method – Still, they're happy enough now.' She and Emily began to walk up the church path, Marcia taking Emily's arm. The memory of the story seemed to have shaken her. 'Ever since then, I've never believed in confetti,' she added. 'It's a dangerous thing, though every Saturday of the year you'll find it thrown at brides all round the country.'

At the church door she tried to persuade Emily to come in with her. But Emily refused. She'd had enough of God for one day. With the patient sigh of one who is used to failing to convert, Marcia clamped her marigold hat closer to her head and gave a reverent push to the studded door.

'Very well, then. I shall look forward to seeing you later.'

Emily turned away. She couldn't think why she had been so against Marcia Burrows' visit. Really, she wasn't at all a bad old thing, for all her funny ways, and if having her to stay meant that Papa could be at home, then that was worth it.

Emily decided to take Wolf's advice and question Fen about what was going on. She felt a natural reluctance to do so, but worry and curiosity were stronger than that reluctance. During the three days that Marcia Burrows was staying with them she was disinclined to ask anything, and indeed on the face of it there seemed no reason for questions. Normality was assumed. Idle and Miss Burrows spent many hours in the study each day, Fen was preoccupied with a patchwork quilt which she would work at hard and often but never for long. When the grown-ups were together, at mealtimes, they appeared cheerful enough, though Emily noticed, long before Idle drew attention to the fact, that Fen's appetite seemed to diminish daily.

Her chance came soon after Idle and Marcia Burrows had left for London. Emily was at the kitchen table doing her homework. The telephone rang. As Fen had her hands in a bowl of flour, Emily went to answer it. Kevin. At the news, Fen's pale face flushed scarlet. She rubbed at her forehead, leaving a trail of flour on her hair. Then she banged her hands on the side of her long purple skirt, marking it with white streaks, not caring, and ran from the room. Emily closed her books.

When Fen returned she seemed calmer.

'You've been *ages*,' said Emily. 'You talk on the telephone to

Kevin as long as you used to talk to people when we were in London.'

'Do I?' Fen smiled and plunged her hands back into the flour. 'I never know why you *mind* my talking on the telephone. Go on, get on with your prep.'

Emily remained immobile, thinking. She decided first to try a roundabout way.

'Do you think we could have a dog?' she asked at last.

'A *dog*? From the way you talk about Gran's dog, and Aunt Tab's, you hate the things. Besides, it would chase the bantams.'

'That would be quite funny.'

'I don't think it would be very funny.'

'Well, I'd like one for my birthday, please.'

'I'm sorry, but you can't have one.' Fen's tone of voice indicated she would never change her mind.

'All right then, I'll borrow Stover. Wolf says I can.'

'I don't want Stover here, whatever Wolf says. You certainly can't borrow him. He's got a mass of fleas and practically no charm.'

'Oh, stew,' said Emily. Aware that this plan had utterly failed, was not worth pursuing, she tried again. A more straightforward approach. 'Are you and Papa going to get divorced?' she asked, in the flattest tone she could manage.

Fen's hands rose up from the bowl. An avalanche of flour fell from them, some of it spilling on the table.

'Divorced? What on earth makes you ask that?'

Emily decided not to give her real reasons. She shrugged. 'Dunno, really. You seem to be different together these days, and not be so nice to each other. Papa's away so much . . .'

'He's always been away so much. That's nothing new.'

'And then you and Kevin.'

'What about me and Kevin?'

'Well, he seems to keep coming here.'

'He won't any more.'

'Good. Doesn't Papa like him?'

'Papa doesn't know him very well.'

'I suppose he must be all right if he's a friend of Uncle Tom's, but it'll be much better if he doesn't come any more.'

Fen smiled a little. She pushed the bowl from her, sat down. 'Are you really worried about all this, Em?'

Faced with such a question, Emily truthfully did not know the answer. She shrugged again.

'Wolf says people get married and divorced, get married and divorced, just like that.'

'Some people do, of course. And very sad that is, too. Especially for the children. But Papa and I have never discussed divorce. Honestly, darling. Why should we?' Fen paused. She was soft now, showing a care she usually liked to conceal. 'I mean it's true, you're right, we've been having a bit of a difficult time lately. Grown-ups do, you know, just as much as children. They get bad-tempered and tired and irritable and things. They hurt each other and even go through funny times of not trusting each other. They let each other down, dreadfully. You see, grow-ing up doesn't necessarily mean getting better at things, it just means gathering together more experience to learn from. And then, usually, rejecting – ignoring – the lessons that are learnt. Do you see what I mean?'

Emily nodded. She didn't, really, and her hands were cold.

'Grown-ups are as imperfect as children,' Fen went on. 'And that's one of the worst things about being your age. It's about now you realise just how far from perfect they are. You realise that even your own parents are as hopeless as anyone else.'

'You're *not*,' said Emily. 'You and Papa are best in the world, and I want you to go on for ever and ever.'

'Oh, Em.' Fen lowered her eyes, her voice unsteady. Emily ran to her, threw her arms round her, buried her face in her neck and hair. Warmth and stephanotis, the unforgettable smell and feel of reassurance. 'Please be for ever, Mama. Don't quarrel any more, will you?'

'We'll try not to. I promise. And anyhow, you mustn't worry.'

Emily stood back from her mother, then, a little weak with relief.

'Are grown-ups ever jealous?'

'Of course. Why?'

'Well, I think Papa's jealous of Kevin, and Kevin's jealous of Papa.'

Fen laughed.

'What makes you think that?'

'I think they both love you. Like Wolf says, everyone loves you.'

'Nonsense!'

'Anyway, do you think they're jealous of each other?'

'Maybe you're right. A little.'

'In that case it's a good thing Kevin's gone away because you're Papa's. So it should be Kevin to go away.' Fen smiled. 'When *I* get married,' Emily added, 'it's going to be for ever and ever and *ever*, and anyhow.'

'Quite right. That's how it should be.' Fen kissed Emily lightly on the cheek and returned her hands to the bowl of flour. 'Now, you just stop worrying your funny old head about things, and help me roll out this pastry. There's enough to make some jam tarts, if you like, and some men with currant eyes. Come on, get one of my aprons.'

Emily shuddered almost invisibly. A smell of baking came from the Aga: it was warm, quiet, wonderfully normal again. And she'd have to tell Wolf. Tomorrow she'd take him up into the loft and tell him. Now, none of his plans would be needed.

The next week the pattern was repeated. Marcia Burrows came to stay for three days so that Idle could work at home. On one of these days Fen went to London. In the evening she rang to say her plans had changed: she was spending the night there, after all, but would be back the following afternoon. As her father was at home, Emily had no complaints about her mother being away for just one night. Marcia Burrows made macaroni cheese for supper. It wasn't at all bad. Afterwards, the three of them played Scrabble by the fire.

*

When Fen came home – no funny stories, this time, of what she had been doing – her first act was to open her post. One letter caused her to look concerned, to frown.

'Em, I've had a letter from Mrs Riley.' Emily's teacher.

'Oh?'

'She says you're not trying this term. That your work's "unsatisfactory in every way". She says you don't concentrate and don't seem interested, and you'll have to do much better if you want to move up in September.'

'*Everyone* hates Mrs Riley,' said Emily. 'She's always complaining, honestly.'

'She's never complained to me before. There must be some truth in it.'

'I simply can't understand maths, so there's no point in trying any more.'

'She says you don't try in anything.'

'That's what she thinks.'

'Is it true? Don't you concentrate?'

'Some of the time. Most of the time she makes it so dull. Ancient boring old Britons and things.'

'But you were doing so well last year. Trying so hard.'

'I don't feel like trying any more.'

'I think you'd better go back to it. Papa won't be very pleased by this letter.'

Emily, who had been playing with the strap of her satchel, looked up in alarm.

'Don't let's show it to him.'

'Perhaps he could explain to you how silly it is, what a waste of time it is, not to work. Perhaps he could explain better than me.'

'*Please*, Mama. Don't show it to him. I will try.'

Fen threw the letter on the fire. Already her mind was elsewhere.

'Well, all right. This time. Any more complaints and I'll tell him straight away.'

'Thank you, Mama.'

*

178

Mr Ragwort, the art teacher, semi-retired and happier breeding budgerigars than painting, came to Emily's school twice a week. Years ago he'd found the easiest way to go about teaching: give the class a subject to paint, and leave them to it. That way, he could have half an hour's peace in which to study his *Manual of Domestic Birds*, only interrupted by one journey of inspection round the class.

Today, however, he had been inspired. Or at least, to be honest – and Mr Ragwort saw absolutely no reason to be honest with his pupils on this point – it was his wife who had had the inspiration. A Summer's Day, she had suggested. A Summer's Day it was to be.

When Mr Ragwort made his announcement, the whole class sighed in unison. Knowing she had the support of everybody behind her, Sandra Buckle voiced their complaint.

'We've done A Winter's Day, A Spring Day and An Autumn Day, already, Mr Ragwort,' she said.

'Then A Summer's Day will nicely round off the whole cycle of the seasons, won't it?' Mr Ragwort, unabashed, took his bird book from his pocket.

Emily had a simple idea. Tomatoes. Nothing but tomatoes. She drew five rows of them, right across the page, taking great care to make them identical in shape and size. Then she painted them thickly scarlet, leaving an oblong highlight on the side of each one. When it came to the time for Mr Ragwort to examine her picture he was, as she had predicted he would be, puzzled.

'Why all these tomatoes, Emily?'

'They're what I think of on a summer's day.'

'Nothing but tomatoes? What about picnics, haymaking, a day at the sea, and so on? Those are the sort of thing come to most people's minds.' Privately, he didn't care a damn what came to Emily Harris's mind when she thought of a summer day, but at the sight of such calculated tomatoes he felt it his duty to protest a little before returning to his chapter on *Rearing and Breeding*.

'I just think of tomatoes.' Emily was sullen. She could hear a few stifled giggles coming from behind her.

179

'Well, it's an interesting thought, I dare say. But where *are* these tomatoes? On a market stall, a plate? In a greenhouse? Couldn't you give me a little background?'

'They're just in my mind.'

'Very well. But it makes rather an abstract composition, doesn't it?' Unable to approve anything he didn't understand, Mr Ragwort shuffled on, confident he'd made his point. Behind him, Emily stuck out her tongue. Mr Ragwort always annoyed her: today he annoyed her particularly. She took the painting from her easel and quickly tore the paper into four pieces. There were sounds of exclamation from the girls nearest to her. Mr Ragwort turned round.

'Dear, dear, Emily. That was a silly thing to do, wasn't it? I hadn't got anything against your tomatoes, you know. As a matter of fact, they were quite well drawn.'

'Stew,' said Emily, so that he shouldn't hear.

At the end of the lesson Mr Ragwort, ruffled by the small scene, hurried out of the class first. He was worried about one of his broody birds: if she was sitting happily on her nest, that would take his mind off such truculent pupils as Emily Harris. The rest of the class followed him, animated with chatter about Emily's tomatoes. Emily herself remained at her easel waiting until they had gone.

When the studio was empty, she took a brush and began to stir a pot of scarlet poster paint. Then she went to the large, bare white wall between the two windows. She raised the brush and quickly wrote, in huge letters: *Goats are smelly*. She hadn't worked out what to write: she simply watched the words flow from her brush, as if they were written by someone else.

She stood back, contemplated her work, added a full stop, and left the room. It was time for Geography now, but she had no intention of going to her class. Instead, slowly, calmly, she made her way to the cloakroom. It was quite empty, rather cold. She sat on a bench, leaning her head back against a pile of mackintoshes. On the floor opposite her was a long row of gym shoes.

180

She began to count them, to give them names, and to divide them into families.

Some time later, half an hour perhaps, she heard footsteps coming towards her. Mrs Riley, no doubt. Mrs Riley, it was, swollen with disbelief.

'Emily Harris! And what may I ask do you think you're doing here?'

'Just sitting.'

'Stand up when I speak to you, girl.' Emily stood.

'Apart from missing your geography lesson, I wonder if you would happen to know anything about the disgusting message written on the art studio wall?'

'Yes,' said Emily, dully, 'I wrote it.'

The admission left Mrs Riley speechless for a moment. One of her fat hands jumped to her stomach, scratched, then crawled on down to a troublesome suspender.

'Well, you'd better come and explain to the Head, is all I can say. She's waiting for you. Follow me.'

Emily followed Mrs Riley's triumphant bottom down a long corridor, across the courtyard and to the Head's study. Mrs Riley knocked, pushed open the door, and Emily went in.

'Here's Emily Harris, Mrs Parker. She's admitted everything.'

The Head, sitting behind a large desk, looked up with a curious lack of interest.

'Thank you, Mrs Riley. Perhaps you would leave Emily and me to it?'

Mrs Riley, silent in her indignation, left the room backwards.

When she had gone, Mrs Parker motioned Emily towards a chair. Emily sat down. In the long silence she glanced about the room, which smelt of years and years of tea and biscuits. There was a picture of a man behind Mrs Parker's desk. He wore military uniform and looked hungry. Emily wondered if he was Mrs Parker's dead husband and, if he was, why his picture wasn't somewhere easier to see than behind her back.

Mrs Parker scribbled on her blotter. She had brown hair with a white wave running right through it, from front to back. The skin of her face was pale orange, but her neck was white. Her downcast eyes showed wrinkly lids thick with blue. As most of the girls' fathers had observed, she wasn't bad for a headmistress.

'So what happened, Emily?' Considering her voice could rap out prayers that reached right to the back of the Hall, her tone was now amazingly soft.

'Mr Ragwort didn't like my tomatoes so I tore them up, then I painted goats are smelly on the wall, then I went and sat in the cloakroom so that I could miss Geography, and Mrs Riley came and fetched me.'

'So I heard. Why did you do all that?'

'Don't know.'

Outside, there was sun. Emily wondered if she dared ask if she might open the window. It was stuffy in here, with the gas fire.

'I hear you haven't been doing your best, this term, in general.'

'No.'

'Anything on your mind? You've plenty of friends, haven't you? Unhappy about anything?'

'No.'

Mrs Parker sighed.

'You know you're one of the girls who can get pretty good results when she tries. It's a pity to waste your brain.' Emily remained silent. Mrs Parker put down her pencil at last and met her eye. 'If you were me,' she said, 'if you were in my position, what sort of punishment do you think I should give you?'

Emily thought for a while.

'I think you should only punish people when they plan out to do naughty things. I didn't plan anything. I just did it.'

Mrs Parker smiled.

'Do you know why you did it?'

'No. Honestly. I just did it.'

'And how do you feel about what you've done?'

'Nothing much. It wasn't *that* bad.' Emily shrugged. Mrs Parker pushed back her chair and clasped her hands, beautifully painted nails, tomato scarlet, on the blotter.

'I tell you what, Emily, I'm not going to do anything about you this time. I believe what you say. I'm sure your acts weren't premeditated – thought out before. But I don't want to hear of anything like this again. Do you understand?' Emily nodded. 'And please try harder for what's left of the term. Your father, if I'm right in thinking, wouldn't be too pleased if you had a bad report, would he?' Emily shook her head. 'Well, then, see what you can do.' Mrs Parker stood up. 'You can go now, unless, that is, there's anything you'd like to ask me.

Emily too stood up. She nodded towards the photograph on the wall behind Mrs Parker's head.

'There is. Who's that?'

Mrs Parker didn't turn round, but raised her chin a little.

'That was my husband.'

'What happened to him?'

'He was killed in the war.'

'How awful. Did you have any children?'

'No. Now enough questions. Off you go.' Emily moved to the door. 'By the way,' Mrs Parker added, 'your father, Emily – does he still go away on those long trips to Africa?'

'Not so often.'

'That must be nice for you.'

'Thank you, Mrs Parker.' Emily ran away.

In the playground, her class crowded round her. They clamoured to know what exactly had happened. What had it been like, being ticked off by the Head? How had she felt?

Emily told them the truth.

'I wasn't ticked off,' she said, 'and I felt nothing. Absolutely nothing. Honestly.'

Since the incident of the tomatoes, Mrs Riley did little to conceal her disapproval of Emily. In her opinion the shocking thing was not simply that the child had been naughty but her message on the art studio wall had revealed that *unhealthy thoughts*, such as Mrs Riley could not and would not abide in the minds of any of her pupils, were planted deep within Emily.

Such a revelation was a strain on Mrs Riley's meagre charity. In spite of the fact that she had to admit that Emily was making a little more effort in the last few days, she found her disapprobation difficult to contain. 'I despair of you, Emily Harris,' she reiterated most days. 'You're not doing credit to yourself or to your family.'

For her part Emily remained passive. Mrs Riley's chidings did not touch her. She was protected from them by a barrier of apathy. Mrs Riley could do or say what she liked: she could not make Emily care.

A week went by. It was a maths lesson. As usual, Emily struggled to understand some problem that the majority of the class seemed to find easy. The problem itself bored Emily profoundly. She did not see that even if she reached understanding it would do her any good. But she made some effort to dislodge the heavy dullness within her, and concentrate. Mrs Riley, however, was unconvinced. To her mind Emily Harris, in her usual stubborn fashion, was not trying. Moreover, her attitude of apparent nonchalance was detrimental to the rest of the class. Emily was sent from the room with a warning of a serious talking-to at the end of the lesson.

As she stood in the passage, leaning against a window sill, Emily remembered the time when any such admonition would have filled her with fear. Indeed, the very act of having been sent out of class would have caused her shame. But now she felt only relief at being out of the class. Threats of punishment held no fear for her: concern about such things was long past.

Time went slowly. Bored, Emily walked down the corridor. At the end of it she turned into another corridor that was out-of-bounds for pupils. A few yards along it she found a cupboard door marked *Stationery and Stores*. Emily looked about. There was no one in sight, no sound. She opened the door. Shelves were well-stocked with exercise books, blotting paper, pencils and blackboard chalk. On the floor stood two pitchers marked Ink. Emily picked one up. Made of brown earthenware, it was heavy and cold. Moving it about, she could hear the gentle slopping of the ink inside. She removed the cork stopper in the neck of the jar, but in the gloom of the corridor it was impossible to see the colour of the ink.

Emily replaced the stopper and walked back down the corridor. She let herself out of the door that led to the playground. The gardener was chipping at the edges of the grass with his hoe. She nodded at him and walked on. The spring sun was warming: she made for a small rhododendron bush, its buds still hard and closed, and sat on the ground behind it. There she inspected the ink once more. The pitcher was almost full. She dipped in a finger: it came out a wonderful royal blue. Next, leaves: she plucked a dozen or so from the rhododendron bush, submerged them in the ink then lay them in a pattern on the grass to dry. All the while a song shrilled through her head.

> *Mean to me: why are you so*
> *Mean to me?*

It was a song Fen often sang, joining in the olden-days lady who sang it on the record player. Ruth Etting, she was called. She had a sad, quavery voice, but when Fen sang with her, holding a pretend cigarette holder and clutching at her breast with comic tragedy, it always made Emily laugh.

Bored by her blue leaves, she peered behind the bush. She could see, through the open window of her own classroom, Mrs Riley at the blackboard pointing at something with her stick. The lesson, Emily calculated, would soon be over. She got up, taking the pitcher of ink with her.

As she walked back across the playground it occurred to Emily everything about her had a peculiar sharpness. Previously, she hadn't been aware of this. But now the sky was blue glass, the sun a glinting coin, the playground a stretch of emerald splinters, while the edges of the school buildings themselves were cruel as blades. The grass ended. She crossed a gravel path. Her feet sank into the soft earth of a flower bed. In the mottled room through the open window one or two heads twitched up

185

from their books. They had no faces, just huge eyes stuck on to one-dimensional white shapes.

Emily lifted the heavy pitcher, hearing for a second the slosh again inside it. There was a lightning pain in her stomach as she reached up. With all her strength she threw it through the window.

She watched the raging of the inky storm only for a moment. She was aware of blue everywhere, splattered like fighting blood on desks, walls, skin, clothes. Girls were screaming, one was crying. Mrs Riley's voice, from somewhere, whipping up the frenzy:

'Duck your heads, girls! It's a *maniac!*'

Emily ran away.

She ran through the garden spurred on by the kind of excitement she had felt on the church tower. Throwing the ink had released something within her: she was light-headed with relief. Quickly, she reached the gate to the walled kitchen garden, another out-of-bounds place that would be safe for a while. It was a peaceful, silent half-acre, divided by tiny cinder paths, smelling faintly of herbs and silvery shrubs, and the warmth of the sun was packed close by the old brick walls. Emily sat on a wooden bench, panting. Her hands were brilliant blue. She tried to wonder what would happen next, but the song was still in her mind, confusing her. She waited, unafraid.

This time, in Mrs Parker's study, all the patience and quiet had gone. Mrs Parker had admonished her in a harsh voice which rose to a shout. She asked no questions, this time: just spelt out in terrible clarity the destructiveness, the futility and the sheer bloody-mindedness of Emily's act. Then, her wave of immediate anger over, her voice subsided into tones of weariness.

'Emily, this is your very last chance. Do you understand? I will give you one more try – against the wishes of Mrs Riley and other members of the staff, I might add. But if there's one more complaint, if I hear of one more misdeed of any kind, I shall have no alternative.' She paused. 'I shall have to ask your parents to take you away from here.' Emily shifted slightly in her chair. Her hands, still unwashed, were in a blue knot on her lap. 'There,' Mrs Parker went on, 'I believe I hear your mother's car.'

Until that moment, Emily had been calm and silent. Now, anxiety rose within her, nauseous.

'Why's Mama coming?'

'I thought it best to send for her, to explain. And to take you home.'

'But it's before lunch.'

'Nonetheless, I think it would be wise for you to go home for the rest of the day.'

'Oh lummy.'

There was a knock on the door. Fen hurried in, untidy and harassed. Emily stood up, hiding her hands behind her back. Mrs Parker told her to fetch her blazer and wait for her mother in the car.

During the long wait the sky clouded over and it began to rain. Emily watched the heavy drops gather into streamers and jostle about the car windows: beyond them, she could see the figures of her friends hurrying across the playground. The red and green stripes of their blazers blurred and ran in the screen of raindrops, making them pretty, flower-like shapes.

Fen eventually appeared, wet and worried. The windscreen wipers made two clear arcs: as they drove away, Emily could see looks of enquiry and astonishment on the faces of the passing girls.

'Whatever made you do it, Em? Please, darling. Tell me.'

'I don't know, Mama. Really I don't.'

'You must have had something in your mind.'

'No. I didn't. Honestly.'

Fen sighed. They were out in the lanes now, high banked with dripping green. She put a thin hand on Emily's knee. She didn't seem at all cross.

'Anyway, I love you. You know that,' she said.

*

The school judged that Emily behaved well for the rest of the term. She was docile, quiet, causing offence to no one. She tried a little harder, even in maths. But it brought no rewards.

On the first day of the Easter holidays she was in the orchard with Fen. They were picking early daffodils to put in the house before Idle and Marcia Burrows arrived for the weekend.

'I've got to go away for a week, Em,' Fen said. 'To the north.' She broke the news lightly.

'*No*? Poor you. Why?'

Fen straightened up, bunching her daffodils together.

'To be honest, I want to go. I hate leaving you, but I want to stay with Kevin.'

'You're going to *stay* with Kevin?' Fen nodded. 'But nobody would want to do that. And anyway, I thought you weren't ever going to see him again?'

'It isn't as easy as that.'

'I don't understand.' A sudden tiredness flowed through Emily. 'What's happening, exactly?'

'Well, we're trying things out. Different things. To make it all right in the end. I know it's difficult for you to understand. I know it is. But you mustn't worry.'

'But I don't like you going away, especially to Kevin.' Emily sighed.

'Oh, darling. I haven't made the decision without a lot of thought. For everyone,' Fen added. 'Come on, let's get a few more. Then we'll go in. Cheer up. A week's not long, is it?'

'Yes, it is, it's ages. And I hate you going away.' Emily's voice quivered, though she felt no danger of tears. She looked at her mother whose face was far away, very bright, very beautiful. 'I hope you have a horrible time,' she said. 'And as for these stupid old flowers.' She threw her bunch of daffodils to the ground.

Nine

*T*he hour between Fen's departure for her Easter holiday, and the arrival of Idle and Marcia Burrows, caused Mrs Charles indignation too overpowering to be contained in silence. She stumped about the house, her face clammy in the mild heat of the spring evening, venting her outrage on Emily.

'And what does some two-penny-halfpenny seck-er-terry know about keeping a house, I'd like to know? I ask you. The betting is I come back on Monday morning to find the place a pigsty. Well, all these irregular goings-on – I don't know what the world's coming to, I really don't. But I shall have to tell your mother when she comes back from her holiday. She's going to have to make up her mind one way or the other.'

Emily, who found Mrs Charles' train of thought confusing, debated whether it was best to say nothing or to support both her mother and Marcia Burrows. She decided that silence might be taken for agreement, and agreement with Mrs Charles on any subject was something she could never contemplate.

'The place certainly won't be a pigsty,' she said. 'Marcia Burrows is very tidy – much more than Mama, in fact. And Mama needed a holiday. She's lost nearly a stone, so there.'

At the tone of her voice Mrs Charles' duster stopped licking at the china on the dresser for a moment, then gave a vicious swipe at a blue china mug. It crashed to the ground, quite shattered. There was an almost imperceptible pause in the writhing movements of Mrs Charles' indignant body before she bent down to gather up the bits.

'And that mug was given to Mama when she was a child by a friend of hers.'

'Was it, just? Well, you'd never catch my mother larking off to Scunthorpe or wherever just because she felt like it. My mother had one holiday in twenty-five years and died of internal abcesses, big as eggs the doctor said they were, as a result.' She thrust the broken pieces of china into her apron pocket and rattled them about.

'What are you going to do with those bits?'

'Throw them out, of course.'

'Leave them on the table and I'll try to mend them.'

'Don't be so daft. There's a thousand and one pieces.'

'All the same, I'll try.'

In the grip of her unbearable vexation, Mrs Charles slammed the pile of fragmented china on the table before Emily. It was obvious that to mend the mug was impossible, but Emily scooped the bits protectively under her hand. She hated the thought of Mrs Charles being the one to throw them away.

'Sentimental rubbish.' Mrs Charles' face across the table was the greenish colour of an old bruise. 'And your father not here on time.'

'I expect the train was late.' Screwing up her hand, Emily could feel the shavings of china digging into her skin.

'You can never trust men. My father, what he wasn't up to, I can tell you. If it wasn't drink, it was the other. Men's all the same, right across the country . . .'

Emily left Mrs Charles to her soliloquy. She went upstairs to her parents' bedroom and threw the remains of the mug in the wastepaper basket. There was a note stuck to the mirror on the dressing table, Fen's large handwriting on the back on an envelope. *Afraid I forgot to get any more soap, E can get some in the morning. Bread being delivered all week, drink organised. Please don't let E stay up too late, lots of love. P.S. I mean that.* Emily read the note several times, hearing the words in her mother's voice.

Then she touched the remaining necklaces that hung from the mirror. Fen had taken the best of them. Only the old ones she never wore were left – two strings of pearly shells, mauve-pink, frail, mostly broken: some emerald plastic beads, and a string of heavy amber lozenges, each one so scratched that its original gleam of yellow was dulled as if by mist. Emily lifted a handful of all the beads, and let them swing away from her. Some of the shells broke at once, scattering minute chips of silver on the carpet. The swing of the necklaces made a soft chinking noise, familiar, the noise they made round Fen's neck on her exuberant, dancing days.

After a while they settled back in their place, hanging still again, dead. Emily turned away. Gradually she absorbed the unusual tidiness of the room. The chaise-longue, without its rubble of clothes, was strangely naked. The books on the table had been moulded into orderly piles, and the old Sunday papers folded neatly. On the table at Idle's side of the bed was a small bowl of narcissi, but the photograph of Emily, as a baby, had gone. Both windows had been left open, but it was not cold. A shaft of evening sun showed up the worn condition of the patch-work quilt on the bed. Emily, kneeling on the floor, ran a finger round the hexagonal shapes of some of the patches – fragments of faded cornflowers, old gingham, calico, satin drained of the quiet colour it had once been. The quilt, where the sun was, had become warm: the bed beneath it sank into a soft and mild valley. Emily climbed into it, keeping her body in the warm part, as a swimmer avoids shadows in the water.

She sat there.

Idle and Marcia Burrows arrived from London with quantities of frozen foods. Idle also brought, for Emily, a new pack of cards. Their backs were patterned like brilliant stained-glass windows, each one different. Almost at once Idle suggested that he and Emily should play a game of Knock at the kitchen table, while Miss Burrows prepared supper.

'Drink, Marcia?' he asked. Emily had never heard him use

her Christian name before. She looked at him. His face was cheerful as he poured two glasses of wine. Marcia, for her part, seemed happy too. She wore a pink silk scarf round her throat which threw a matching glow on to the lower half of her face. She laughed when Idle handed her the glass of wine.

'You're a wicked influence!'

'Nonsense.' Idle turned to Emily. 'Marcia's not going to type a single word this week, Em. Orders. She's going to cook for us, and look after us, and we're going to look after her.'

'Oh.' Emily, shuffling the new cards, was dazzled by their stained-glass backs.

'Now, come on.' He sat down, rolling up the sleeves of his London shirt. 'You're hopeless at that, darling one. Let me do it.'

Emily handed him the cards. Beyond the brightness of his face was the dimmer shape of Marcia Burrows as she filtered from cupboard to cupboard. She seemed to know her way about. She seemed to know Fen's place for everything. She never had to ask, she made no fuss. When she produced dinner, Idle congratulated her on being a good cook and housekeeper. She blushed with disappointed pride. But the kitchen was confused: its normal shape and feel were hidden by her presence, and there were no smells of baking coming from the oven.

In the next few days Emily observed Marcia Burrows quite curiously, and found herself sometimes surprised. The quiet cardigans – they changed each day while the grey flannel skirt remained constant – concealed occasional shafts of spirit that seemed unlikely in so meagre a breast. A neighbouring farmer came in one morning, swinging a rabbit in his hand. Just shot: would it be useful for lunch? While Emily kept her distance from it's already dulled eyes – she hated dead animals – Marcia Burrows slung it eagerly on to a wooden board and at once began to skin it with a lethal knife. She was fast and skilful. Pushing her sleeves above white elbows, she plunged her hands into its guts and drew out the bloody mess with no sense of horror.

'How *could* you?' asked Emily. 'Mama couldn't possibly.'

Marcia Burrows laughed, a little triumphant at last.

'Really? I'm surprised, your mother being so keen on nature. But then we're all squeamish about different things, I suppose. I helped my mother skin rabbits from a very early age – she'd have sent me up to bed if I'd showed I'd minded.' Her hands, which moved most delicately when she whisked, without relish, at custards, now chopped the gleaming body into those pathetic shapes of flesh whose angle only just recalls that once it was a springing thigh, a stretched rib cage. Later, it became delicious stew.

One afternoon Emily found Miss Burrows watching a wrestling match on television. Emily offered to switch to something more appropriate.

'Oh, no, please,' said Miss Burrows. 'If you don't mind. I enjoy the wrestling. I watch most matches.'

'Do you really? Have you ever been to a real one?'

Marcia Burrows smiled, eyes still on the fighters.

'Well, as a matter of fact, I have. I plucked up courage about a year ago. You see, when the odd gentleman has asked me out, a film or theatre is usually suggested. That's a very nice invitation, of course. So I can't very well say: really, I'd rather go to a wrestling match – can I?'

'Why can't you?'

'I suppose I'm not that sort of person. So in the end I went alone. And very enjoyable it was, too, shouting with the crowd for the winner. A lovely evening. Now, I go quite often. Think nothing of it.'

'Gosh.' Emily felt some admiration. She broke the news to Idle later on.

'Did you know Miss Burrows goes by herself to wrestling matches, Papa? She loves wrestling. She knows lots about it. She knew all the time who was going to win the match we watched this afternoon.'

'No?' Idle's incredulity equalled Emily's.

'Well . . . if I can't get a seat at Covent Garden, it's the next best thing.' Marcia Burrows was suddenly demure in front of

Idle. It was as if she suspected a show of enthusiasm might embarrass. Caught off guard, she could admit some of it to a child, but in her adult world it was essential to hide all but her most superficial feelings. Better still, by denying them, to conceal them from herself as well. She blushed.

Wolf and Emily talked about Marcia Burrows at one of their meetings in the loft.

'She's not too bad, really, is she?' Wolf asked, when he too had heard the rabbit story.

'Not too bad. Sort of stiff, though, usually.'

'How do you mean?'

'Dunno, really. The way she does things. Except typing and cutting up rabbits. *Then* she's fast. You should have seen her this morning. But she's slow at everything else. Her hands and feet seem to move slowly, compared with Mama.'

'I thought the plan was for her to fall in love with your Uncle Tom.'

'She hasn't met him yet, but Mama and I are going to arrange it. I don't think she's his type, really, but she'd be an awfully good wife to him. You know what? She cleaned Papa's shoes last night. Mama'd *never* do that. I think Uncle Tom would like her.'

'Perhaps we'd better make a plan to get him all, you know, *feeling* towards her before they ever meet.'

'How could we do that?'

'Write him a letter saying how lovely she was and everything.' Wolf giggled.

'Ooh, yes, and I could make her wear her best cardigan when he comes, with all the patterns on. And he might think she was much better than all his silly old girlfriends.'

'Well, I mean, she is in a way. She wouldn't want to be sleeping all the time, would she? Come on. Let's write the letter now. Let's type it.'

'Wolf! You've such good ideas. But we mustn't tell Papa. We must let it be a surprise if Uncle Tom wants to marry Miss

Burrows. We could just tell them at the wedding we'd arranged it all. I think Mama and Papa'd be very pleased if they got married, actually. Except Papa would lose a secretary.'

'Stupid! Once she was a relation she could go on typing for no money. Come on. We'll have to get in through the study window and put newspapers under the door so's they won't hear the typing.' He started to climb down the ladder. Emily followed him.

'It's quite safe,' she said. 'Papa's gone out somewhere and Marcia Burrows is upstairs washing her cardigans.'

Easter Sunday, to Emily's amazement, Idle agreed to go to church with Marcia Burrows. To please him, Emily said she would go too. Marcia wore her marigold hat again, and navy gloves. Idle wore his London coat and looked very handsome. Emily walked down the road between them. Above her head they talked about the Prime Minister, shouting their remarks several times over against the pealing bells. At the three rough steps that led up to the wooden porch Idle moved closer to Marcia Burrows and put his hand beneath her elbow, helping her, although she looked as if she could have managed the climb quite well on her own. Then he left his hand on her arm all the way up the church path.

Inside, the church was lit with white April sun and huge bunches of daffodils, whose heads trumpeted against the multi-coloured Biblical scenes in the windows. On the altar the two copper urns had been polished to a white glare and the organ played quietly. Emily thought if church was always like this she wouldn't be so against it. She knelt down in the pew, the red hassock scratchy beneath her bare knees. Covering her eyes with her hands, she made a cavern of blackness that was shot through with dancing lights. *O God, please bless Mama and Papa*, she said into the darkness, feeling her lips move against her hands. Then she made a crack in her fingers and peered through. Papa wasn't kneeling, but sitting, his forehead resting in one hand, eyes hidden, mouth a peaceful and unmoving line. Beyond him, Marcia Burrows rested her chin on her navy hands. Sandy eyelashes lay short and straight on her cheeks and her marigold hat, dazzled by a ray of sun, had turned into a golden halo. *O God, please bless Mama and Papa*, Emily repeated, eyes open this time, *and make them be married for ever and ever, Amen.*

A thunderous chord and the congregation stood. The six choirboys, washed and ironed, began to move up the aisle with one gliding motion, all together like a small boat. At their helm came the old vicar holding up a cream silk sail, embroidered with a gold cross, his eyes fixed on the horizon of the altar.

Jesus Christ is risen today, Alleluia!

Everybody sang. Marcia Burrows knew the words by heart. She didn't even bother to open her hymn book. Emily, looking up at her, saw that she glanced about with some kind of private exultation, just as she had the day she had been searching for God in the trees. Finally her eyes came to rest on Idle's white head, and a smile flickered at the corners of her mouth. Idle was unaware of her attention. Bass voice ringing out, he concentrated on his hymn book. His free hand lay on the pew in front of them, as if to steady himself. Emily put her own hand next to his, so gently he didn't notice. *Alleluia* . . . she sang with all her might.

A few days later Idle formally took Marcia Burrows' arm again. This time they were climbing a slope in the Cumnor hills, looking for a picnic place. This time Emily did not let the gesture go unobserved.

'Papa, really! Miss Burrows isn't an old woman, you know.'

'*Marcia*, Emily, please,' said Miss Burrows, blushing.

'Marcia's wearing slippery shoes,' said Idle.

'Silly me, I didn't bring any proper ones,' said Marcia.

Emily said no more, but gave Wolf a look. He returned it knowingly.

They chose a place about half way up the hill and spread out two rugs. The children sat a couple of yards from the grown-ups. It was a warm, breezy day, intermittent sun among the clouds. Marcia Burrows was especially appreciative of the view. She sat, legs straight out in front of her, upright with admiration. She had tucked her hair under her angora beret, so that it looked like a bathing cap, and her face was flushed from the climb.

'Well, I never,' she said. 'It's wonderful up here.'

Emily thought that sometimes Miss Burrows wanted to say quite clever or interesting things about what she saw and felt, but was incapable of producing anything but the most ordinary observations. Sometimes she looked as if she was annoyed by her own inadequate words, and snapped her mouth shut after they had come out, too late, quite crossly. Emily watched her now, carefully. Nobody responded to Miss Burrows' remark about the view, and she lowered her head over the picnic basket in shame. She began to unpack the plastic picnic boxes. Emily saw to her dismay that they were full of matching sandwiches: sardine, tomato, egg. Crisps, cheese biscuits, orange juice. Not at all the sort of food she liked. She was used to Fen's picnics – a wild mass of impractical things, chickens that leaked mayonnaise through the foil paper, ice cream that had melted, quiches crushed beneath careless bottles. Hopeless and delicious. Picnic-wise, Fen never learnt from her mistakes and Emily was glad. Far rather . . . than these boring sandwiches. She chewed one without relish, her day suddenly destroyed.

'What's the matter?' Wolf was lying on his back, his knees in the air.

'Nothing really.'

'When's your mother coming back?'

'That's nothing to do with it.'

'Who said it was?'

'She's coming back soon.'

Wolf didn't seem to mind the sandwiches. He had a pile of them by his side and ate them one after the other. Emily turned away from him. She looked up at her father, on the rug beside Marcia Burrows a little higher up the hill. Their heads were inclined together, Idle's hands cupped over hers, one thumb stabbing at his lighter. Suddenly, he drew back, and a thin line of smoke (which didn't smell even indoors) petered up from Miss

Burrows' small, thin, tipped cigarette. A cloud rolled up behind Idle's head, white as his hair, so that for a moment it became part of his head – an enormous, cartoon bulb of hair.

'Right, Em. Time to fly the kite?' Emily shook her head. 'But it'll be perfect higher up. There's just the right amount of wind.'

'Don't feel like it.'

'Wolf, how about you?' Idle's eyes were frowning.

Wolf agreed. He and Idle began to climb, Idle with the large dragon-fly kite beneath his arm. Marcia Burrows started to clear up the picnic things.

'What's come over you, dear? I thought it was your idea to fly the kite in the first place?'

'Changed my mind.' Emily sat with her back to Miss Burrows.

'Well, we're all at liberty to change our minds.' Her voice was bewildered. She looked a little desperately at Emily's hunched shoulders. 'Would you like us to play a game of I-Spy, or noughts and crosses, or anything?'

'No thank you. Not if you don't mind.'

'I don't expect I can make picnics as well as your Mummy, but then I'm not so used to them, you see. I haven't been on one for as many years as I can remember.'

'Oh, it was very nice. Really.' Emily stood up. 'I think I'll run down the hill and wait in the car.'

'You run on down, then, and enjoy yourself. It's getting quite chilly up here. I hope your father and Wolf won't be too long. I worry about your father, sometimes. He takes so little care of himself.'

'Oh, I shouldn't worry about Papa,' said Emily. 'He's very strong.'

'So it seems. And he enjoys himself, at least. I like to see a man enjoy himself despite . . .' She paused. 'Despite his work.' Marcia Burrows, surrounded by the empty plastic boxes and screwed-up paper napkins, gave a small shiver and a friendly smile. Emily felt quite sorry for her.

She ran down the hill without looking back. She would have liked instead to have been flying the kite with Papa and Wolf.

But somehow she hadn't been able to, not after the disappointment of the sandwiches. It wasn't Marcia Burrows' fault, of course: she was doing her best. But from time to time, moments like these, the very fact that *she* was there, not Mama, was so horrible that running like this, fastest ever, so that the earth spun and tumbled under her legs, was the only thing to make the horrible thoughts go away.

Emily sat on the edge of the bath while her father shaved. This had become her daily habit since Fen had been away, and the ritual had become a long, comforting one. Idle had kept to his word: there was no typing, little work, and consequently no hurry.

'Papa, have you ever been to the north?'

'Not often. Why?'

'I wondered if you liked it.'

'Quite.'

'I wonder if Mama likes it.'

Idle grimaced slowly into his magnifying mirror, distorting his face into shapes of soap and reddish skin.

'I think she probably does.'

'I thought it was horrible.'

'You had bad weather up there.'

'Even if it'd been sunny I would have thought it was horrible. Kevin's flat was about the nastiest flat I've ever been in.' It was the first time she had mentioned Kevin's name to Idle since Fen had been away. 'Is Mama staying there?'

'I'm not too sure of her plans. Perhaps she's gone to a nice hotel.'

'I wonder why she wanted to go when she could have been here with us?'

Idle's mouth, half disguised by a froth of soap, turned down.

'Sometimes people need to get away for a while, even from their families.'

Emily listened to the scraping of his razor for a while.

'Only two days till Mama comes back, anyway,' she said. 'What will happen then?'

'How do you mean, what will happen then? She'll be here for the rest of the holidays.'

'And what about you?'

'Well, I'll have to do some work, won't I? We've been having a lovely time this week, haven't we, but I haven't done a stroke. So I'll have to go to Brussels for a while, where I should be at this very moment.'

'Oh.'

'Well, that's reasonable, isn't it?'

'I suppose so. But won't you be here at all together? I like it best when everyone's here at the same time.'

'I'll do what I can. I'll be here most weekends, I dare say.'

Emily slid from the bath on to the floor. She leant up against the bath. The steam from the hot water made bubbles on the ceiling. It was very warm. Sun outside.

'Papa, shall I tell you something? A few weeks ago on the top of the church tower I told Wolf I thought you and Mama might be getting divorced. Wolf said it wouldn't matter all that much because people got divorced all the time – he'd *like* his father to divorce his horrid old stepmother. But I think it would matter.'

Idle turned to her, one half of his face freshly rinsed, shining.

'Whatever put such ideas into your head, darling?'

Emily shrugged. Papa looked so amazed that comfort, warm and thick as treacle, flowed through her limbs.

'Don't know, really.'

Idle put down his razor and came and sat on the edge of the bath. He ruffled his fingers through Emily's hair. Sighed.

'When you grow up, Em, you'll discover all marriages are different. Some married couples like being together all the time and never get bored. Others like parting for a little while, then having all the excitement of coming back together again and swopping their news. One way suits some people, the other way suits others. Do you understand?'

'Yes, but it's nicer for the children if they're the people who like being together all the time.'

200

'Could be, could be not. If they're together all the time just for the children's sake, but wishing they could get away sometimes for their own sake, then they might become bad tempered and resentful and irritable, and the children would suffer.'

'But which kind of couple are you and Mama?'

Idle paused.

'To be quite honest, in the beginning we were together most of the time, and we loved it. For two years, I think it was, we never spent a night apart. Then you were born, and my work changed and because of that I had to keep going away. But funnily enough we found that suited us, too. We were sad about the partings, of course, but looking forward to meeting again was terribly exciting. Mama always used to come and fetch me at the airport or station, no matter how late at night or early in the morning, and each time, for years, it was always exciting. Marvellous.'

'Is it still?'

'Of course.'

'Good.'

'And it always will be.'

'But I wish Kevin didn't seem to love Mama. It makes it so complicated, when she's really ours, doesn't it?'

'Kevin's just a friend, darling. Mama has lots of friends. She's so lovable. It'd be surprising if people didn't love her.'

'Do girls love you like Kevin and men love Mama?'

Idle smiled.

'According to Mama's theory, there are hundreds of girls about desperate for a man on almost any terms. I'd say she's probably right. Some of them are remarkably pretty. Even intelligent.'

'Do they love you, some of them?'

'What funny ideas you have! I don't know. There's been no need to find out. There *is* no need.'

'But it's nice to know they would if you let them, isn't it? Say Mama got run over or something. I mean, Wolf's father, I bet not even the most spinstery girl would love him. He's so silent, compared with you. Kind, though. Do you love Marcia Burrows?'

'Marcia Burrows? You've got a long way to go in understanding grown-up love, Em. It isn't something you just cast over anyone who happens to be good to you. It's a thing that catches you out, like a cold, at the most inconvenient and unlikely times. And if it goes wrong, after a good spell – well, you wrap yourself up well against it, if you see what I mean, so that you're not so likely to catch the disease so easily again.'

'Marcia Burrows ought to be loved by more people, I think. Then she'd be gayer and prettier. What do you think of her?'

'She's very nice, and very kind. She's looked after us very well.'

'That's what I think, too. And I think that banana custard was the best thing she's cooked.'

'It was lovely. Just like I remember it at school on Sundays.'

Emily looked up at her father and laughed. The shaving soap on one half of his face had dried, an unbroken white skin. She put up a finger to feel it, touching gently.

'You look so funny, Papa, You've got a funny clown's face.'

Idle smiled, and the dried up soap cracked across his cheek.

The morning Fen was due home Marcia Burrows insisted on leaving early for London. Idle tried to persuade her to stay and drive up with him in the afternoon, but she was adamant.

'You've been very good to me and I've enjoyed my week no end,' she said. 'But I'm not part of the family, and families should be together on their own.'

Emily went up to her room to help her pack. Predictably, everything was laid in neat piles on the bed. Emily sensed something in the way Miss Burrows put the clothes into the case very slowly – that she was a bit sad to be leaving. She wondered what her life would be like back in London.

'I mean, what will you be doing *tonight*?'

Marcia Burrows slipped trees into a pair of highly polished shoes and put them in an embroidered bag.

'I shall be tidying up my little house. It'll need a good going over after a week away.'

'Poor you.'

'Not at all. I enjoy getting things straight again. And then tomorrow there'll be a lot of work for your father after all this holidaying.'

'Where do you work for Papa?'

'In his office. It's a nice room overlooking the Park. You must come there one day. Sometimes, if I know I will be late finishing something, I take it home, and he comes round to fetch it so that he'll have it first thing next morning. I think he's quite fond of my house, although his head almost touches the sitting room ceiling.' She smiled to herself. 'One night, he was so tired, he fell asleep in the armchair watching television. I was typing upstairs so as not to disturb him. I came down and there he was – sound asleep. I hardly liked to wake him.' She shut her case, pressing down upon it with small white hands. 'This week I've got to get through a report in record time. I worry a little about it. I wonder if I can manage it? Anyhow, your father he said to me, he said: "Marcia, if you get through that by Friday night I'll take you to the opera." Well! I must get through it, mustn't I? With that invitation dangling. I love the opera. I haven't been for years.'

'Mama hates the opera,' said Emily. 'She says she can't like it however hard she tries, so Papa's given up taking her.'

'So I hear,' said Miss Burrows.

She left very quietly, waving a gloved hand. The excitement of Fen's arrival, soon after, banished further thoughts of Marcia Burrows from Emily's mind.

Fen was less pale but no fatter. She seemed very pleased to see both Emily and Idle, and to be home. But she hadn't been in the house long when she noticed that the flowers – the bowls of narcissi she had arranged all over the house before leaving – were dead, and had not been thrown away. This made her inexplicably cross.

'You *know* how I hate dead flowers,' she said to Idle. 'They're so depressing.'

'I'm sorry, darling. It's entirely our fault, isn't it, Em? We simply didn't notice.'

203

'I should have thought Marcia Burrows would have noticed.'

'She had a lot to do,' said Idle.

'Throwing away flowers doesn't take long.' Fen pulled a bunch of brown daffodils from a vase on the dresser. She seemed really cross, and upset. Her uncontrolled irritation provoked unusual lack of sympathy in Idle. He spoke angrily.

'For God's sake, the bloody flowers aren't that important.'

'But supporting Marcia Burrows seems to be.'

'What on earth can you mean? You can't mind her coming here if you go away?'

'I suppose I mind less than if some of your more flamboyant admirers had mucked about in my house. But if her greatest quality is housekeeping, then she should have noticed the flowers.'

'There are more essential things.'

'I'm glad you found her so satisfactory.'

'You're crazy.' Idle's voice had swooped down again. Emily, alarmed, took the bunch of dead daffodils from Fen.

'We're sorry, Mama,' she said. 'Don't be so cross now you've just got home. Let's go and get some more straight away. There are millions in the orchard.'

With an effort Fen smiled at her, took her hand. They went out into the garden. Idle followed them. There, while they stood by their favourite apple tree admiring the tide of flowers in the orchard, Idle stood close to Fen and put his arm round her shoulder. He grasped her firmly and forgivingly, quite unlike the hesitant way he had touched Marcia Burrows. Fen smiled up at him briefly, then shrugged off his hand and bent down to sniff at a cluster of yellow heads.

She had brought with her from London boxes of rich patés and spicy Greek things for lunch. As it was so warm, for the first time that year they ate in the garden. Fen rolled her bread into small pellets and threw them at the bantams. Emily and Idle told her stories – funny versions that made her laugh – of what had happened during their week, and nobody mentioned either Kevin or the north.

While her parents drank their coffee, Emily pushed back her chair and drew her knees under her chin. She watched them, relaxed and sparkling, as she would always remember them best, and thought back to her conversation with Idle. Perhaps it *was* best that they came and went as they did, because though the partings were sad, as Papa said, the coming together again was like this. Like this the house, the garden, was utterly theirs, its normal shape, its normal feeling again. A sensation of well-being began to seep through Emily, so intense that it made her drowsy, and her parents' voices became distant chimes, a simple music with no meaning. But she roused herself to say goodbye to Idle, who had to leave far too soon. Still, he was coming back on Saturday, four days from now. Something to look forward to. They'd all be together for the weekend – have a real picnic, per-haps, and fly the kite. Mama loved running along the tops of the hills, her long skirts puffed up by the wind. It made Papa laugh: he said she'd be blown right away one day. If she was, no doubt Papa would fly after her, chasing her through the clouds, and catch her, and bring her back.

'See you Saturday.' Idle was kissing Fen's cheek.

'Saturday, early as you can. We'll have a picnic lunch.' Fen was touching his face. Emily was right. All was well, all was well.

For the rest of the week Fen made a great fuss of Emily, who was in her element. There was nothing she liked more than to be alone with her mother when Fen was in this mood – funny and gay, and full of interesting ideas. A hot spring sun shone every day, and they spent most of the time out of doors, doing ordinary things: picking flowers, sowing a patch of herbs, tidying up the ground floor of the barn, going for walks on the common and picnic teas (with wonderful squashed cakes) in the hills. Wolf came with them most of the time, and although she liked his being there, to Emily the best part of the day was when he departed after tea, and she and her mother were left on their own for the lengthening evenings. They had begun reading *Great Expectations*, but after a page or two neither of them could concentrate any more. Fen would get up and begin to cook, almost in a frenzy, with great energy: different coloured pale mousses – 'cloud food', as Emily called it – and store them in the cool of the larder. Emily would help her, standing at the thick scarred wooden board, chopping slowly and carefully, listening all the while to Fen's stories about her wicked childhood. There was only one thing that puzzled Emily in this idyllic routine: every evening, when they had finished supper, Fen asked Emily to be quiet for half an hour while she wrote a letter.

'But you never write letters,' Emily complained, the first evening.

'I do now, it's my new craze. I write letters every day instead of a diary. We have such nice days I feel I have to write about them, or they'd be wasted.'

'But who wants to know about our days? Who do you write to?'

Fen shrugged. She was bent over her paper, hair all over her face, so that Emily couldn't see it.

'Oh, people. Shush now, Em, till I've finished. Then we'll do whatever you like.'

And every morning Fen was up unusually early, and had breakfast waiting on the table by the time Emily came down. Each morning at the same time they would hear the thud of letters on the floor by the front door. Fen would leap up with a start, almost as if she had been waiting for the postman, and dash away to collect them before Emily had a chance to do so. She would come back more slowly, splitting brown envelopes as she walked, complaining about bills. But on two mornings, Emily noticed, she had put a fat unopened letter in the breast pocket of her shirt, and on those mornings she wasn't hungry and only drank black coffee.

Every evening, Idle rang them from Brussels, and every night, much later, the telephone went again, after Emily was in bed. But through her open door, she could just hear the rise and fall of her mother's voice, and the frequent laughter. The conversations went on a very long time, till she fell asleep. The next morning she always forgot to ask who had rung. There were so many other more important things to think about: a donkey, perhaps. She and Wolf had planned to save up for a donkey to pull the old cart in the barn, and to eat the thistles in the field. That part of the reasoning might appeal to Fen, they thought. She might help them out with the money. Then there was the bird town to think of again – Fen had revived their enthusiasm with an idea of making one of the houses into a night-club for the birds who came to life after dark. Nightingales, for instance. Why shouldn't they have as much fun as the sparrows and blue tits? They would decorate the club with a small string of Christmas tree lights, and stick sequins round the windows. Tomorrow they were to go to Woolworths in Oxford to choose the lights and sequins.

With so many plans, the days went very fast.

Idle returned on Saturday for lunch, and, surprisingly to Emily, Uncle Tom came too. For once he was without a girlfriend, although Emily understood a certain Amabel with curly hair was hastening to join him on Sunday. Today, it seemed, a plan had already been made which Emily was told about at lunch. She was to spend the afternoon with Uncle Tom in Oxford, where he was rehearsing a student production of *Twelfth Night*. It would be good for her education, Idle explained, and Fen said she was very lucky to have such a chance. Privately, Emily had been looking forward to getting on with the night club with Wolf. But she always enjoyed doing things with Uncle Tom, and quickly readjusted her anticipation.

They left Fen and Idle sitting at the kitchen table, a new bottle of wine between them, wearing serious faces.

'You two look as if you're going to have a talk about money,' said Emily, and they both smiled weakly.

Tom had taken the roof of the car down. They drove slowly to Oxford, to prolong the pleasure of sun and wind.

'Had a letter from you and Wolf,' he said. 'What's she really like, this Marcia Burrows?'

'Like we said, fabulous.' Emily put her hand over her mouth so that Uncle Tom shouldn't see her smile.

'You spelt fabulous wrong.'

'Well, anyway, she is.'

'What makes you think I'd like her?'

'Like her? You'd *love* her. She's quiet and gentle, and she doesn't want to go to sleep all the time, and she does things like clean men's shoes. She'd look after you very well, and I'm sure she'd like you to teach her about poets and things.'

Tom laughed.

'You'd better arrange a meeting.'

'Wolf and I are going to do that, as soon as possible. We're going to have this restaurant up in the barn in the summer holidays. Mama and Papa are going to come – we'll make Papa pay. And we'll keep a table for you, reserve it, you know. And when you come in, there'll she be at your table, all waiting.' This plan had come to Emily on a sudden inspiration. She felt sure Wolf would approve.

'What happens then?'

'Easy, silly. You'll talk about marrying – she's longing to get married, so she won't argue at all. Then you just get on with the wedding.'

Tom put his foot on the accelerator.

'Just one other thing, Em. Very important. Is she sexy ?'

Emily looked at him. He seemed quite serious, so she braced herself for seriousness too.

'I should think she's probably the sexiest woman I've ever met, that's all.' Wolf would be very pleased with her when she told him what she had said. She was quite sure Tom was encouraged.

They arrived at one of the colleges and walked through its gardens. Glossy lawns curved through stately trees: all was newly green. A group of students sat waiting by the side of a lake, wearing identical jeans and tee-shirts. Looking like younger versions of Tom, they clustered about him, laughing and gesturing, flicking their cigarette stubs into the water, which confused the swans. One of them threw his book high into the air and caught it on his head: another, for no reason, did a somersault. Tom didn't seem to mind. Emily stood a little apart from the group, forgotten.

But suddenly all their revels ended, at the same moment. They moved away across the lawn, a serious group, ready for work. Tom came over to Emily, stood with his hand on her shoulder.

'You want to be an actress, don't you, Em? Well, one of the first things you have to learn about is getting to know your fellow actors. Really getting to know them, so that you feel you can do anything in front of them, uninhibited. In this little session this afternoon, we're just going to loosen up a bit, get to know each other. Sit on the grass and watch for a while. We won't be long.'

He went back to the group and spoke to them quietly. Emily could not hear what he said: from where she sat he seemed to be conducting them in silence. And they responded beautifully. Beatific expressions illuminating their faces, they leapt about the grass like young rabbits. With some kind of natural order they skipped and wrestled, somersaulted, and twirled each other about. Uncle Tom clapped his hands and they paused to rest.

'*Now* we're getting somewhere,' he said.

They nodded. Behind them was a willow tree, a clear sky, three Oxford spires. The mysterious process began again. This time the actors shut their eyes and tiptoed about: on bumping into a fellow member of the group they stopped and, eyes still shut, let their hands rove over each other's body.

'*Super*,' said Tom, waking them from their trance.

Emily shifted on the grass, puzzled, amused. If this was life in the theatre, she would definitely be an actress. She longed to join in but dared not say so.

The actors were now bending, stooping to touch the grass, eyes shut again, fingers stretched out like antennae. Soon as they touched earth their hands sprang back, as if scorched by the daisies: then began the gentle bending towards the grass once more. They seemed to like this exercise particularly, and repeated it several times, till Tom called a halt.

'*Really* exciting,' he shouted, and stretched out his arms to them.

Emily reflected upon her Uncle Tom's world. If the subtleties of this afternoon's performance had evaded her, the mood at least had inspired its lone audience. Whatever it was the actors had been trying to do, their silent gestures had conveyed to her a recognisable spirit. Like a fan waved in hope, they had fluttered for a moment the common air, making it tremble with a myriad of reflections. When Uncle Tom gave a small, rather heavy leap himself, Emily knew why, and she loved him. In a way, she hoped the plan for him to marry Marcia Burrows would fail. She didn't want the magic he could induce all to be taken up by her.

The rehearsal over, they walked back through the gardens. Uncle Tom asked if she had enjoyed herself. Emily nodded, unable to say why.

'That was just a beginning,' he explained, 'but worth it, I think. One day, perhaps, I'll direct you in something.'

'I hope so.' Unimaginable distances stretched before Emily, a stage with rising curtains at the end, her parents in the front row. She took Uncle Tom's hand.

He drove her to an ice-cream parlour and ordered strawberry ice-cream sodas. They sat at a counter on high stools, sucking the cold pink froth through straws. It was altogether a good afternoon.

'Do you take your girlfriends out for ice-creams?' asked Emily.

'Not many of them.' Tom smiled. 'They're not really ice-cream girls. And I'll tell you something else, there's not a single one of them I would have taken to that rehearsal this afternoon, either.' The compliment made Emily splutter through her straw. 'Kevin, now,' Tom went on, 'he's a different matter. I would have liked him to have been there. He would have been interested. In the old days he used to do the same sort of thing himself. He should never have given up, you know, Kevin. He's a marvellous actor.'

'We don't see him any more,' said Emily.

'Well, he's like that. He's inclined to disappear.' Tom put some money on the counter and swung himself off the seat.

'Do you mean once he's disappeared he doesn't come back again?'

'You can never really tell with Kevin. Now, come on. Fen and Idle must have finished their talk by now. We must go back.'

'Do you think it really was about money?'

'I expect so.'

'They looked quite worried, didn't they? Hang on – wait for me. And thank you for all my treats.'

They drove home fast in the open car.

The brilliant spring turned into a hot and rainless summer, a time of increasing work, apparently, for Idle. Although not abroad, he seemed to have to be in London almost constantly, even weekends. Emily returned to school, and an anonymous present of a camera was sent to Fen. She instantly took up photography and, encouraged by early results, decided to study the subject with some seriousness. This meant that she, too, was away frequently. Going to classes, she said, in London. She explained that the absences wouldn't last long, and it was all worth it if in the end she could do something to earn a little money – something she enjoyed. Emily saw the reasonableness of her argument, and felt it would be churlish to object. But she did wish less of her own evenings were spent in the unstimulating company of Mrs Charles.

Whenever Fen and Idle were at home together for the weekend it seemed that always, this summer, other people were there too. Uncle Tom and different girls; Fen's mother, who none of them had seen for years; a middle-aged married couple from the Foreign Office; students from Oxford introduced by Tom. They were never alone. Emily complained to her mother.

'Oh, darling, with a house and garden like this it's so lovely to be able to have people down, isn't it?'

'Yes, but not all the time.'

211

Idle said nothing. But in his silence, Emily felt, he perhaps agreed with her.

Then several mysterious events took place. One week in early June Fen announced she was off to Wales for a few days to photograph the mountains. She maintained that the trip was absolutely essential – 'before high summer', as she put it – but she promised to be back by the weekend, when Idle and Tom were coming down. The night she left for Wales Idle telephoned and asked Emily if he could speak to Fen. Emily explained she was away. Idle sounded surprised for a moment. He paused, collected himself, and went on to say how silly he was to have forgotten her plans. Emily did not repeat the conversation to Mrs Charles who, in her fury at having to spend two nights in the house, had retired to a deck chair in the sun.

Idle arrived home late Friday night. An hour earlier Fen had rung to say she wouldn't be able to get back till the following morning. A shadow passed over Idle's face at the news, but the moment passed in a flurry of broken eggs – Uncle Tom, transporting them to the frying pan, let them crash to the floor.

When Fen did arrive, just before lunch, there was no disguising the fact that she had been crying. She hardly stopped to kiss Emily, then dashed upstairs. Idle followed her, looking concerned. They shut their bedroom door. Downstairs, Tom and Emily played a desultory game of cards. The time went very slowly.

Eventually Idle returned, saying the plan was to lunch in Oxford, to save anyone cooking. Emily went upstairs to find her mother. She was making up the bed in Marcia Burrows' room.

'What are you doing, Mama? Who else is coming?'

'No one. But Papa and I sleep so badly in one bed, this very hot weather, we've decided we'll get more sleep apart.' Her face was calmer, but her eyes, without make-up and still swollen, were dim reflections of their normal selves.

'But it's not that hot at *night*.'

'Oh, it is in our room. We toss about.' Fen dropped a blanket

212

on the floor and came over to Emily. She put her arms about her and rested her chin on Emily's head. Instant, stephanotis smell. Emily sighed.

'Are you all right, Mama?'

'Um. It's nice being back with you.'

'Didn't you like Wales?'

Fen returned to the bed. She smiled.

'The photography didn't go very well,' she said. 'Maybe I'm not a very good photographer after all.'

'I should give it up,' said Emily.

Later, they lunched in a pub garden on the banks of the Thames. Tom did his best to amuse and divert, but it was impossible to disguise the fact that something was wrong, and a thought so horrible occurred to Emily that the food stuck in her throat: she could eat no more. It suddenly seemed very likely that both her parents would have good reasons for not turning up at Sports Day.

In the school calendar the importance of Sports Day, to the children at least, was second only to the Nativity Play. The tireless practising of team races, the endless striving for yet greater records in the high and long jumps, all became worth it when a bank of cheering parents lined the lawns, dressed in all their frippery, and bellowing for their own child to win. Last year, the Harrises had had a family triumph. Emily had won the egg-and-spoon race, Fen and Idle had won the Parents' Wheelbarrow race. As a new girl, this feat had stood Emily in good stead. She was thumped on the back with cries of 'Good old Harris', and even a snooty prefect, whose wiry parents had won the race for years, managed to give her a smile.

Parental failure to turn up at Sports Day, from the participants' point of view, was total betrayal. There were always some girls who could only count on one parent turning up: they were considered unlucky. A very few knew that no one would come. For them, the greatest pity was extended. Until this year Emily had never really considered their plight. She had always been one of the lucky ones. Apart from the Nativity Play – not Papa's fault, after all – both her parents had always made a point of turning up for all school functions. Now, doubt had gripped her mind, and as the weeks went by the picture of Sports Day without them became a torment.

Since lunch in Oxford Emily's appetite had never returned, and sleep was difficult. Eventually Fen questioned her. What was wrong? Emily, uncomfortable in the hot garden, answered in a monotone.

'I just thought perhaps you and Papa with all your work wouldn't be able to come to Sports Day.'

Fen paused. Then laughed.

'Is that all that's troubling you? I thought you must be sickening for something. Of course I'll come, definitely. And we'll try to persuade Papa to take a day off work. All right? I'm sure he'll do his best.'

Emily nodded. She was consoled, but not entirely convinced.

It thundered the night before, but Sports Day itself was glassy bright. Fen had finally promised Emily that both she and Idle would be there. In her clean shorts and Aertex shirt, along with the rest of her excited friends, Emily crowded the window of her classroom to watch the parents arrive. Fen came in good time, dressed as a magnificent tomboy, lithe and dazzling. Several of the children wolf-whistled at the sight of her. She was indeed different from the general run of mothers. Emily was proud: but there was no sign of Idle.

She left the window and went to the back of the class. Sat at her desk and screwed her hands into her eyes to stop herself crying. How could he be so mean as to let her down? Papa! He'd promised. Now he wasn't here, and she had no energy to run, to jump, or to enjoy the day.

'Emily Harris! There's a man who looks like your father looking for you.'

Emily's heart soared, confused. She ran to the window, pushing past her classmates. There, indeed, was her father, in a cream linen suit and silk tie and brown-and-white shoes. He smiled and waved at her. And then she understood. He had come in a separate car, direct from London. She leapt in the air, shouting with delight.

Later, from the children's side of the lawn, while others ran races, Emily kept an eye on her parents. Even from a distance they were beautiful, outstanding in the crowd of dumpy mothers in stiff dresses, and lumpish fathers with balding heads and short-sleeved shirts. They stood quietly side by side, not speaking, watching the races intently, and when Emily ran she could hear their cheering.

The children's races over, the Parents' Race was announced. This year it was to be three-legged. Emily ran through the crowd to find Fen and Idle. She wanted to make sure they would enter. They hugged her in turn.

'You did very well.'

'Only third.'

'But you were against a pretty fast lot. They all seemed bigger than you.' Idle smiled down at her, his skin remarkably brown for someone who had apparently spent so many weekends in London.

'Come on, now. They're all lining up over there. You've *got* to win again this year.'

Neither of them moved. Both looked at her.

'Oh, Em,' said Fen at last, 'do we absolutely have to go in for it this year? I mean, winning last year, aren't we entitled to retire?'

'Of course you've got to! Hurry up or you won't get a good place.'

Idle gave in.

'Oh, all right. Tie us up, then. But I warn you, I'm not in a running mood, and I'm hardly dressed for the occasion.'

'You certainly aren't,' Fen snapped. Her brittle eyes ran up and down his body.

'But you used to like these clothes . . .' His voice was hesitant, bewildered. 'You chose this suit.'

Fen snatched the scarf from Emily's hand, thrust her ankle against Idle's, and bent down.

'That was a long time ago. And not for *Sports* Day.'

She pulled the scarf into a severe knot round their ankles and Emily felt a chill over her flesh. She watched them put their arms round one another's waists, leaning a little away from each other, awkward.

'Hurry up,' she said, 'please.'

They walked away from her to the starting post, stiff wooden figures, all their ease of last year gone. Emily knew they wouldn't win. It didn't look as if they would even enjoy it.

She cheered them on, of course. She shouted till her throat was sore and blue spots gathered before her eyes. But their co-ordination was never any good: they stumbled, almost fell, leant away from each other, shouted at each other. They weren't in the first three, or even last: merely in the insignificant middle of clumsy runners. But Emily was determined to hide from them her disappointment.

'You did very well.' Their ankles were unbound at last. They walked a few yards apart. The stuff of Idle's coat was creased where Fen had clung to it round his waist. 'Most of them were cheating, pushing like that,' Emily went on. 'The wheelbarrow race was much better.'

They collected glasses of iced coffee and plates of gingerbread, the school cook's speciality, and sat in a small triangle under the willow tree. Near to them sat other groups who, last year, had caused them much laughter: the conventional middle-class parents with their braying voices and expensive cars. This year, it all seemed much less funny, and to ease the silence Emily kept up a mild chatter about the hopelessness of the gym display they were about to see.

The sky by now was mulberry, and the grass an alarming yellow.

'I think we'd better be off, really,' said Fen, 'and not wait for the gym. You'd better drive home with Papa, darling, as he's going straight on to London.' Emily could see by their faces there was no use in trying to persuade them to stay for the gym, and anyhow, she didn't really mind.

She went with Idle to his car. They drove the short way home in silence, watching the sky grow darker. The house, the garden, the drive were alert with that mushy quietness before a storm. They sat in the car, in mutual silent assent not to get out, waiting for Fen. They watched the first drop of rain – a single drop that spread on the windscreen, then shimmered down it in long threads.

'Wish you could stay here,' said Emily. 'There's no one coming this weekend.'

'Wish I could, too, my Em.'

Emily's throat was tight.

'Papa, I think you looked by far the best.'

'Thank you, darling.' Fen's small car chivvied into the drive. Idle put his hand on the ignition key, then bent over to kiss Emily. 'Bye, fat one. Be good.'

'Bye, Papa.'

Ten

The summer, which had begun with several weeks of untrammelled sun, became temperamental. Although there was no rain, storm clouds edged the days. Gathering their bright darkness each evening, they thickened the night sky when it came to cover them. In the orchard, trees scarcely flickered. Their shadows had a winter stillness, and the ground they fretted was patched with burnt grass.

It was very hot. It was as if some natural form of central heating had been turned too high, and in the closed walls of the earth the air was stifling. Only a storm could open a window. But there was no storm, in spite of the repetitive pleadings for one from Mrs Charles, whose overalls were stained with pungent sweat – and at night Emily, too, lay awake hoping for thunder. Every day the back of her neck, under her long hair, was wet and sticky, and all movement was an effort. After school she watered parts of the garden, spraying the parched flower beds with an arc of silvery drops that she would then trail over her own bare feet and hands and face, and find comfort for a moment. Fen alone, it seemed, was unaffected by the heat. Her long skirts changed to thin cottons, shadowy legs beneath them, and she tied wispy shirts in a knot under her breasts, leaving an expanse of brown ribs. Her hair, like Emily's, clung in tendrils to her face, which gleamed a little damply. But she was not enervated by the heat. Rather, in contrast to the lethargy all round her, she seemed to move more dartingly than usual, and set herself to endless tasks of preparing fruit, whisking cream for syllabubs, or polishing the copper pans. Idle, during this thundery time, remained in London.

But one Friday evening he arrived unexpectedly – Emily, at least, hadn't known of his coming. When she heard him she was lying on her bed, without thought, without energy, in that smudged world between consciousness and sleep, where the shapes of a room are doubly exposed upon the abstract patterns of the mind. She did not move, but waited for his voice in the garden. She heard it: low, enquiring, solemn. She listened to the tone of Fen's answers – brisk, cold. Then there was silence and Emily, without meaning to, slept.

It must have been two hours later when she woke – shivery, in spite of the heat, a little dazed. She went to the window. There was a dun sky, as on many previous evenings. Though no sun was visible, the grass and trees were a troubled yellow. In these still, violent colours, Fen and Idle paced the lawn, side by side, not touching. Backwards and forwards, backwards and forwards, a distance of not more than ten yards. It would seem from their rhythmic steps they had repeated their journey many times. They were talking quietly, but from Emily's room their voices were now impossible to hear.

She watched them. The chill she had felt on waking had left her. She was too hot again. Shifting restlessly, she wanted to shout down to them, but resisted. At that moment Fen paused, looked up at Idle, shrugged, and laughed. Emily could just hear her laughter, and observed Idle's silent surprise. Then Fen turned and tripped towards the house, smiling to herself. Idle remained where he was, his eyes on her. Both their forms were outlined now with the yellow of the grass. The colour blasted the edges of their clothes, their hair, their arms, making them illusory figures. Fen stopped at the wall of the house beneath Emily's room, half-hidden by a climbing rose. Emily leaned a little further over the window ledge. She could see her mother, arms raised, plucking at the odd dead head among the great

219

moony faced roses, the white petals falling apart in her hands and spilling over her shoulders. Then Fen cracked the stem of a live rose and turned away from the house, offering it to Idle. But when he made no movement, just stayed watching her, she held it to her cheek, symbolising for a moment the aestival creature that she was, glowing in the stormy light, passive, still.

'So many dead heads.' Her voice like flags in the silence. Idle began to walk towards her.

'Mama! Papa!' Emily called down to them at last.

They both looked up. In spite of the threatening air, they appeared unaffected – there was a strange relief in their look, some lightness about them that defied the electric garden.

'Em! Come on down. We've something to tell you.' Fen stuck the rose in her hair, a gesture of triumph, and turned into the house.

'Been asleep? I've been waiting for you.' Idle was under her window now, crinkly face smiling up at her, arms folded over his dark silk tie.

'Are you *staying*, Papa?'

'For the weekend.'

'*Good.*'

Emily ran to the stairs.

In fact they had two things to tell her. The first was that there was to be a treat tomorrow night: they were all to see Uncle Tom's production of *Twelfth Night*. The second was that the first week of the summer holidays Emily was to go with her father to France, while Fen went off on some photographic exhibition of the greatest importance. Wolf, it had been arranged, was to be included in both plans.

Emily, curled up in an armchair picking at her toenails, was torn by the combination of pleasure and disappointment in the news.

'But *why* do you have to photograph just in my holidays, Mama?'

'It can't be helped, darling. Really. Something's come up that's

220

a chance for me to try out being a professional photographer. I'm to be paid – imagine that!'

'Where will you be ?'

'Edinburgh. That part won't be much fun, in August. I've got to photograph a play there. It's only for a week, Em. Don't look like that. You and Wolf will have a lovely time looking after Papa.'

'I think it's unfair. It'd be much better if you came too.'

'Well, things don't always work out right, do they? Timings. I'm sorry.'

'It's a good chance for Mama,' added Idle. 'You wouldn't want her to miss a chance like that, would you?'

If they had once been apart, Emily thought, they were together now – against her. They both seemed to think the arrangement was quite reasonable, and were therefore not inclined to understand. She said no more.

Emily watched her parents laughing at Malvolio. And indeed, dressed as an old-fashioned butler, an inspiration on Uncle Tom's part, he was being very funny. So were Sir Andrew Aguecheek and Sir Toby Belch, tumbling about with their huge stomachs and striped socks. This *Twelfth Night* was a pantomime, with much rolling about on the grass (as practised in those early days) and winsome music and witty songs. Wolf, whose reluctant study of Shakespeare had produced nothing but scorn for the boringness of the old bard, was laughing so loud that tears rolled hard upon each other down his freckled cheeks.

By some lucky chance the heaviness of so many previous evenings had evaporated. The air was light and clear, leaves stirred in a warm breeze. The actors frolicked about the lawn, the lake flecked with swans behind them; the audience was mounted on raised seats under a striped canopy. Fen was her most beautiful. She wore a dress of long white pleats, a lilac gauze scarf plaited through emerald beads at her throat: her hair, half piled up, was escaping its ribbons. Her face was restless with laughter, her brown hands flew constantly in delight to her cheeks. Idle, too, appeared happy, his eyes flicking from the lawn to Fen, imitating her laughter. If it hadn't been for the thought of France, it would have been a perfect evening.

In the interval, when the audience gathered under the chestnut trees, Tom brought them plates of strawberries and cream, and goblets of mead. Emily and Wolf tried it: liked it. They drank a whole goblet between them.

Tom was surrounded by admirers. One particular girl, tall with a dull pretty face, stuck relentlessly to his side. Wolf noticed her at once. He urged Emily to walk a few yards away with him so that his speculation would not be heard.

'Reckon Marcia Burrows has had it as far as your uncle's concerned.'

'What do you mean?'

'Nobody, especially Miss Burrows, would get past *her*.'

'Perhaps not.' Warm and melancholy from the mead, Emily felt within her the dying fall of a plan that is struck with little future.

'As for your parents' – Wolf nodded his head towards them – 'I've never seen two people less divorcified. I don't know what you were talking about.'

Emily looked over at them too. They were listening to Tom, faces intent, smiling.

'Oh, *that*,' said Emily. 'I think that's all over. They seem to be all right now.' The gold and green leaves on the lower branches of the trees confused her with their dancing. Her knees felt weak. She wondered if she was going to be sick. Concentrating hard, she noticed Wolf put on his most philosophical face.

'Oh, well, it's difficult to tell sometimes. Grown-ups decide on divorce like we decide on a game of marbles. Heads we do it, tails we don't. That sort of thing.'

'You're right, Wolf,' said Emily. She put her hand on his arm because she felt unsteady. He let her leave it there until they reached their seats.

The sky darkened during the second half of the play. Stars

222

appeared, the first for weeks, and lanterns were lit in the trees. When the lovers finally sailed away in a creaky punt across the lake, the band played a wild haunting tune, and fireworks showered down through the sky till they met and drowned with their own reflections in the water. Emily felt better. She took her father's warm hand, leant against him. Although so much was going on before them, they both turned to look at Fen. She was shining in her whiteness, her laughing face against the moon.

'I don't like treats being over,' whispered Emily.

'There'll be others, from time to time. France could be fun, you know.'

France. Without Mama. Papa a bit lost sometimes, like he was without her.

Emily joined in clapping with the audience. She clapped till her hands were stinging, and the fireworks and the stars and the swans and the leaves shimmered like the last act of a dream. She felt reluctant to leave this luminous night place. It was easier, here, not to think about France.

There was one further piece of news kept from Emily till the day they left. Marcia Burrows was to come with them. She met them at the airport.

Emily, already dulled by a disloyal reluctance about going on the holiday at all, was hardly surprised, hardly interested. She assumed her father would explain how much Miss Burrows needed a holiday, how she could keep him company while she and Wolf played, and how, with her there, they might even do some essential work. Emily judged his explanations accurately: he said precisely those things.

At the airport Marcia Burrows seemed a little flustered. Dressed like an eager novice traveller, in white linen coat and matching hat, she kept tapping her small new suitcase as if to check she still carried it. Idle, superb in dark glasses, led his small dazed herd of travellers with great authority. Instinctively he understood the ways of the world's airports, and Miss Burrows' eyes glittered with admiration.

Brittany was their destination. A small, unpretentious town on the coast full, it seemed, of children with middle-aged French parents in espadrilles and sailcloth trousers, but who nonetheless eyed the sea with some suspicion and lay in firm rows on the sand. The shops, cluttered with Brittany china, found an avid buyer in Marcia Burrows. As one who had never adventured beyond a landlady cousin in Bognor for her holidays, she was enchanted by everything she saw, and spent most recklessly on postcards and ashtrays. The sun shone, local gulls screamed furiously at the annual disruption of their quiet habitat, and fumes of fresh fish rose in the narrow streets. Down at the harbour, nets were strewn along the quay to dry, and there was a dried-sea smell of sunbaked sails, faded rusts and cobalt blues, that lay rolled in the fishing boats. Emily, who always expected anywhere new to be disappointing, was nicely surprised by the place, and Wolf, who had once had the misfortune to spend a day at Nice airport with Coral, admitted it wasn't bad compared with the South of France. They did little to resist the temptations of the local *patisserie*, and Marcia Burrows' attempts at French – nothing could stop her – kept them giggling like old sophisticates.

But their real pleasure was the hotel: built of white wood at the end of the last century, it threw an aristocratic shadow over the beach, a magnificent and chipped monument to more glamorous seaside days. Its long wooden terraces leapt beneath the feet of running children, and the older guests were not disturbed: perhaps because of the dampness of the wood all sound was muted, muffled, no sharper than the soughing of the waves. There were no carpets. The lino floors were newly streaked with sand each day, so that every evening guests were aware of a slight crunching underfoot. Two unhurried waiters served drinks to vast parties of grown-up relations on the terrace, while the children played ping-pong in a room behind them. The dining room smelt of fish and fried herbs, and the checked tablecloths and napkins were always slightly damp. Idle had arranged a window table: it was during their long, delicious meals, looking out upon the spumous sea and wide sands, that Emily most missed her mother. *She* would have liked this: the baby lobsters, the icy white wine, the funny shouting French families in their man-made fibres. She should have been there.

But Idle made great efforts to entertain the children. Late mornings in bed, reading, were his only selfish pleasure. Eleven onwards, he was theirs. He drove them to heathery cliff tops for proper picnics – provided by the hotel – of melon and runny cheeses, and croissants and chocolate. He climbed over the rocks with them, stepping in and out of warm shallow pools: he swam, and played *boules* on the beach, making an effort, it seemed, to consume as much energy as he could. Marcia Burrows was a contented spectator to these activities. She would sit on a rug, legs straight out in front of her, linen hat with a floppy brim on her head, a white hand always sheltering her eyes. Sometimes she would look anxiously at Idle and warn him not to overdo it – he would laugh at her to conceal his irritation at her anxiety, and tell her not to worry. He was enjoying himself, he said.

One evening, after dinner, Idle agreed that they should go to the local discotheque for an hour. Emily was delighted: friends at school had been to discotheques. The experience would be new to her. But when they arrived, her excitement vanished at once. She wished they hadn't come. The music hurt her ears, and the strobe lighting, slashing everything as it did into strips of livid colour, was unnerving.

They sat at a dark table, an incongruous foursome. Idle and Marcia Burrows looked twice as old as anyone else in the place. Emily wished they were younger. She also wished that Miss Burrows would stop holding her hands up to her ears in that pained fashion, and that Idle would stop grinning round at everybody as if determined to enjoy himself. Wolf, who had always thought dancing was stupid, and whose mind was in no way changed by the writhing creatures before him, blew patient bubbles into his Coca-Cola, longing to return to the hotel. Then the thing that Emily most dreaded happened: Idle suggested that he and Marcia Burrows should dance. Miss Burrows leapt up, all of a dither in her keenness, saying she didn't know if she could manage this kind of thing, but she would like to try.

In the violent lights that ripped about them, the grown-ups were absurd. Idle moved with stiff-hipped enthusiasm, and held up his hands in a position of surrender. Marcia Burrows bounced about with small skips, quite out of time with the music, like someone used to maypole dancing. Her sunray pleated skirt, printed with snakes and ladders, flicked about her knees, and her face was radiant with effort. Emily noticed the strange glances the couple were receiving from the other dancers. She wondered if her father was aware of the mirth he was causing . . . And if he cared.

'They look bloody loony,' said Wolf, embarrassed as Emily by the performance. 'Your *mother*, now, if you don't mind me saying so – if she was here they'd all be looking because she dances the best I've ever seen.'

'Oh, shut up,' said Emily.

She looked once more at her father. Behind his grin, as he watched his frolicking partner, his eyes were dull. *Mama: I can't bear for them to go on.* It was suddenly clear to Emily what she must do. In order to get Marcia Burrows off the floor, she must dance herself. She must dance as she did with her mother, as her mother had taught her. Her best. She stood up.

'Where are you going?' Wolf was puzzled by Emily's determined look.

'To dance.'

'You can't expect me to.'

'Don't want you to.'

Emily danced her best. Slowly at first, bending her body to the sounds, stretching her arms, feeling the weight of her head and the swish of her hair as she rocked her neck from side to side. Through the squalls of music, she heard Marcia Burrows' shriek of amazement, her giggle. Then dimly Emily saw her cavorting back to the table. Idle was now before Emily, hopefully practising a kind of rhythmic bow, like a courting pigeon. But she swung away from him, impatiently. So he, too, shuffled back to the table.

226

Emily was left on her own among tall, teenage strangers. Some of them, tanned boys with dark eyes, divided from their partners, danced opposite her for a while. The music, encouraging, grew faster, louder. Emily became a totally pliant thing, wild but never uncontrolled, intoxicated now by the flashing lights that turned her movements and the shadow of her movements into a quivering film. She was oblivious to the attention she caused – didn't notice for some moments that she was alone on the floor. Her only thought was that she had to dance her best for Mama. It didn't matter, really, that Mama would never know . . .

When the music finally subsided, Emily returned to the table. Applause, like rain, splattered the newly still darkness. Sweat pricked everywhere on Emily's body. Her tee shirt was damp, all the fire had left her.

'That was pretty good, Em.' Idle was proud, sad.

'What a little dancer!' Marcia Burrows was still clapping her feathery hands. Wolf sniffed.

'Let's go, shall we?' Idle was paying. The music had started again – strange, distant sounds now that Emily had climbed down from them. 'That was quite fun, wasn't it? There was gooseflesh on Idle's arms.

'No,' said Emily, 'it was horrible. All wasted.' Too late to take back what she had not meant to say. Apologies would confuse.

'Really,' said Idle, 'I don't understand you.'

'Your father and I thoroughly enjoyed ourselves, didn't we, Idle?' Miss Burrows enthused. In reply, Idle merely sighed.

The next day the sky clouded over. Emily, tired and irritable, found nothing to enjoy. Idle suggested that everyone should rest that afternoon, and if the evening was fine they would go to their favourite beach. But Emily remained hot and alert on her bed, unable to read or sleep. Eventually, she decided to go along to her father's room, suddenly wanting to see him on his own, unsure what she should say to him.

She knocked on the door, opened it without waiting for an answer. The room was dusky behind drawn blinds. Idle was lying on the bed, dressed in a both-robe. Marcia Burrows stood beside him, a glass of water in her hand. She, too, was in a dressing gown. On hearing the door she made a clumsy pirouette towards Emily, swatting the dressing gown around her knees.

'Oh, dear. Is there anything the matter?' Her face was a deep plum.

'No.' Emily shut the door. Stood watching them. 'I wanted to see Papa.'

'I was just insisting he took his pills.'

'Are you ill, Papa?'

'No, darling. I've probably been overdoing the good food.' His voice was tired. One hand rested on his stomach.

'It's your ulcers, Idle, whatever you may say.' Marcia sat down on the end of the bed and patted one of Idle's ankles. It was stuffy in the room in spite of the open window.

'What are ulcers?'

'He should be having lots of milk. That's what they always recommend for ulcers. But the French milk . . .' Marcia Burrows clacked one of her leatherette slippers against her heel. Emily's head ached.

'I'm all right, Marcia.' Idle gently twitched his foot from out of her grasp.

'Shall I go away?' Emily asked.

'No. Stay.' Idle smiled, half in pain.

'*I'll* go. I'll go and carry on with my siesta.' Marcia Burrows stood up, her face lively with offence. 'It was only remembering your father's pills made me leap out of bed.' She addressed Emily in some confusion, then left the room quickly. Idle seemed amused by her manner of departure.

'What's the matter with her?' Emily asked. Papa was closer now Marcia Burrows had gone.

'I dare say she doesn't like her nursing routine to be interrupted. She's a woman of inflexible habits. The sort of thing you and I aren't entirely used to.'

'Sorry.'

'Don't be silly. Come here.' Idle patted the bed beside him.

Emily sat down. 'You all right? Enjoying yourself?' Emily nodded silently. 'Only two more days. Funny how the time goes so fast. I think it's been a good time, though. Being with you so much.'

'But I wish . . .'

'I know.'

A small breeze shifted the blind, making it tap at the window ledge. Emily swung her feet on to the bed and rested her head on her father's chest. From this position she could see half her mother's face – half her smile of a few years ago – in the photograph on the bedside table.

She cried. Quite suddenly, surprising herself by the tears.

'Don't, darling. Don't, my Em.' Idle's hand was gentle on her head.

'I don't know why I'm crying, Papa.'

'You're tired from last night.'

'Yes.' Her body heaved. 'But I hate crying.'

'You hardly ever do. You're a pretty brave one, you know.' His voice was medicine. Emily lifted her head. Idle dabbed at her eyes with a corner of his bath-robe. His London smell had absolutely gone, now.

'You smell of the sea,' Emily said, 'and there's sand in your hair.'

Idle smiled.

'Tell you what, we'll never get to sleep now, will we? Shall I read to you?'

Emily nodded. Warm, better.

'*Great Expectations*. Mama and I got to page sixty-eight.'

'You go and get it for me, then later we'll go out. Look: I think it's getting brighter.'

But when the time came, although her spirits were temporarily restored, Emily felt disinclined to join the beach party. Wolf was desolate at her lack of enthusiasm. He kicked moodily around her room.

'We've been stuffing in all day.' Why don't you want to come now it's sunny?'

'Don't know.'

'Gloomy old Emily. Emily gloomily gloomily Emily. I could make a tongue twister out of it. Do you want to be on your *own*?' He was sarcastic.

'Yes.'

'Women and girls always want to be on their bloody own. Stupid spoilsports, I think. Well, anyway, your father – he's not a spoilsport, at least – he said he'd help me fly my model aeroplane.'

In the end, Emily went with them. Although the sun had broken through the cloud, it was a cool evening. The cove they went to was deserted. Idle and Wolf flew the plane on the cliff top. Marcia Burrows, in a new cardigan to protect herself from the light breeze, watched them patiently. She wasn't a bad old stick, really, Emily thought. Kind, and not much trouble. But brittle, somehow. Frail. Good but uninspired. The sort of woman who, if she married, and had children, would make an easy grandmother. But rather an embarrassing mother.

All the same, she looked a bit out of things, sitting here. Ill at ease.

'Don't you want to help the others fly the kite?' asked Emily.

'I wouldn't be much good at that.'

'Mama loves kiting.'

'Your mother and I have different kinds of stamina. She's physically energetic – admirably so. I'm, well, more of the persistent kind. Privately persistent, so that you'd never guess.' Her eyes, blurred from the wind, were on the horizon. She seemed to be speaking to the elements rather than to Emily.

'But are you just going to go on and on being a secretary, for ever and ever, until you're old?'

Marcia Burrows roused herself a little.

'I don't see what that has to do with anything, but probably not. Who can say? One thing you learn when you're as middleaged as I am' – she smiled to herself – 'is your exact role. And you accept it, even if it's second best. You accept your role in the lives of other people. There's no use in reaching for some sort of unobtainable heaven if you've been born equipped only with a step ladder. So very persistently you stick to your minor role. – That's not to say you can't imagine, sometimes.'

'I don't understand what you mean.'

'Well, I can't explain myself better than that.' Marcia Burrows stiffened herself against a new gust of wind.

'Then can you tell me what flamboyant means?'

'You ask so many questions! Wherever did you pick up such a word?'

'Mama said Papa had flamboyant admirers, but you weren't the most flamboyant.'

'Oh. Did she? She's right, of course.' Marcia Burrows crumpled a little. 'It means – showy, decorative. Not dowdy. Not a secretary for life. People like your mother and father are flamboyant in the best sense of the word. They attract other flamboyant people. They always will. It's a sort of luxury. Perhaps well deserved, perhaps unfair,' she added. 'Now, Emily, do leave me, will you? I like to look at the sea without all this chatter.'

'All right.'

Emily, shivering in her bathing trunks, wandered away. She had the feeling there was no longer any need to feel sorry for Miss Burrows. In spite of all the laughable things about her she seemed to be quite happy on her step-ladder, whatever that was, persisting away privately in her own peculiar world. Emily scrambled down the cliff to the beach – a long, shell-shaped curve of sand. It was windless down here. Quiet, except for the distant rasp of the breakers. The sand was soft warm ridges under her feet, cold if she wriggled her toes more deeply.

She walked towards the sea, wondering at its sadness. Perhaps it was just because it was evening. Perhaps the waves don't like the end of days, the coming of night, the lighthouse flash. And yet it was lucky, the sea. Because even if it was quite boring, millions of years of swirling up the beach and slipping back again, at least it was always the same. The tides would go on till the end of the earth, you could count on that. Whereas with people,

231

even the people you knew best, you could never tell. Their ways, in fact, were much more mysterious than those of the oceans. Most peculiar, sometimes. Put out if you went to see your own father in the middle of the afternoon. And . . . oh! Here was a cluster of shells, lying in the sand like a family. Such pretty ones. Emily stooped to pick them up. She would take them home as a present for Mama. Mama would like them. She could make them into a new necklace. Papa, of course, being a man – well, Papa wasn't much interested in shells.

They returned to England. Idle and Marcia Burrows stayed in London: Emily and Wolf went home. Fen was already there, welcoming and gay. In a mood of capricious energy, she had arranged bowls of cream and white roses in most rooms, and trailed honeysuckle, already dying, across the mantelpiece in the kitchen. She had made summer puddings and left them to cool in the larder: and in the evening she threw lavender on to the fire so that the house itself became infused with the peaceful smell of summer gardens. Emily wondered at her happiness.

Fen asked questions about France but hardly seemed to listen to the answers. She sat at the kitchen table, a yellow chalk in her hands, shuffling through a pile of large photographs. Emily, too, looked at them, with less interest than her mother. Pictures of some theatre, some play: shadowy men in long robes, girls in togas and sandals, garlands of flowers on their heads.

'Do you mean this was your job, photographing this play?'
Fen nodded.
'I told you. What d'you think of them?'
'They're good.' Emily sighed. She studied one particular picture. One of the actors with a long beard looked very familiar. She looked again at the wild eyebrows. Of course. 'Is this Kevin?' she asked.
'Yes.'
'Was he in the play ?'
'Yes.'
'But I thought he wasn't an actor any more.'

'He missed it too much. He's going back. He's going to sell the factory. He had awfully good reviews – you know, the critics were nice about him. They said the play wasn't up to much, but his performance was marvellous.' Fen had no hope of containing her smile. Emily let the photograph fall on to the table with a click.

'So that's why you were asked to take the pictures?'

'It could have had something to do with it.'

'So Kevin was there all the time?'

'Rehearsing.'

'Did Papa know? Did he know Kevin was in the play?'

'Of course. He was pleased it was a chance for me . . .'

'I wish you'd told me.'

'Oh, Em. Why? I didn't think it was important.'

'All the time in France, I imagined you being sad in Scotland, just working.'

'You silly old thing. I was having a lovely time. Whatever are you looking like that for? Come here and tell me which of these you like best.'

Emily moved closer to her mother, who was far away, absorbed in the photographs. And the pleasure of being home again, for all the warmth of the evening kitchen, and the flowery smells, was a little dimmed.

A few days later Emily remembered the restaurant plan. Before reminding Wolf she would, she decided, make one positive move and buy the candles. She would act upon his advice and get the night-light type of candle, so that there should be no risk of the barn catching fire. The idea of the restaurant was something to look forward to – it would be arranged for one of the weekends when Idle was home. Marcia Burrows might be there, too: it wouldn't matter one way or the other, and Wolf's father. Coral was the only problem.

Emily bought four night-light candles in the village shop and, carrying them in a paper bag, walked home. It was midday, very hot. Everything bright with high summer. Soon, it would be early autumn, the best time, when she would feel more energetic. Now, she felt enervated. Walking was an effort. She was glad to be on her own because she could not have bothered to talk to anyone. Not even Wolf. Though she would ring him as soon as she got home, and make a plan for this afternoon.

But halfway down the drive the shade of the barn tempted her. Anything to shelter from the hard sun for a moment. Wolf could wait.

Emily walked through the wide, doorless opening to the barn. Its cool shade flung over her like water: the familiar smell of warm musty hay bristled round her and the pigeons, chiming on their high rafters, fluttered a little, ghostly fans in the half-light. Emily leaned against the old dog-cart, panting. Its high iron wheel dug into her back. She turned, and read the carved message once again: *Ada loves Charlie*. Tracing the words with her finger, she wondered if the cart had belonged to Ada or Charlie. Ada, most probably. She was a girl with old-fashioned hats tied on with veils, and a small waist and a secret smile. She owned a glossy pony and a tall whip, and she drove through the country lanes hoping to run into Charlie. But Charlie had a huge black hunter: *he* galloped across ploughed fields and jumped the hedges. Ada, racing along the lanes, could never hope to catch him. Perhaps they only met at church, Sundays, where, after the service, Charlie would hold the pony's head while Ada climbed into the cart. She would give him a smile, and drive away filled with a love she could never mention. Perhaps it was only *years* later she had sold the cart, a poor grandmother by then, married to some man who said *why don't you get rid of that junk?* And so she had inscribed the message in loving memory before letting it go to a local auction.

Emily climbed into the cart. One of its hard seats, split, frothed with white stuffing. Part of an old rein was looped over the side of the cart, the cracked black leather quite stiff. Emily held it, bending it gently, wondering if she could ever make it pliant again, as it must have been in Ada's hands.

From the darkness of the barn the scene outside was a huge, oblong picture, very bright: part of the house, its mossy roof

234

dazzling green, on the left: an apple tree on the right. Fen walked by, a whicker basket over her arm. Looking for more roses, perhaps. She couldn't want *more* roses. Emily called to her. Fen stopped, peered into the barn. The folds of her long corn-coloured skirt shifted gently about her ankles. Perhaps Ada had stood just like that, once, looking for Charlie.

'I'm here! In the cart.'

Fen came towards her. She crossed from the brilliant light outside to the barn shadows, and as she did so the summery essence of her figure seemed to evaporate. Suddenly, though still warm and gold, she was a harbinger of autumn: summer had quite fled from her shape, leaving her beautiful but melancholy.

'What are you doing here? I was wondering where you were.'

'Why don't you come up in the cart?' Emily swung open the small door and Fen climbed in. The cart rocked for a moment, till Fen sat on the split seat opposite Emily. 'I was thinking of Ada and Charlie.'

'It's sad they had to sell this. They'd probably had it for years,' Fen said.

'Do you think they married, then?'

'Oh yes. They're grandparents. Living in a little cottage in a wood somewhere. They've got sepia photographs of themselves in this cart, don't you think?'

'I thought Ada *lost* Charlie. I mean, never got him.'

'*No*. You are an unromantic one. They sit by the fire, remembering.'

'I hope so.' Emily watched her mother shifting on her seat. Her smell of stephanotis fused with the greyer smell of hay. Emily wanted to touch her, but she kept her hands on her paper bag. 'I bought the candles for the restaurant,' she said. 'You know, Wolf and I are going to make a restaurant one night in the loft. For you and Papa and Wolf's father and perhaps Marcia Burrows. We wondered if we could borrow a tablecloth and if you could help us a bit with the food, secretly . . . We're going to make the menus this afternoon. When do you think it should be? Mama?' She paused. 'What's the matter, Mama?'

Fens' eyes met Emily's. They were bleak in the shadows. And fear, like a shawl, seemed to have wrapped round her, making her cower down on the seat. Her long silence was alarming.

'Em,' she said eventually. 'I don't think you had better make plans for a restaurant. You see, Papa and I aren't going to be here together, any more.'

Miles above them, in the dark, a pigeon twirled and tumbled. Its friends cooed their appreciation.

'Why not?' The sides of the barn lurched like a ship in a storm. Emily held on to the frail sides of the cart.

'Well . . . Oh God, I didn't want to tell you any of this till the end of the holidays, Em. Then we wanted to tell you together. But with all your plans . . .' Her voice wavered away.

'But I bought the candles. What shall I tell Wolf?'

'You'll have to tell Wolf the truth. We're not going to be married any more, darling.'

'But I bought the candles, Mama.'

'I know. But it's all over, really. Papa and I can't live together any more. We've tried, but we can't.'

'Why not? Don't you love each other any more?'

'Oh yes. I expect we'll always love each other. For ever and ever and ever, like we'll always love you.'

'I don't understand. If you love each other . . . and except for that time Papa was cross with Kevin, you've never had rows and things.'

'No.'

'So I don't understand.'

'I wish I did. I wish we did. I wish I understood why things go wrong, and then they can't be mended again, no matter how hard you try. It's hard to explain. But something dies, and you can't bring it to life again. So if you stay together, it's a kind of – living death.'

'I still don't understand.'

'And you find yourselves loving other people in the old, alive way.'

'So you mean you're going to get divorced?'

'Divorced?' Fen sat upright at the harshness of the word. 'I suppose we shall get round to that. There's no particular hurry.'

'And what else will happen? What will happen to here? To me?'

'Oh, darling. We haven't thought out the details. We've just agreed to part. We've got to discuss everything.'

'But what will happen to you?'

'To me? I'll be all right. The plan is that I shall leave at the end of the holidays . . . and go and live with Kevin, follow him wherever he goes in the theatre. I'll see you a *lot*, of course. As many weekends as you want. Wherever I am, I'll come for you.'

'And Papa?'

'Papa hasn't been very well, as you probably know. He's been working too hard for too many years. He's given himself ulcers. So he's not allowed to work so much any more. He's going to be here most of the time, looking after you, and you don't need to move school. One day, perhaps, you'll move to a smaller house.'

'But who will look after Papa and me?'

'Who will look after Papa and you?' There was a long silence. 'I believe Papa said something about Marcia Burrows . . .'

'*Marcia Burrows*?' The pigeons made dizzying arcs of white in the barn dusk. 'Will Papa *marry* her?'

'I don't know.'

'But he can't *love* her.' Marcia with her toes pointed to the sky on picnics, her fear of the cold, her grey neatness, her sad willingness to please. 'Papa *can't* love Marcia Burrows, he can't, he can't . . .'

'I daresay he doesn't,' said Fen. 'But people often substitute the habit of loving for just plain habit.'

As birds and barn, lightness and dark encircled her in their spinning, Emily was supported by the warm familiar place of her mother. They slipped, arms about each other, into the corner of the cart, their hearts pounding at the horror of all prospects. And even as the first nightmare blazed through Emily, the second began to formulate.

'Mama, you and Kevin – *you* wouldn't get married, would you? You don't love Kevin, do you? *You couldn't!*'

Emily felt the huge movement of Fen's sigh.

'I don't know about marriage, Em. Honestly. We haven't discussed it. We'll see what happens. For the moment all we know is that we're happy when we're together . . . and we want to make *you* happy as possible in the circumstances.'

Emily listened to herself laughing, or it may have been a pigeon noise.

'Why did it have to happen to you and Papa, after all these years?' She must have asked out loud, because she heard Fen's answer.

'I don't know. Sadly, it happens to a lot of people.'

'Couldn't it ever be all right again, if you tried?'

'No.'

Emily released herself from her mother's hold. Somewhere in all the turmoil was a small flicker of hope.

'I think it could be. If you really tried.'

'No, darling. There's no point in thinking that. Really.' Fen's wan voice fluttered down, chilling. Emily took her hand.

'Then please tell me *why* it happened.' Emily glanced at her mother: Fen's head was high, her eyes bright as she looked out at the garden.

'What can I say to you, Em? Sometimes you do things without meaning to, not guessing at the risk you're taking. Strong as you may think you are, you're not strong enough to stop what happens. You stand, looking at the whole disaster from a long way off, terrified by your own actions, but unable to stop.'

'You mean, like when I threw the ink at school.'

'Like when you threw the ink at school.'

'But everyone forgave me for *that*.'

'It isn't just a question of forgiveness. We all forgive each other. Papa and I . . .'

'Don't cry, Mama.'

'Of course I shan't cry. I never cry, do I?'

238

'No.'

'And you're not to *worry*. I promise we'll see to it you'll have the best life possible, given this has happened. We'll see you a lot together, Papa and I – we'll never fight, or be difficult, like some separated parents. In a way, it might be quite fun, having two lots of families . . .' Her ridiculous voice, almost breaking, strained on. 'Mightn't it? Don't lets think about it any more today . . . I couldn't bear it. Em, Em. It'll be all right, honestly. You'll get used to it. It'll just be different.'

Already the speckled dusk in the barn had changed its tone. The garden outside was no longer merely brilliant, but cruel. The pigeons mocked – had their cooing ever been a comfort? Fen, with her shrill voice, remained the only familiar figure in the landscape. But soon she would be gone. It was different already. Quite, quite different. Emily flung her bag of candles on to the floor. Perhaps, if she had never got into the cart – perhaps if Ada and Charlie had kept their stupid old cart . . .

'Help me get some more roses, Em,' Fen was saying, climbing down the small step. 'They're almost the last.'

She crossed the floor of the barn, came to the glitter of the sun outside. It tore at her silhouette like flames. She turned back to Emily, beckoning, not noticing the flames. Not noticing she was on fire.

Mama!

Emily followed her.

Coral had made an effort with the tea. She had arranged small plates of different kinds of sandwiches and coloured biscuits, and had bought an iced cake. But Emily hadn't the energy even to pretend she was hungry. She sat in silence, tearing a piece of bread into smaller and smaller bits. Coral chattered on in a cheerful voice, as if nothing had happened, as if nothing was wrong. But she received no answers to her silly questions. Wolf, in deference to Emily, kept silent too.

Tea over, the children went out into the garden. They just stood there, a few feet apart, not talking. Toys were strewn over

239

the lawn, but Wolf knew it was useless to ask Emily what she wanted to play.

'What do you want to do?' he asked, at last.

'Go home.'

'But you're meant to stay here till . . . till your father comes to fetch you later.'

'I know. But I'm going now. You can't stop me. Do you want to come?'

Wolf looked at her, worried by the sharpness of her voice. She stood very stiff, arms by her side. When a breeze blew a strand of long hair across her face she tossed back her head. Suddenly she looked much older than he felt. He nodded. Of course he would go with her, no matter how cross it would make Coral.

It was nearly six weeks since Emily and Fen had sat in the cart in the barn. Six warm, busy weeks. They had done so many things, mostly with Wolf, spinning out the days, not wanting them to end, going to bed late and getting up early. Idle had been down once, just for lunch. And for those few hours the madness to come had seemed unbelievable: they had been *happy*, hadn't they? Talking, laughing, just like so many other times. But when Idle said goodbye, Fen had turned her head away, quickly, not waving, and ran towards the house. Emily, left between the two of them, had remembered, then. It was like waking up to bad reality after a good dream. All her life, till now, she had been used to it the other way round.

It wasn't till two days ago that Fen began her packing, and then she did it at night after Emily was in bed. She stored the packed suitcases in the spare room, but Emily saw them. She also noticed, although Fen was careful about what she removed, the disappearance of small things: the necklaces that seemed to hang from every mirror, the quill pen that lived on the dresser, a Victorian mug, some of the bright wools, some of the battered cookery books. Irreplaceable things, peculiar to Fen.

The curve of the summer had begun its downward slope, and the heat had gone out of the days. There were early mists again that dulled the apples, morning and evening: the roses browned

240

and died, and the sunflowers, much taller this year, stood like childish paintings of the real sun, their primitive faces dazzling in the sky. Inside, Emily's new gumboots and new mackintosh, ready for the new term, were in the hall. Fen, unused to sewing, had sat by the fire one night struggling with a name tape, and Emily had prayed that the cotton would never run out, the task would never end. But it was soon over, like every precious action these days, and Fen returned to her cooking. In the last few days she had cooked wildly, extravagantly, fast filling the deep-freeze with things Emily felt there was no hope of ever wanting to eat. Sometimes, making pastry or sieving gooseberries, she would talk vaguely of future plans: what fun it would be when Emily joined Kevin and her on their trips round the country . . . But then she would break off, distracted, and write a note about the milk or the forwarding of letters, and pin it to the dresser. Sometimes she looked sad, and fell silent. But Emily discovered that talking about Kevin's new play soon cheered her.

Fen had said goodbye to Emily this morning, and sent her over to Wolf for the day. She herself was to leave later, collected by Kevin. Then Idle and Miss Burrows would arrive in the evening, for the weekend. The following week Idle would take Emily back to school, and he and Miss Burrows would stay at home. He had, it seemed, almost retired. He planned, he had told them that day at lunch, to write a book. Anyhow, he'd be *there*. Nearly always.

So the plans for the parting, now it had come, were simple and easy. So unbelievably simple, quite possibly they were not true. It was to check this that Emily now walked back home, contrary to all orders to stay at Wolf's house: she wanted to make sure, finally.

Kevin's car was in the drive, one door open, a stack of things on the back seat. Emily and Wolf slipped into the orchard and climbed an apple tree. From the protection of its thick leaves they watched Kevin emerge from the house, a suitcase in each hand. Emily, who hadn't seen him for some time, was shocked at his height. Also at the ugliness of his face and the blackness of his hair. She watched while he wedged the suitcases into the boot of the car, then stretch himself, scratching his ribs. He called out impatiently to Fen.

Fen came out of the front door, slamming it behind her. She seemed to be all in orange – something new, a dress Emily didn't know – scarves flying from her neck, her face pale. Unsmiling, she checked the door, then let her hand run over the stone wall of the house. She tweaked at a curl of honeysuckle as if to break it off, but then left it. Slowly she walked to the car, looking at the ground. When she reached him, Kevin put his arm round her. Still she didn't smile, just brushed the hair out of her eyes. She got into the car, not looking at anything. Banged the door.

Kevin started the engine. Turned. They drove out of the gate. If Emily leapt from the tree, ran very fast across the lawn, climbed the wall, jumped down into the road in front of the car . . .

'*Mama!*' She heard her own cry as she scrambled down through the branches.

'They've gone,' said Wolf.

'I know.' On the grass, Emily didn't try to move.

'You'd better come back to us.'

'I'll stay here.'

'You'll get into trouble.'

Emily shrugged.

'You go, though.'

'Sure you don't want me to stay with you?'

'No.'

Wolf glanced at her face. It seemed smaller than usual, the eyes bigger. Not surprising, really, all this divorce business. Perhaps they should have tried out his plan after all, the plan that day on the church tower. But Emily had seemed so certain it was all right, then.

'Come up any time, won't you?' Wolf said. He'd have to go: he couldn't bear to stay with her, looking like that.

'Thanks.'

'Tomorrow or something.'

'All right.'

Wolf walked away, hands in his pockets, whistling.

Alone in the garden Emily wandered towards her old hiding place in the long grass. She sat there, looking at the silent house, the shut windows of the kitchen. The church clock struck occasionally, but she didn't count the chimes. It began to feel like evening: cool, fading. The grass was no protection. She was cold, cold, as if caught by a sudden dew. After a while – a long time, perhaps – she heard a car. It drew up at the front door. Marcia Burrows got out first – through the window of the car Idle handed her a key. She began to walk up the front path, her head making uncertain pecking movements. She was wearing her customary grey flannel suit, and carried a number of small boxes. At the door she fumbled for a moment, then went in.

Now Idle got out of the car. He wore a blue London shirt, no coat. Folding his arms over himself, as if he felt suddenly chilled, he looked up at the house, and then across the garden to Emily's hiding place. She leant back, trying to hide completely for a moment. But then she remembered that particular game was over. It belonged to last year. Peering through the grass, she saw her father coming towards her, as she knew he would. She stood up.

'Papa!' she said.

He couldn't have heard her, so far away, but he smiled. Emily waited for him. She wondered if he would carry her on his shoulders, so that one last time she could lose her head in the clouds.